PICARD STOOD HIS GROUND . . .

. . . as the dragon closed in on him, striking out with one huge claw.

He threw himself to one side, hacking out with his sword as he fell. The talons whistled over his head, and he felt a shudder in his arm as the sword struck the tough skin.

The dragon roared again and stomped down, barely missing Picard.

Picard fought to regain his breath and senses. The dragon's head shot toward him, and Picard found himself watching huge, saw-edged teeth heading directly for him. . . .

Look for STAR TREK Fiction from Pocket Books

Star Trek: The Original Series

Ashes of Eden
Federation
Sarek
Best Destiny
Shadows on the Sun
Probe
Prime Directive
The Lost Years
Star Trek VI: The Undiscovered Country
Star Trek V: The Final Frontier
Star Trek IV: The Voyage Home
Spock's World
Enterprise
Strangers from the Sky
Final Frontier

#1 Star Trek: The Motion Picture
#2 The Entropy Effect
#3 The Klingon Gambit
#4 The Covenant of the Crown
#5 The Prometheus Design
#6 The Abode of Life
#7 Star Trek II: The Wrath of Khan
#8 Black Fire
#9 Triangle
#10 Web of the Romulans
#11 Yesterday's Son
#12 Mutiny on the Enterprise
#13 The Wounded Sky
#14 The Trellisane Confrontation
#15 Corona
#16 The Final Reflection
#17 Star Trek III: The Search for Spock
#18 My Enemy, My Ally
#19 The Tears of the Singers
#20 The Vulcan Academy Murders
#21 Uhura's Song
#22 Shadow Lord
#23 Ishmael
#24 Killing Time
#25 Dwellers in the Crucible
#26 Pawns and Symbols
#27 Mindshadow
#28 Crisis on Centaurus
#29 Dreadnought!
#30 Demons
#31 Battlestations!
#32 Chain of Attack
#33 Deep Domain
#34 Dreams of the Raven
#35 The Romulan Way
#36 How Much for Just the Planet?
#37 Bloodthirst
#38 The IDIC Epidemic
#39 Time for Yesterday
#40 Timetrap
#41 The Three-Minute Universe
#42 Memory Prime
#43 The Final Nexus
#44 Vulcan's Glory
#45 Double, Double
#46 The Cry of the Onlies
#47 The Kobayashi Maru
#48 Rules of Engagement
#49 The Pandora Principle
#50 Doctor's Orders
#51 Enemy Unseen
#52 Home Is the Hunter
#53 Ghost Walker
#54 A Flag Full of Stars
#55 Renegade
#56 Legacy
#57 The Rift
#58 Faces of Fire
#59 The Disinherited
#60 Ice Trap
#61 Sanctuary
#62 Death Count
#63 Shell Game
#64 The Starship Trap
#65 Windows on a Lost World
#66 From the Depths
#67 The Great Starship Race
#68 Firestorm
#69 The Patrian Transgression
#70 Traitor Winds
#71 Crossroad
#72 The Better Man
#73 Recovery
#74 The Fearful Summons

Star Trek: The Next Generation

Star Trek Generations
All Good Things . . .
Q-Squared
Dark Mirror
Descent
The Devil's Heart
Imzadi
Relics
Reunion
Unification
Metamorphosis
Vendetta
Encounter at Farpoint

#1 Ghost Ship
#2 The Peacekeepers
#3 The Children of Hamlin
#4 Survivors
#5 Strike Zone
#6 Power Hungry
#7 Masks
#8 The Captains' Honor
#9 A Call to Darkness
#10 A Rock and a Hard Place
#11 Gulliver's Fugitives
#12 Doomsday World
#13 The Eyes of the Beholders
#14 Exiles
#15 Fortune's Light
#16 Contamination
#17 Boogeymen
#18 Q-in-Law
#19 Perchance to Dream
#20 Spartacus
#21 Chains of Command
#22 Imbalance
#23 War Drums
#24 Nightshade
#25 Grounded
#26 The Romulan Prize
#27 Guises of the Mind
#28 Here There Be Dragons
#29 Sins of Commission
#30 Debtors' Planet
#31 Foreign Foes
#32 Requiem
#33 Balance of Power
#34 Blaze of Glory
#35 Romulan Stratagem

Star Trek: Deep Space Nine

Warped
The Search

#1 Emissary
#2 The Siege
#3 Bloodletter
#4 The Big Game
#5 Fallen Heroes
#6 Betrayal
#7 Warchild
#8 Antimatter
#9 Proud Helios
#10 Valhalla
#11 Devil in the Sky

Star Trek: Voyager

#1 Caretaker
#2 The Escape

HERE THERE BE DRAGONS

JOHN PEEL

POCKET BOOKS
New York London Toronto Sydney Tokyo Singapore

This book is a work of fiction. Names, characters, places and incidents are either products of the author's imagination or are used fictitiously. Any resemblance to actual events or locales or persons, living or dead, is entirely coincidental.

An *Original* Publication of POCKET BOOKS

POCKET BOOKS, a division of Simon & Schuster Inc.
1230 Avenue of the Americas, New York, NY 10020

ISBN: 0-671-86571-4

First Pocket Books printing December 1993

10 9 8 7 6 5 4 3 2

Printed in the U.S.A.

For my wife, Nan

Historian's Note

The events in this story take place before the sixth-season episode "Rascals."

HERE THERE BE DRAGONS

Chapter One

COMMANDER WILLIAM RIKER eased forward, gently pushing aside a handful of the huge swamp weeds as he did so. Even this slight motion sent ripples through the dark green water and released bubbles that broke with noxious effect by his legs. Fighting back an urge to cough his lungs up, he strained his ears for the slightest indication that *they* had heard him.

Nothing.

Then again, according to legend, you *never* heard a *'tcharian* warrior unless he wanted you to—and that was as he delivered your deathblow. But it *had* to be just a legend, or else how would anyone know it and remain alive?

Riker tightened his grip on the hilt of the double-edged sword he carried, then shifted his other foot forward. More disgusting bubbles broke on the surface of the water in front of him. For his money, this holodeck simulation was getting much too uncomfortably real. It was harder to restrain the cough building up inside his raw throat.

Behind him, Alexander moved with greater ease. The water came up to the Klingon boy's stomach, so he didn't cause as many ripples as he walked. The bubbles of swamp gas didn't seem to bother him; to his Klingon nose, Riker thought, they might even have the fragrance of perfume. He held his smaller thrusting sword over his head to keep it dry. There was a faint smile on Alexander's dark face. He was enjoying himself.

Typical, Riker thought. Only a Klingon would think of this as *fun*. Alexander might only be a child, but he was a *Klingon* child, and they were born to fight. Riker had long ago come to the conclusion that *he* was a lover, not a fighter. And there was nothing in this benighted swamp to love. Another step and he stopped to listen. Still nothing but the gut-searing stink and the icy water, up to his thighs to make him uncomfortable. Despite this, he *knew* the *'tchariani* had to be around here somewhere. Three experienced warriors couldn't have been put off their trail this easily. Riker reviewed what he knew of the species as he edged his way through the weeds and around the thick treelike growths. Each branch seemed to trail a sticky liana, and avoiding them was a major hassle. He couldn't afford to get caught on one, though. It would shake the trees and alert the *'tchariani* for certain.

The warriors were a grim bunch of characters who loved to fight more than anything. Their idea of a pleasant evening was to sit around a blazing campfire and toast someone's feet. If that person screamed, he was immediately killed for displaying less than warriorlike behavior. If he didn't, he had to learn to get through life minus his feet. The *'tchariani* were so humorless they made even the Borg look like a race of stand-up comedians. Their favorite food was the heart of a *ichkhari*—a kind of armor-plated lionlike monster—which they ate not merely raw, but freshly torn from the chest of a dead beast they had personally slain seconds before lunch. And here I am with three of these warriors tracking me, Riker thought. Maybe Beverly Crusher was right, maybe I am way overdue for a mental checkup.

Riker cast a quick look over his shoulder to make certain that Alexander wasn't falling behind. It must have been the slight loss of concentration that the warriors had been awaiting.

The reeds beside him exploded outward as a *'tcharian* hurled through them. The warrior scream howled from its double throat as it raised its weapon for the kill. This was not just to terrify its prey but to let the other warriors know it had located Riker—and warn them to stay back until one of them was dead.

Riker threw himself to the left, heedless of the stench and frigid waters. As he did so, he swung his sword up in a backhanded blow that intersected the downward sweep of the *'tcharian* spear. The force of the impact almost broke his arm.

Hissing in fury, the warrior leapt back several paces to ready another attack. Riker was half-submerged now, thin, puke-green weeds trying to cling to him. He pushed down at the cloying mud to right himself. Another bout of noisome bubbles shattered on the surface of the swamp. Their stench burned his nasal passages as he gasped for breath.

The *'tcharian* balanced on its four legs and held its spear flat in both hands. It wasn't simply a stick with a point—instead, the pole was capped with a curved edge, like part of a sickle. The idea was to catch your prey with the thrust, then twist so as to disembowel it. It made the prey's death much more agonizing and therefore more entertaining for the warrior. It was looking for an opening to gut Riker.

Now what? Riker thought. Should he wait for it to attack again—and hope he could defend himself? Or should he attack and try not to leave himself open for a thrust? Which was better? Another clutch of bubbles erupted behind him as Alexander drew closer. Their stench helped Riker to decide—he *had* to get away from it. Whirling his sword, he leapt toward the warrior.

It danced aside with astonishing agility for a creature of its mass. Damn those four legs! As Riker halted his charge, he realized he was in a bad position. Then the *'tcharian* struck. It didn't have the time to reverse its spear and use the cutting edge, but it made do. The hard wooden edge slammed across Riker's ribs, knocking him from his feet and back into an even harder tree trunk. A sharp dagger of agony buried itself in Riker's side, and his back was a searing fire of pain. His sword hand slumped numbly, and great red flashes filled his vision.

Sensing victory and death, the *'tcharian* threw back its lizardlike snout and keened the deathsong.

With all of his remaining strength, Riker jerked back his arm and threw his sword.

The warrior had time for a startled look of astonishment as the blade ripped out its throat. It coughed up blood. Its legs spasmed in agony, then it fell lifeless into the water.

That was the good news; the bad was that Riker's sword fell in a tangle of tree roots with a loud splash. There was no way for him to find it again in time. . . .

The second warrior whipped from the reeds, its own spear at the alert. Riker tried to move aside, but he stumbled over something in the dark waters. He twisted as he fell, and fresh pain whipped up his entire side. The fall saved his life. The blade of the spear slashed through his jacket, leaving a foot-long blood-red trail across his back, and adding fuel to the fires of his pain.

Riker fought to remain conscious. The body of the first *'tcharian* had stopped thrashing, but its blood was still gushing into the filthy swamp waters. It was bound to attract predators, most of which had mouths overfilled with long, sharp teeth. And he wouldn't be able to see them coming. . . . Ignoring the pain, he grabbed the dead warrior's spear and wrenched it from the lifeless grip. Then, with as much speed and agility as he could muster, he turned to fight.

Alexander had beaten him to it. The warning he wanted to cry died unuttered in Riker's throat. It was too late and would only distract the Klingon youngster. His thrusting sword held firmly and proudly, Alexander darted in for the *'tcharian* before it could take advantage of Riker's clumsiness and finish him. The warrior twisted to meet the new foe. It let go of the spear with one hand and swung it in a lethal arc toward Alexander's head.

Possibly the warrior was unused to striking at so small a victim. Possibly Alexander was faster on his feet than Riker had ever imagined. Either way, Alexander shot forward, ducking under the darkness of the foul swamp waters, and the spear blade missed him by several microseconds.

The *'tcharian* reared back slightly, obviously puzzled by this maneuver. When Alexander failed to surface, it began stabbing at the water with the nasty end of the spear. Riker took advantage of the distraction to get the butt of his spear into the mud and use it to lever himself to his feet. Pain zigzagged up his side. It felt as if his back had been snapped in at least two places. Fighting down a wave of nausea, he stumbled a step forward. His vision wavered and it took every ounce of concentration he could summon up to make his other foot slurp forward through the mud and water.

The sound made the warrior snap around to face him. It hesitated in mid-thrust, wondering which foe to tackle. That second of uncertainty was sufficient.

Like a dolphin leaping from the sea, Alexander shot out of the filthy swamp, his sword held firmly in front of him. His whole body was as part of the weapon, and he lunged below the guard of the *'tcharian.* The blade of his sword struck home below the creature's breastbone. There was the scrape of metal on bone, and the warrior reared back, its forefeet flailing wildly. The spear fell with a splash from its nerveless fingers. It screamed and then fell, dead, into the water.

And then there was—

A wild howl filled the air as the final warrior hurtled out of hiding. Alexander was too startled to react in time. The sword was wrenched from his grip by the falling *'tcharian,* and he was left defenseless before the onslaught of the final warrior.

Riker pushed himself into action. With a primeval yell of his own, he staggered forward, grimly ignoring the pain. He lifted the spear and thrust as hard as he could. The point lanced home in the *'tcharian's* side, slicing a great gash that fountained blood onto the weapon. Gritting his teeth, Riker threw his remaining strength into twisting the blade.

The warrior screamed as the weapon dug in and eviscerated it. Riker screamed, too, because his ribs were a blaze of agony from the effort he had made. Completely drained, he fell forward into the embrace of the cold, disgusting waters.

"Terminate program," came Worf's voice, apparently out of nowhere.

Instead of breathing in the fetid swamp waters, fresh air filled Riker's lungs. His face hit the padded floor of the holodeck. He barely felt the extra pain it caused. With the termination of the program, all of the physical aspects of the battle vanished. The swamp was gone, replaced by the dark walls of the holodeck and the faintly glowing golden squares set into the walls and ceiling. The stench of the swamp was replaced by the scrubbed air of the *Enterprise.* The noises of water and combat gave way to the subdued humming of machinery.

It was a shame that none of the aching and stiffness went with the rest of it. It was almost impossible to tell the difference between the holodeck's environment and reality while a program lasted. Once reality was restored, however, the energy spent was real.

Riker was absolutely exhausted. He managed to roll over onto his back, gasping in lungfuls of cool, clear air.

"Did you see me, Father? Did you see me?" Alexander was almost hopping up and down in his eagerness.

"Yes, my son," Worf said with a grim smile on his lips and unmistakable pride in his voice. "I saw all. You acted very bravely and fought as a Klingon should." Then he glanced at Riker, almost embarrassed. "You fought well, too, Commander."

"That was my first kill!" Alexander beamed with pride and self-confidence. "I took him well!"

"Very well," agreed Worf. "You are progressing well. But now it is time for you to prepare for classes."

Alexander's face fell. "Aw, do I *have* to? I want to fight some more."

"Yes, you have to." Worf's stern tones couldn't mask the affection he felt for his child. "A Klingon must be prepared for his duty mentally as well as physically. Go and take your shower now. I will be along shortly."

"Yes, Father." Alexander gave Riker a big grin and bolted from the room.

The ceiling was finally slowing down its wild gyrations now. The ache in Riker's side was almost down to being simply unbearable. Any year now he'd be able to get back on his feet again. Riker frowned as a dark blotch floated across his vision. Then he managed to focus his eyes a bit and saw that it was Worf's face, gazing down at him.

"I am very grateful that you agreed to help my son with this simulation, Commander," he said. "Normally, it is one that Alexander would undertake as a class exercise in a Klingon school with other youngsters of his own age. But as he is the only Klingon boy on the *Enterprise* . . ."

"Think nothing of it, Worf," Riker said with some effort. "I'm glad to be of help."

"Thank you, Commander." Worf's face twisted slightly into what *might* have been a smile. "I would have felt very embarrassed had I been forced to be his partner in this program. It is of a level reserved only for children. No offense intended, Commander."

Please don't rub it in any more, Riker thought. "None taken," he said aloud.

Worf inclined his head slightly. "Do you require assistance standing?"

"No, no." Riker waved his hand feebly. "I kind of like it down here."

"As you wish." Worf turned and left the holodeck.

Riker rolled his eyes. Only a Klingon could make a *thank you* sound like an insult. Though he was happy to help Worf with Alexander's education, he rather doubted the use of a combat simulation like this. The Klingons placed a great deal of stress on hand-to-hand combat, but it was an outdated mode of fighting. Nowadays starships and phasers were the more customary weapons to use. A man with a phaser could stun a *'tcharian* warrior without mussing his hair. Why bother with obsolete arms like swords and spears? He sighed. No matter how hard he tried, he never really understood the Klingon mind.

The computer chimed softly. "Do you require medical assistance?" it inquired in its pleasant but unemotional tones.

"Don't you start!" Riker groaned.

He had a feeling that this wasn't going to be his day. . . .

Chapter Two

CAPTAIN JEAN-LUC PICARD sat back in the command chair, his fingers inches from the cup of tea (Earl Grey, hot), a feeling of deep satisfaction within his soul. Moments like these never failed to remind him why he had applied to join Starfleet in the first place. On the huge viewscreen that dominated the main bridge of the *Enterprise* was perhaps one of the most beautiful sights in all the universe.

The ship was cautiously approaching an interstellar cluster, and the screen showed the view ahead in all its majestic glory. The cluster was an immense cloud of gases, all tendrils and thunderheads, like some cosmic Rorschach test fresh-dripped from the fingers of God. It was out of matter like this that stars were born, as gravity and other forces acted upon the microscopic particles that made up the dust. The tiny particles and molecules would be drawn together, layered, and shaped until in one blinding instant they would explode with light and energy—the microsecond of stellar birth. Picard felt like an expectant father, waiting in the wards for news of a fresh arrival.

Dozens of stars had already begun their lives within the cloud. Light streaming from them danced and diffused off the particles of gas, casting strange and exotic hues into the cloud. Salmon pinks, intense magentas, glowing ochres, startling chartreuses, vivid sapphires—they all swirled and streaked and demanded attention. Rarely did such violent and savage forces as existed here come together to result in so much beauty. The individual particles were caught in the grips of fields of such strength that they were snatched from their paths and dragged into the embrace of their fellow particles in a process that was almost a flicker on the cosmic scale. Yet the view that now entranced him would barely change in the next thousand or even ten thousand years. The cloud was so huge, the forces so slow by human standards that only their most delicate instruments could detect any changes at all.

Picard wasn't the only one affected by the sight on the screen. Chief Engineer Geordi La Forge, standing beside Picard, murmured softly: "Man, oh, man, oh, man." Picard couldn't resist a smile—and a flicker of envy. Geordi had been born blind, but the VISOR he wore over his sightless eyes more than compensated for his lost vision. Its technology enabled Geordi to "see" far more of the electromagnetic spectrum than the normal human eye. If the cloud looked this gorgeous to Picard, how much more wonderful did it appear to Geordi?

"When I was a boy," Picard said softly—to speak

any louder would be unforgivably intrusive in the presence of this scene—"I was given a book by an aunt. It was some text on astronomy that my father said was far too advanced for a boy my age. He was right, too. But it had a section of color photographs that stole my heart. I loved looking through them and dreamed of being out here, amongst objects of such rare elegance." He looked again at the screen. "And here I am."

From his station at Ops in front of Picard, Data glanced around, an expression of childlike innocence on his face. "Maintaining our position, sir," he reported. "Scans confirm that the shields can easily withstand the forces we are now experiencing."

"Thank you, Mr. Data." Picard sighed slightly. Data could always be relied upon to bring even the grandest vistas down to practical reality. Lacking human emotions, the android tended to respond inappropriately at times.

Geordi shook his head ruefully. "Data," he said softly, "it's a shame that view out there doesn't mean anything to you."

Data looked back at the screen, then at Geordi, a slight frown on his face. "It *means* a great deal to me," he replied in all seriousness. "It means that proto-star formation is entering a scientifically interesting stage. It means that we are in an excellent situation to check Zingleman's Theory of Beta Tachyon Decay. It means that we must keep our shields raised as long as we are this close to the formation zone. It means—"

"Mr. Data," Picard broke in before the android could list every pertinent fact, "I think Mr. La Forge is referring to the *beauty* of the view."

"Ah." Data glanced at the screen once more. "It *is* aesthetically interesting."

Seated beside him at Navigation, Ensign Ro Laren snorted. "Trying to discuss beauty with an android is like trying to discuss business ethics with a Ferengi," she said. "No common ground."

"On the contrary," Data replied. "I have a great appreciation of aesthetics. I merely do not have an emotional response to beauty."

Knowing Ro's own appreciation of a good argument, Picard broke in. "Thank you. Mr. La Forge, perhaps you'd be kind enough to let the science teams know that they can begin launching their probes as soon as they are ready."

"Aye, sir."

As the turbolift door to the bridge hissed open, Picard glanced up. His first officer, Will Riker, entered. "Ah, Will," Picard called in greeting. "Come to enjoy the sights?"

Riker looked up at the screen, and his face creased into a smile. "It's certainly worth a long, hard stare," he agreed. He seemed to wince momentarily as he took his seat at Picard's right hand.

"Are you all right, Number One?" asked Picard, concerned.

Riker shot him a pained look. "It's just a . . . twinge," he replied. "Nothing to worry about." Before Picard could ask for details, Riker called out to Data: "What are the tachyon levels like out there?"

"Within predicted parameters," the android replied. "At this distance we will have no problems. Shields are holding at five percent carrying capacity."

Riker nodded. "And if the science teams want us closer in?"

Data cocked his head slightly as he performed the calculations in his positronic matrix. "We could go another light-year closer before the shields begin to show strain," he reported. "Two light-years would definitely overextend their capacity."

"Well, there's little chance we'll have to worry about that," Picard said. "This is a nice, routine examination, and science section will just have to be happy with whatever they get from this distance."

Riker couldn't resist a grin. "Aren't you at all interested in getting some answers to the mystery of beta tachyon decay?"

"I might be, Number One, if I knew what it was!" Picard was willing to let him have his fun at the captain's expense.

Riker stroked his beard. "Data's been explaining it to me," he said. "Apparently a maverick scientist named Zingleman from Benecia has this theory that the forces at the heart of a stellar cluster like this are sufficient to funnel not merely alpha tachyons but the beta version as well. And beta tachyons seem to undergo some form of decay that nobody's been able to measure or explain exactly. They *should* have all evaporated or something when the universe was half its present age."

Picard was intrigued despite himself. "And yet they haven't?"

Riker nodded at the android. "Data?" he prompted.

Data swung about in his seat to face them. "No, sir, they haven't. There are a number of hypotheses that might account for this, but Professor Zingleman's theory is the most intriguing. He posits the idea that they may create a kind of space-time tunnel that leads from their moment of creation to their eventual destruction—a form of very localized distortion that allows them to live on far after they theoretically should have decayed."

Struggling to grasp this, Picard asked: "You mean a kind of time warp reaching back to the instant of the Big Bang itself and then forward to the eventual end of the entire universe?"

"Precisely." Data raised an eyebrow. "An intriguing possibility, is it not?"

"Think of the ramifications," Riker urged. "If such corridors through time *do* exist, it might be possible to actually send probes back through them to the very instant of creation itself—and to the other end of time as well. . . ."

Ro had stayed silent longer than she liked. Ever practical, all the talk of theory rankled her. "Except that we *know* that tachyons can rip normal matter apart in seconds," she pointed out. "If the *Enterprise* tried to enter a tachyon funnel, we'd be annihilated instantly and our atoms scattered from the Big Bang to the Last Flicker." Then, recalling herself, she added: "Sir."

Picard and Riker exchanged smiles. When she had first been assigned to the *Enterprise,* Ro Laren's records had labeled her a malcontent and habitual troublemaker. Picard, however, considered her a valuable addition to the crew—not at all the problem that her previous commanders had rated her. What some officers had considered to be her weaknesses—

questioning orders, offering unasked-for recommendations, and sometimes simply acting without proper authorization—Picard felt were strengths that simply needed channeling in the right directions. She had proved her worth many times over.

"Then we had better be certain that our shields remain at full strength for this survey, hadn't we?" Picard said mildly. Then he noted that Data had swung back to study new readings on his board. "Mr. Data?"

"Sir," the android reported without turning his head. "I am receiving some very anomalous information from sensors." Ro busied herself checking the incoming data.

"Clarify, please." Picard leaned forward. What could possibly be happening out there that would register on the sensors? In a stellar cloud such as this, events took place over cosmic periods of time, not minutes.

"It appears to be another vessel, Captain," Data replied.

Riker frowned. Starfleet didn't have any other ships in this sector—which was why the *Enterprise* was taking these readings in the first place. "Where is it, Data?"

"Inside the stellar cluster, sir."

"What?" Picard jumped to his feet. "But that's impossible." He moved to stand behind Data at Ops, scanning the incoming readings with his own eyes.

"Nevertheless, it *is* there," the android insisted.

"On screen," Picard ordered.

As Data obeyed, the image of the cloud focused

down tighter to a section of the wispy matter. Nothing was visible except the stellar matter.

"Confirmed," Ro announced. "I'm reading a distortion in the space-time fabric ahead of us at two oh three mark seven."

"But *nothing* could survive inside there," Riker objected.

"*Something* apparently can, Number One," Picard replied. "Intriguing, isn't it?"

Geordi had returned to stand beside them all. The five of them stared from the screen to the instruments, waiting. "There she is," Geordi said.

A small shape appeared on the screen, flitting out from an arm of the stellar gas. Data instantly magnified the view, and the shape leapt into sharp focus.

Picard was stunned. Had the vessel been a Klingon bird of prey, or even a Cardassian science ship, he would have been puzzled, but it would have made some sort of sense. A ship like that *might* have been built and tested on the quiet. Or if the ship they saw emerging from the lethal cloud was some new and previously unidentified alien vessel of mysterious technology, that would have been fascinating but explicable.

What they were looking at literally made no sense at all.

"It *can't* be," Riker said, shaken.

"Confirmed," Data announced, the only one of them incapable of being shocked. "The vessel is an Earth pleasure cruiser, Damascus class."

"There's no *way* they could have survived that," Geordi complained.

"A blasted *tourist* vessel?" Picard growled. "Gentlemen, I want some answers! Who are they? How did they survive? What the blazes are they doing here?"

"Presumably sightseeing," said Ro, straight-faced.

From his station toward the rear of the bridge, Worf called: "Captain! They're firing on us!"

Chapter Three

"THEY'RE *WHAT?*" demanded Picard, incredulously.

Worf looked up from his board, a savage smile on his face. "They're firing on us," he repeated. "Phasers only, two of them." Even as he spoke, the ship gave a slight—barely noticeable—judder as the bolts hit the *Enterprise's* screens. "No loss of shield strength," he added.

"They've got to be kidding," Riker ventured. "A pleasure cruiser trying to take on a starship?"

"A one-sided fight like this is hardly going to put them in the history books," Ro muttered. "They don't stand a chance."

"Precisely," agreed Picard, frowning at the screen. "That much should be obvious even to a Denebian slime devil. So why are they firing on us?"

Geordi scratched the back of his neck. "And what's

a leisure vessel doing equipped with phasers anyway?" Another blast hit their screens as they conferred.

"No loss of shield strength," Worf called out.

Picard sighed. "I think we can take that for granted, Mr. Worf," he replied. "This situation is getting more baffling every moment."

A happy gleam filled the Klingon's eyes. "Shall I fire back, sir? Phasers are on line."

"I'd feel rather like a bully, Number One," Picard muttered to Riker. A starship firing on a pleasure cruiser . . ."

"We can't let them keep this up, though, Captain," Riker pointed out.

Picard nodded. "Noted." To Worf, he ordered: "Open hailing frequencies, Mr. Worf."

Worf nodded and bent to his work. After a moment he announced: "No reply on any channel, Captain. They *are* receiving our message but refuse to respond." The ship rocked slightly once again. "No loss of—" Worf cut himself off.

Shaking his head in despair, Picard said: "All right, Mr. Worf. One shot across their bow." To Riker, he added: "Maybe that'll knock some sense into their heads."

"Firing," Worf reported. On the screen they saw the searing ray of their phaser flash past the craft. It was a hundred times stronger than the ones the pleasure ship was using. The other ship promptly changed direction but continued to fire.

"All right, Mr. Worf," Picard decided. "Take out their engines."

Worf smiled eagerly. *"Aye,* Captain." He tapped the figures into his panel.

On the screen they saw the small ship rocked by two beams that passed through their shields without pause. The phaser fire sliced off both engine nacelles and then vaporized them. The inertial dampers on the vessel stopped it dead in space.

It continued to fire at them.

"Captain," Data said. "I have been scanning the vessel since we first saw it. I am now recording seven life-forms aboard the craft. When I began my scan, there were nine."

"Did we kill them?" asked Riker, concerned. None of them liked having to kill, even though the other ship had commenced hostilities.

"No, sir. The two fatalities occurred within their lower decks, not near the engine room."

Riker's puzzled frown matched the one on Picard's face. "What is going on over there?"

"Maybe their captain doesn't take failure lightly?" suggested Ro.

"Then they should never have begun this insane attack," snapped Picard. "Mr. Worf, that continuous phaser fire is getting on my nerves. Can you take their cannons out without injuring anyone?"

"I believe so, Captain."

"Then—"

"Sir!" Data broke in. "I am now registering further activity on the lower deck." He looked up. "They have launched a life pod, with a single being inside it."

"What?" Picard felt like a swimmer going under for the third time. "This is getting more damned puzzling every minute. Put a tractor beam on it as soon as it clears the ship. I want it brought aboard now. Maybe we can get some answers from whoever is in it."

As they watched, the tiny teardrop-shaped pod rocketed away from the battered space yacht.

"Captain," Worf announced. "They have ceased firing at us."

"Oh, good," Ro snickered.

Worf looked up, a heavy frown on his face. "They are now shooting at the life pod."

Picard spun around to the intercom in his command chair arm. Triggering it, he called: "Mr. O'Brien!"

"Aye, sir," the transporter chief's voice answered him. "I've already locked on. Beaming the passenger aboard—now."

"Good man." Picard glanced across at Worf. "Get a couple of security men down to transporter room three," he ordered. "I want whoever is beamed aboard escorted to the briefing room."

"Understood," acknowledged Worf.

As Picard turned back to stare at the screen, there was a brief flare of light as the life pod was vaporized.

"Not very good shots," Ro observed. "It took them eight tries to get it."

"But why were they firing at it at all?" Geordi wondered. "And why was it launched in the first place?"

"An escape," Riker said. "Whoever was in that thing chose the right moment to make a break for it." He scratched at his beard. "Do you think they know we got the passenger out of it?"

Before anyone could venture an opinion, Data announced: "Sensors are picking up an increase in energy readings from the other craft. It is about to—"

The automatic dampers on the screen cut in, lowering the image almost to black. Then, with a blinding flash, the pleasure ship detonated.

Shocked, Picard turned to his security officer. "Mr. Worf, did *we* do that?"

"No, Captain," Worf replied grimly. "They did it to themselves."

"They self-destructed," Data added, somewhat unnecessarily.

Picard stared at the screen, which had reverted to the beautiful view of the stellar nebula. None of this made any sense at all. "I want answers," he said firmly. "Will, get the reserve officers to the bridge immediately. Mr. Data, Mr. Worf, Mr. La Forge, and you, Ensign"—he nodded to Ro—"will join us in the briefing room as soon as your replacements are here." He tapped the intercom on his chair arm again. "Dr. Crusher, would you please join us in the briefing room at your earliest convenience?"

"I'll be right there, Captain," her voice replied.

"Excellent. Picard out." He turned to Riker. "Will, I believe Counselor Troi is resting at present."

"I'll wake her, Captain," Riker promised. "I don't think she'd forgive us if she missed out on this one."

As Picard strode into the briefing lounge, Dr. Beverly Crusher was waiting for him. Over her blue uniform she wore her inevitable medical robe. On her face she wore a puzzled expression. Picard knew he must have a similar one on his own face.

"What's this I hear about us being attacked, Jean-Luc?" she asked. "I didn't hear a red alert, and nobody warned Medical."

"There really wasn't any need for either, Doctor,"

he replied. "We were attacked by a blasted *yacht* that was using slingshots against our phasers. We were in no danger whatsoever of suffering casualties."

"Are you joking?" she asked, and then answered herself immediately: "No, of course you wouldn't be. Not about matters like that. But it doesn't make any sense."

"Doctor," Picard said with frustration, "I don't need you to tell me that. I'm sorry, I don't mean to sound rude. But eight people died out there a short while ago, and I don't have the slightest idea why."

The briefing room doors opened again, and Counselor Deanna Troi entered. She looked tired. "Captain, Doctor," she acknowledged. "I was just getting ready for bed when Will called me. What's this about us being *attacked?* I didn't feel a thing."

"None of us did," Picard replied. "There was one survivor, being escorted down here right now."

"And we'd better hope he has some answers," the doctor added. "Or else our captain may become apoplectic from sheer frustration."

He had to smile at that. "I'm sorry if I sound grouchy."

"You're forgiven."

The door hissed open and the bridge crew trooped in to take their places. Only Worf was missing. Picard, Deanna, and Beverly moved to the conference table to join Riker, Data, Geordi, and Ro. For the final time the door opened. Two security officers entered, taking their places beside the door. Behind them came the survivor, and Worf brought up the rear.

The man from the yacht seemed to be at his ease. He glanced about the room, then fastened his gaze on

Picard's collar insignia. "Captain," he said, extending his hand. "I'm pleased to meet you."

Ignoring the offered handclasp, Picard studied the man. He looked to be in his early forties, and definitely of Terran stock. His thick brown hair hung long about his shoulders, and he had a firm, muscular build. His face was long and lean, his eyes blue and clear. He wore casual clothing, including what looked to be a hunting vest. There were several pockets, all empty.

"Who are you and what the devil is going on?" Picard demanded.

"I understand your confusion, Captain," the man replied with an affable grin.

"Fine. Then help me to relieve it. Your name?"

"Castor Nayfack," the man announced. He stared at his hand and then tucked it behind his back, matching Picard's pose. "May I have the pleasure of knowing yours?"

"I am Captain Jean-Luc Picard of the Federation starship *Enterprise,*" Picard snapped. "Now perhaps you'd be kind enough to explain what the deuce happened here?"

"Enterprise?" Nayfack mused. "I wasn't told you'd be in this sector. Then again, the less I know, the less I can reveal, eh?"

"What are you talking about, man?"

Nayfack tapped his chest. "I'd better explain. I'm a Federation security agent, working undercover."

Chapter Four

PICARD STARED AT NAYFACK and then managed to crack a slight smile. "I had thought that you might clarify matters, not muddy the waters further."

Worf leaned forward on the table. The surface creaked under the added stresses. "You can, of course, prove what you are claiming?" he challenged.

"Don't be absurd." Nayfack stared at the Klingon distastefully. "If I went into my assignments with my credentials in my pocket, how long do you think I'd last?"

Worf settled back in his chair, his face twisted in what passed for a knowing grin. The table didn't quite sigh with relief. "A convenient excuse," he stated.

"The truth," Nayfack countered.

Picard held up his hand to prevent further argument. "What you say," he told Nayfack, "does have a certain grain of truth to it. However, I'm sure that you will appreciate that we are not willing to take your statement entirely on faith at the moment."

Nayfack sighed rather theatrically. "I'm afraid you'll have to do just that, Captain Picard. I assure you that once you hear my reasons—"

"Surely," Riker interrupted, "you have a supervisor that you report in to from time to time? All we need is a name, and we can check with Starfleet and est—"

"No!" Nayfack's poise slipped for a moment. He turned to Picard, urgently. "Captain, you haven't tried to report any of this to Starfleet yet, have you?"

The whole matter was making less and less sense to Picard as it continued. "No," he replied cautiously. "I wanted to have something solid to report first."

Nayfack sighed with relief. "Thank the seven Dark Lords of Polimedes," he breathed. "Captain, I urge you to hear me out before you even consider filing any kind of report about this incident. I assure you that when I finish you will do as I say."

Picard raised his eyebrow. When he spoke, his voice was deceptively mild. "I will hear you out, Mr. Nayfack—but on this ship, *I* give the orders."

"Of course," agreed Nayfack quickly. "I didn't mean to challenge your authority on this ship, Captain Picard. But you must understand that I am very concerned about completing my mission."

"I may well sympathize with your mission," Picard agreed, "once we have been enlightened. If you please . . . ?"

The long-haired man considered for a moment, then nodded. "Normally I'm attached to the Federation Bureau of Conservation," he explained, "assigned to investigate illegal hunting and any other factors that might endanger the well-being of indigenous species across Federation space. About a year or so ago we received confidential information that there was a group of criminals that had begun to offer—ah —*sportsmen* who didn't possess well-developed moral scruples the chance to go after some really big game. Our informant suggested that this game was *extremely* large indeed and not native to any known Federation world. I was given the assignment of tracking down the truth of the matter.

"I managed to make friends with one of the wealthy hunters we were certain had to be involved. After a few meetings our suspicions were confirmed very forcibly. The man took me to his trophy room in the heart of his mountain fortress. It was filled with animals that he had killed and placed into stasis fields for the purpose of display.

"I can't tell you how appalling that room was, Captain. He had specimens of at least thirty critically endangered species that he had murdered. There was an Earth mountain gorilla, a Vulcan nightclaw, a family grouping of Aldebaran sand eels . . . Well"—Nayfack shrugged—"I'm sure you get the idea."

Data inclined his head slightly. "As you say, each of those is on the prohibited list of animals. There are fewer than five hundred of each surviving anywhere in the known galaxy."

"Exactly." Nayfack concentrated on Picard once more. "I had to pretend enthusiasm for his *skills,* and I admired his trophies. Then he showed me the one that we had been tipped off about. It was in a separate room—it needed to be. The creature was some eighty meters long and thirty high. The thing it most closely resembled was a dragon from Earth folklore."

Riker leaned forward. "A *dragon?*"

Nayfack shrugged. "Something like that. It was obviously of some kind of reptilian stock. A sort of super-dinosaur, I guess you'd say. It was built something like a triceratops, with four massive legs, a long tail, and a thick hide in a kind of camouflage green and brown mottle. But it had a long, fanged snout, bony crests to the head, and spinal ridges running to about halfway down its long tail. The thing had claws that could tear duraluminum apart. If he'd told me it could breathe fire, I wouldn't have been too surprised.

"Well, I'd convinced him I was a rich sportsman, too, in search of fresh game. He asked me if that creature interested me. When I assured him it did, he put me in contact with the ring. For several million credits I was offered the chance to kill one of the creatures for my own trophy room." He grinned. "Naturally, the department had to furnish the fee for me, but we figured it would be worth it if we could discover where the monster came from and then round up the gang. I expected to be taken somewhere off the beaten track, but I was not prepared for *that.*" He gestured at the nebula visible in the briefing room window. "Captain, at the heart of that cloud there is a planet where these dragons dwell."

"According to all known theories," Geordi interrupted, "there can't even be a planet inside there, let alone an inhabited world. The tachyon streams would rip every living cell apart."

"Believe me, such a world *does* exist," Nayfack insisted. "I was just as astonished as you would be, but I was taken inside the cloud, and we made planetfall several weeks ago. As the organizers promised, I was given the chance to shoot one of the dragons. Naturally, I turned out to be somewhat . . . inept with my phaser cannon and missed my opportunity. We were leaving the cloud when the *Enterprise* was sighted.

"The gang that runs this whole business isn't really very smart, Captain. They—"

"Not very smart?" Geordi laughed and shook his head. "Man, if they could build a field generator that enabled them to penetrate the tachyon clouds out there, then they have to be absolute *genius* material."

"They built nothing," Nayfack informed him. "They *stole* what they were using. I'd say that the entire gang probably has the collective IQ of a wombat. They're secretive and well-established, but they are really not very bright. They fell into this deal, and knowing that their income depends on keeping the location of their hunting grounds a secret, the captains of the two yachts that bring the sportsmen in to the dragons' world were under strict orders to destroy their craft rather than be captured. The instant that the *Enterprise* was sighted, the captain of the vessel I was on gave the computer the self-destruct command and then attacked you, knowing his battle was hopeless. It was clearly a foolish course of action and gives you some idea of how idiotic this gang is. Anyway, I managed to make a break for their escape pods—"

"Killing two of the crew on the way," Riker said.

"I had no option, Commander. If I stayed on the ship, what I knew would die with me. I killed the men when they tried to kill me to prevent my escape. I then ejected and the ship self-destructed."

Picard leaned back in his chair, studying Nayfack

thoughtfully. "Your story is very interesting," he agreed cautiously. "But if what you say is true, then surely you will wish to contact Federation security as soon as possible and have the gang rounded up."

"No!" Nayfack almost jumped to his feet in frustration. "They monitor all transmissions. They were smart enough to slip an agent into the Federation's Earth communications post. If they know they've been discovered, they'll simply cease operations for a while. Then they'll begin again when we leave them alone. We couldn't patrol the entire cloud indefinitely. No, we must strike, and strike fast. The yacht makes the run to Earth in three weeks. When it does not arrive, the gang will know that something has gone wrong. Before then we must capture the members of the gang on the planet at the heart of the cloud."

"Not wishing to stress the obvious," Geordi told him, "but there is no way that the *Enterprise* can get into the cloud. The forces would rip us apart."

"Of course they would," the agent replied. *"If* you simply forced your way in. But you don't have to do that. There's a small tunnel through the tachyon storms and into the heart of the cloud."

"I find that difficult to accept," Data broke in. "There is simply no chance of such a tunnel occurring naturally. And no race in the galaxy possesses the technology to confine beta tachyons or to exclude them from such a tunnel."

That didn't seem to faze Nayfack at all. "I'm sure you're right," he agreed. "But the tunnel is there. You'd never detect it, of course, but I have the coordinates memorized. I can take you through it. There's a device inside the cloud that creates the tunnel. If the gang is alerted to our presence here, they will simply turn the device off. Without the generated tunnel, we couldn't go in after them. They could then open a fresh tunnel when they feel secure, and in any direction to either escape or begin operations again."

Geordi spun in his seat to face Picard. "If what he claims is true, Captain, then this I gotta see! A tachyon confinement field is theoretically impossible."

With a smile tugging at the corners of his mouth, Riker said: "But you've performed your own share of the theoretically impossible."

"Not this!" Geordi assured him. "I wouldn't even have the vaguest idea how to go about it."

Picard held up a hand. "This is all very interesting," he said slowly. "But I really don't think we can oblige you, Mr. Nayfack."

The long-haired man looked stunned. "But . . . Captain," he protested. "Don't you care about what these villains are doing?"

"Of course I care," Picard countered. "I dislike the selfishness of any man who feels that the whole of creation has been placed here merely for him to exploit. And I commend your zeal in seeking their arrest and punishment. But you must understand that our mission here is scientific, and not one of law enforcement. I sympathize with your concerns, but my responsibility in the matter is limited to reporting it to Starfleet and delivering you safely to Starbase Three Two Nine when we proceed to our next assignment."

"Captain!" Nayfack was practically on his knees, begging. "You *must* reconsider! You have to help me capture these . . . murderers!"

Picard shook his head slightly. "Believe me, I wish I could. But I cannot risk this vessel and its crew in an attempt to penetrate this cloud simply to round up a few crooks. That is not the function of this ship."

"Captain," said Ro, "if I may offer a comment?"

"By all means, Ensign," Picard agreed. "Your views are always interesting."

"This technology that the gang appears to have somehow come by is clearly of a very advanced order. If our Chief Engineer says it's beyond his understanding"—she nodded at Geordi—"then it is surely vital that we investigate it. What if these criminals were to decide to sell the technology, fearing that they couldn't use it any longer? Imagine what would happen if the Cardassians or the Ferengi were to get their hands on the field generator."

"She has a valid point," agreed Riker. "It's bound to occur to them as a way to make money sooner or later. They could practically hold a bidding war for such technology."

"If the Romulans were to get their hands on such technology," Worf stated, "then the Galaxy might well errupt into another war. If their ships were equipped with such devices, they could hide in any nebulae, and the Federation would be unable to follow."

"Possibly even inside a star," agreed Geordi.

It was obvious that Picard was reconsidering his decision. Nayfack slammed his fist down on the table. "Perhaps I can convince you, Captain." He glowered at Picard through his long hair. "There are a few things I haven't yet told you about the planet."

"I doubt that it will influence my decision at all," the Captain replied. "But I am willing to hear you out.

I should also be interested in hearing just where this gang of poachers laid their hands on such novel technology."

"The two matters are linked," Nayfack said. "First —the planet in that cloud where the dragons dwell is inhabited. By *humans.*"

"Humans!" Riker exploded. He stared at his captain, who was obviously as startled as he was by this outrageous claim. "That's impossible. There have been no human settlements out this far, for one thing. And no human could have penetrated those tachyon fields."

"I agree," said Nayfack calmly. He was clearly happy to have regained the attention of everyone in the room. "I did not say that they had made it here themselves. Tell me, ladies and gentlemen, have you ever heard of the Preservers?"

Chapter Five

"THE PRESERVERS!" Picard stared around the table. Riker, Geordi, Beverly, Deanna, and Ro looked as astonished as he felt. Worf merely glowered, as ever. Data had inclined his head slightly, the closest he ever came to showing surprise. "Of course we have," the captain added gruffly. "Everyone in Starfleet knows about them. They're one of the biggest mysteries of the galaxy."

"How would you like to solve that mystery, Captain?" Nayfack gave a sly grin. "This is your opportunity."

Picard didn't answer immediately. Instead, he turned to his android second officer. "Mr. Data, perhaps you'd be kind enough to bring us all up to date on what is known about the Preservers?"

"Everything, Captain?"

Picard shook his head. Knowing Data, that could take hours. He was extremely thorough. "Just the essentials, if you please."

"As you wish, Captain," the android agreed. "The Preservers first came to Starfleet's attention in 2302. Very little is known of the race, save that it apparently set itself the goal of seeding uninhabited worlds with small groups of people from threatened societies. Their motivations for this remain unknown. The first Preserver planet is now known by the designation *Miramanee* and was located by NCC 1701—the original *Enterprise* under the command of Captain James T. Kirk."

"Kirk," murmured Riker. "I'd forgotten that part."

Data waited to be certain that the interruption was over, and then continued. "The Preservers had selected a group of Native American Indians to be seeded on the world, where they had then developed unhindered. As a large meteor was due to strike the world, the *Enterprise* attempted to assist the natives. The Preservers had, however, planned for such an occurrence, and their own mechanisms dealt with the intruder. Since this initial contact with a seeded world, two more have been discovered, but we still know very little about the Preservers themselves."

"Thank you, Mr. Data." Picard turned to study Nayfack again. "So you claim that the world in the heart of this cluster cloud is another seeded world?"

"Exactly." Nayfack shrugged. "I gather it was originally a small cluster of villages taken from thirteenth-century Germany. They were in a plague zone, and the Preservers must have taken them knowing the natives would not be missed. They were settled here and have stagnated ever since."

"Stagnated?" asked Riker. "Do you have any idea why?"

"Yeah. The Preservers must have thought they were being smart, I suppose. They took a small group of people who firmly believed in things like dragons and plopped them down here where there *were* dragons, of a sort. But the dragons are very dangerous—if you don't have a phaser cannon to skewer them with. The original half-dozen small villages had to put up defensive walls, and the people mostly stay inside them. There's not much cross-contact, so no real progress."

There was a moment of silence, then Deanna asked: "And how did this group of hunters you were looking for stumble across this world?"

"Right," agreed Geordi. "They can't have just poked around in the tachyon clouds on the chance that there was something here."

"They didn't," Nayfack replied. "They had a map. You see, this hunting business was just a sideline until it started to really pay off for them. The people involved here were originally just a small gang of six or seven people. They were archaeological raiders—going into dead worlds, skimming whatever artifacts happened to be there, then selling them on the black market to collectors. Minor stuff, really, and hardly important enough for Starfleet to have bothered with them. Then the raiders hit the jackpot. On one of the worlds they plundered, there were a few Preserver ruins. It must have been one of their worlds that failed to make a go of it. And in the ruins there was a map of their other seeded planets."

"What?" Riker leaned across the table. "A map? Of how many worlds?"

"I don't know," Nayfack said, irritated. "I wasn't

allowed to see the thing. They were happy to take my money, but they weren't prepared to trust me."

"I can't imagine why not," Ro muttered.

"All I know," the agent continued, "is that the head man of this ring on the planet here has a map showing the location of all the other Preserver worlds in the galaxy. This one was the only one that he apparently felt they could really exploit. The leader of the gang is a trained archaeologist, and he managed to decipher the Preserver language on the map. It took him six years, but it finally paid off for them." Nayfack smiled, slowly and slyly, knowing he had them hooked. "Now, Captain, do you agree that we *must* go in?"

Picard thought for a moment. "Well, Mr. Nayfack, I must admit that the picture has changed considerably with this new information. If there is a Preserver world at the heart of the cloud, then we do have to become involved. This gang is breaking the Prime Directive rather seriously."

"Not to mention that if there is a Preserver map, then we must recover it," added Riker. "To be able to trace their path . . . ! Who knows, maybe even to meet them one day . . ."

Picard stood up. Tugging his uniform into order, he looked down at Nayfack. "If you would be good enough to allow me to confer with my officers, I promise you a decision on the matter within thirty minutes, Mr. Nayfack. And until then, I will maintain subspace silence, as you requested."

The agent climbed lazily to his feet. "Good enough, Captain," he agreed.

Picard turned to the security guard at the door. "Why don't you show Mr. Nayfack where Ten-

Forward is?" he suggested. "I'll contact you there when we've reached a decision."

"Aye, sir." The guard gestured with his head for Nayfack to precede him.

In the doorway Nayfack paused. "I'm sure you'll make the right decision, Captain."

"I wish I had your confidence," Picard replied. "But I shall certainly make the best decision that I can."

"That's all I ask." The door hissed shut behind him and the guard.

Picard returned to his place and studied his team. "Comments?" he invited.

"I do not trust the man." That was, naturally, Worf. As both a Klingon and the Security Officer, Worf's suspicions were part of his nature.

"Nor do I," agreed Ro. Again, this was no surprise: the Bajoran was a good officer, but she tended to distrust everyone. Given her background, it wasn't unexpected.

Riker grinned slightly. He'd expected the comments, too. "I don't see why we *should* trust him," he agreed. "He's got a very glib story."

"Perhaps *too* glib?" asked Picard.

Riker's grin broadened. "He let us have snippets of information as it suited him," he pointed out.

Picard raised an eyebrow. "If he is what he claims, then secrecy will naturally be a part of his nature." He turned to Deanna. "Counselor?"

As a half-Betazed, Deanna Troi possessed acute and trained powers of empathy. Picard trusted her judgments implicitly.

She looked worried. "He *is* being devious," she agreed. "But that is in the nature of the job he claims to have. There were times when I sensed he was lying, but most of the time he was telling at least partial truths. Some of what he told us is definitely accurate, at least as far as he knows it. The other parts are a jumble of things, ranging from exaggeration to outright lies."

"Can you be any more specific?" asked Riker. "What parts were completely true?"

"I can't be certain." Deanna looked frustrated. "He's trying to manipulate us, Captain. That much is certain. But his attitude colors everything I read from him. If I were a full Betazed, perhaps I could sense more. As it is, his deviousness clouds his every response. He is using the truth to achieve his purposes. But I can tell you that he certainly does want us to go after the gang."

"All of which *could* be explained if he is what he claims," Picard summed up. "He wouldn't tell us more than he thinks we need to know." He snorted. "People in the security field rarely trust others with all they know. Mr. La Forge, what about his claims that there is a planet at the center of this nebula?"

Geordi laughed. "Captain, ordinarily I'd say the man had bloodbats in his belfry. There's no possible theory that could even begin to deal with the kind of energies you'd need to drive a tunnel through a tachyon emission field."

"But?" prompted Picard.

"If the Preservers *are* involved," Geordi said, "then we may as well throw the science book out the nearest airlock. We know that they can do what seems to be impossible to our sciences. If anyone could punch a hole in that cloud, they get my vote as most likely."

"If I may suggest, Captain," Data offered, "there is a simple way to make a decision."

"Is there really?" asked Picard. "Well, I'd be more than happy to hear it."

"Mr. Nayfack *was* on a ship that came out of the cloud," the android explained. "That strongly suggests that some form of tunnel must exist. The vessel was an Earth ship, which could not possibly have created the tunnel. In which case, we must postulate the tunnel's creation by another race. The Preservers may well possess such technology, so that part of his tale is indeed plausible."

"Granted," Picard admitted. "But how does this help me with my decision?"

"If Mr. Nayfack can indeed locate the tunnel for us, then we could conceivably traverse it. If he cannot, then the question of intervention becomes academic."

"But if he's lying," Worf growled, "then he might lead us into a trap. If we diverge from the safe tunnel, the ship will be torn apart by the tachyon fields. We must consider the possibility that Nayfack came aboard our ship precisely to make certain that we do not report our discovery back to Starfleet. Leading us astray would be an effective way to do that."

The thought was definitely not a pleasant one. Picard saw the faces of the team tense at the idea. The effects of the beta tachyon particles on living tissue was not pleasant. There *were* nastier ways to die, but not many. "Could we send a probe into the tunnel first?" he asked Geordi.

The engineer shrugged. "Hard to say, Captain. In field strengths like that, we'd probably not be able to monitor it for any useful distance."

"There is," Picard added, "another aspect to all of this." Everyone focused on him. "If Mr. Nayfack is telling any particle of truth at all, we are obviously looking at a very severe breach in the Prime Directive. And I am certain I do not need to remind any of you of our duty in that case." He was understating the case, as was his habit. It was quite clear from the expressions on everyone's face that his team understood the problem here.

"I wish it were that simple, Captain." Beverly Crusher put in. The Prime Directive prevents interference with the natural functioning of a viable planetary society." She gestured at the glorious cloud outside the viewport. "The planet that Nayfack is talking about may not exactly qualify. It is an artificially seeded world, for one thing. And, second, the society was placed on a world which appears already to have stunted its natural evolution. The Preservers obviously don't obey the Prime Directive."

Picard smiled; he might have known that she'd pick up on the one crucial point. "Precisely what I was getting to," he told her. "Is this world under the Prime Directive or not? If so, are the activities of this gang of mediocre crooks really harming it? I am inclined to accept Mr. Nayfack's estimation of their capabilities as being somewhat on the poor side. Everything suggests that they have found themselves in a situation where they are completely out of their depth. To take a valuable find like the Preserver map and the field generator and then to utilize it merely to reap a profit from unscrupulous hunters! It is evidence of a lack of imagination on a staggering scale."

"But if it should occur to the gang to try and sell this technology to one of the Federation's foes . . ." said Geordi. He didn't have to complete that thought: The implications were obvious.

"There is still a further complication," Data added. "If Mr. Nayfack's account is correct, then these dragons he speaks of are presumably an endangered species. We are bound by the Federation charter to protect them from outside exploitation."

"But not from *internal* exploitation," Geordi pointed out. "If the world is Prime Directive material, then we cannot impose our conservation laws on the natives."

"Are we even going to think about protecting an animal species that preys on humans?" asked Ro. "Surely that's something for the natives to decide and not us."

"We have to *think* about it, Ensign," Picard said gently. "These . . . dragons were native to this world, it seems, before the humans were. To simply allow them to be exterminated is not an option any of us would willingly consider." Picard sighed. "In short, gentlemen and ladies, we have a ghastly mess. There does seem to be only one possible course of action: We must have further information. Therefore we must investigate." He rose to his feet, signalling that the meeting was at an end. "If this Castor Nayfack can indeed lead us to a tunnel through this dust cloud, then we must penetrate it and then investigate this planet. Mr. Worf, please contact your security representative and have him escort Mr. Nayfack to the bridge. It is time for him to prove at least the first part of his tale."

The Klingon officer looked even gloomier than normal. "You intend to trust this man, Captain?" He quite obviously was not as willing.

"I think we should give him the benefit of the doubt for the moment, Mr. Worf." Picard watched the others file out of the room, returning to their posts on the bridge. Beverly remained behind. She smiled at him, but there was no humor in it. "Is something troubling you?" he asked gently.

Her face twitched for a moment. "Have you ever seen the effects of tachyon fields on the human body, Jean-Luc?" she asked.

"No. But I have read up on them."

"I'm sure you have," she agreed. "But I had to stand by and watch three people die as a result of a small slip in a laboratory accident. There was nothing I could do to save them. Nothing *anyone* could do. The tachyons ripped apart their molecular structure, basic particle by basic particle. They died in terrible agony."

Picard gently took her elbow. He knew that Beverly took every death as a personal loss. "I promise you," he assured her, "that my ship will not enter that cloud unless I am convinced that we will all be safe."

"I know that, Jean-Luc." She gave him a real smile this time. "And I'm not trying to influence your judgment in any way."

"Yes, you are," he replied good-naturedly. "And if you didn't, I'd have much less trust in you than I do. Do you want to watch this from sickbay or the bridge?"

She shrugged. "The bridge, I guess. If anything

happens, there's precious little point in trying to prepare sickbay anyway. We'd have at most thirty seconds before we all died."

Picard nodded solemnly. Whatever lay ahead for the ship, they were skirting the edge of disaster. One false step could kill every single person aboard in a horrifyingly painful manner.

Chapter Six

The shifting tendrils of color writhed in the huge viewscreen on the bridge. Picard, seated in the command chair, was fascinated by the patterns and whorls in the cloud. It was so easy to become so lost in the beauty of Creation that one could sometimes forget the savage fury that often underlay it. Furies that could shred his vessel and crew into shattered subatomic particles in microseconds.

Still, it *was* beautiful.

Ensign Ro was back at her seat in navigation. "Course set and on the board," she reported. "Holding steady at two-thirds impulse."

"Sensors show no evidence of any tunnel so far," Data reported from beside her.

Nayfack winced under the look of distrust that Riker shot him. "If it *were* visible at this distance,

Captain," the agent responded, "then it would have been discovered before now, wouldn't it? Believe me, you can't detect the thing until you're right on top of it."

Beverly stared at the screen in awe. "I have to confess, it seems a little hard to believe. Why would the Preservers go to all this trouble over one small planet? Driving a hole in the protocloud and building a tunnel like this? It seems like a tremendous waste of time and effort."

"Who knows why the Preservers did anything?" Deanna answered her. "Perhaps simply because they *could* do it."

"Or to ensure that this world was left strictly alone," Riker suggested. "A kind of controlled experiment, cut off from the rest of the galaxy?"

"Well, it's not alone now," Nayfack said bluntly. "You'll see."

"Indeed we will," agreed Picard. He continued to watch patiently as the *Enterprise* moved slowly along the coordinates that Nayfack had supplied. The cloud shifted shape as they approached it, and the colors danced throughout the spectrum.

"No change," Data reported.

Picard could see the tension of all but the android in every move they made. Data's lack of emotions made him immune to the undercurrent of nervousness that everyone else felt. While Data was just as likely to be destroyed as the flesh-and-blood members of the crew, he simply could not worry about it. Everyone else could—and did. There was a knot of tension in Picard's own stomach. One mistake as they approached the cloud . . .

"Coming up on the target," Ro reported. Her voice was even, but there was strain showing. The ship was far closer to the raw, primeval forces than anyone had expected to go.

"Shields holding," Worf called out. Not that they would be able to withstand graviton pulses if Nayfack's information was inaccurate.

Slowly the cloud drifted on the scanner.

Data suddenly inclined his head slightly. "Sensors are detecting an anomalous reading," he reported.

"Clarify!" Picard snapped. This could be the first sign of trouble, or—

"It appears to be a dilation in the substance of the cloud."

"It's the tunnel!" Ro said, grinning widely.

"I believe I just said that," Data told her.

There were audible sighs of relief all around as the screen focused in on Data's anomaly. It did indeed resemble nothing as much as a tunnel. The colorful swirls of the gasses in the clouds looked as if someone had bored a long, narrow hole straight into the heart of its substance.

"Sensors show zero tachyon activity in the anomaly," Data reported. "It appears to be safe to proceed."

Picard held back the order for a moment. He caught himself strumming his fingers on his chair arm and forced himself to stop. It was a bad habit he was given to in times of great stress. This was a way in—if the tunnel didn't suddenly collapse. There was no reason why it should—and just as little reason why it shouldn't. As the *Enterprise* hung in space directly aligned with the tunnel, Picard asked: "Data, can you probe inside the anomaly at all?"

Data shook his head. "My instruments can only penetrate about a quarter of the way in. They show nothing beyond that at the moment."

"Would there be any point in launching a probe?"

"Negative," replied the android. "It is unlikely to increase the depth of our scanning ability."

"Any sign of what is holding the tunnel open?" asked Picard.

"It would appear to be a tachyon funnel of some kind." Data gave him a very serious look. "Which is, according to current thinking, impossible, of course."

"Of course," agreed Riker with a slight smile. He looked at Picard. "Shall we investigate the impossibility, Captain?"

"Ensign?" Picard called to Ro.

"Course laid in," she reported. "Straight line math—very simple and direct. Awaiting the command, Captain." Her fingers hovered over the keyboard.

Now was the moment. Picard stared at the cloud and the tunnel. "Make it so," he ordered. "Ahead, one quarter impulse."

"Aye, Captain." Ro's fingers danced across her board. "One quarter impulse."

On the screen they all saw the tunnel growing in size as the ship approached it. They were closing in on a vast stellar nursery. The forces giving birth to stars within were perhaps the strongest since the Big Bang that began the whole process of Creation. And they were venturing inside.

"Entering the cloud perimeter . . . now," reported Data. "Tachyon activity is completely absent from about the ship."

"Shields holding at full strength," Worf added.

"Keep probing ahead," Picard ordered Data. "Let me know the second you show anything at all ahead of us. Ensign, increase to one half impulse."

"Aye, sir."

Beside Picard, Beverly breathed gently. "It's incredible," she whispered.

The tunnel extended into the cloud. On the screen Picard could see the whirling madness of color surrounding them. The tendrils of the cloud were dancing feverishly outside of the anomaly. The energy fields out there were astounding. But here, within the tunnel, they were completely safe from that raw savagery.

He hoped.

It was as if the whole ship were traveling down the tube of some kaleidoscope of the gods. No other starship crew had seen such sights. It annoyed Picard to think that a ragtag bunch of small-time crooks was withholding such a sight from the rest of the Federation.

It was several minutes before he could bring himself to say anything. Even then, he was the first to speak. Everyone else was lost in his own thoughts, staring at the wonders on the screen. "Mr. Data," he said softly, unwilling to jar the mood too much, "is there anything showing on your sensors yet?"

Data, of course, had been silent simply because he had nothing to report. Though he could admire the aesthetically pleasing configurations and colors of the cloud, he was unable to feel the awe that touched everyone else. "No, Captain," he replied. "There appears to be no incoming information at all." Puzzled, he summoned up a diagnostic on the sensor array. "Captain," he reported, "I am experiencing some form of instrument malfunction."

Picard anxiously leaned forward in his chair. The last thing they needed here was for their sensors to go down! "What kind of malfunction?"

"Unknown."

"Blast it, Data—*speculate!* We can't afford to lose our sensors."

With a slight bow of his head the android acknowledged the problem. "I would guess that the tachyon fields are affecting the instruments, Captain. The wave-fluxes are of an extraordinarily high level. We may indeed lose almost all of our sensory input."

Picard caught the anxious glance Riker gave him. His face twisted into a scowl. Of all the times for this to happen . . . Should he have Ro back them out? Without sensors there would be no warning if the tunnel collapsed about them. But he knew that he couldn't retreat now, not without some real threat to the ship. He had to know if there really was a planet at the heart of this cloud. "Keep me informed of sensor status every two minutes," he ordered gruffly, then turned his attention back to the screen.

They were completely immersed in the cloud now. It was several light-years across, and they had to be at least a third of the way into it. It was fascinating—as well as frightening.

"I am getting a very sketchy reading, Captain," Data called out. Had it been two minutes already? "There would appear to be an object directly ahead of us."

"An object?" Riker managed to speak first. "What *kind* of an object? A ship?"

"Unknown, sir," replied the android. "My readings are broken up by the interference, and the object matches no known configuration."

"I can tell you what it is," Nayfack offered. He seemed unaffected by the sights on the screen. "It's the orbital station that generates the tachyon-warping fields of the tunnel."

"Interesting," Picard said. The picture on the screen was changing now. It looked as if there was more than light at the end of *this* tunnel.

As the starship emerged, they were all struck silent by the sight ahead of them. Close by and completely visible was a huge construction, spinning slowly in space. It had to be over a mile across and was coin-shaped. A large fin jutted out of the upper surface. It reminded Picard of an immense sun dial. Beyond it . . .

Beyond it lay their target. In a spherical clearing burned a pair of stars. They were a binary pair consisting of a larger reddish member and a smaller, slightly blue one. There were pinpricks of light about it that had to be planets. It looked as if they had entered some cosmic womb, and there ahead of them floated a strange child, awaiting its birth.

"Mr. Data?" he prompted.

"Fascinating, Captain." The android spun about to face the command circle. "Though the tunnel is evidently generated by this device, this area of the cloud seems to be swept through some unknown natural phenomenon. This region of space is completely devoid of all beta tachyon infestation."

Riker frowned. "You mean that the device made the tunnel but not this bubble?"

"Correct, Commander. And the stars we are approaching are a purely natural phenomenon also. It is a common binary pair, with seven planets in orbit around the blue dwarf. There are a further two worlds orbiting the red giant. My sensors are showing a great deal of interference because of the artifact, and I am unable to scan the planets. I am certain that the two worlds orbiting the red giant cannot be the abode of life. Both are far too close to the corona and must be bathed in solar radiation."

Nayfack gestured. "The planet we're after is the closest to the blue star."

"Ensign," Picard ordered, "lay in a course for that world."

Ro glared at him. "It's easy to say that," she answered. "But when I can't get any reliable position for the damned thing . . ." Her voice trailed off. "But you want results, not excuses, right?"

"I believe you understand me," Picard said, resisting the urge to smile. "Please carry on."

"Aye, sir." She set about doing her best, muttering under her breath in her native tongue. Picard was glad he couldn't speak Bajoran; he was certain he'd need a very good grasp of invective and bodily functions to follow what Ro was saying.

Geordi's voice came over the intercom from engineering. "Captain, I'd love to go over and find out what makes that sweet piece of machinery tick."

"I'm sure you would, Mr. La Forge," Picard replied. "But considering that that machinery is holding open our only means of egress from this place, I doubt that would be wise."

"I know that, Captain. But I can wish, can't I? I can't even get any good readings of it from the sensors."

"We all have our crosses to bear, Mr. La Forge." Picard knew how frustrated Geordi had to be—to be this close to an alien artifact and completely unable to get any hint as to what made it function.

Data called out: "There is no improvement in our sensors, Captain. We are going to be relying almost entirely on visual observations here."

Picard rubbed his chin thoughtfully. "Will this interference affect communications between the ship and an away team?"

"Almost undoubtedly," Data replied. "The fields are not constant, so communications will be possible, but not at all times."

Beverly leaned forward. "You're sending a team down there, Captain?" she asked.

"No," he replied. He knew there was going to be considerable argument from everyone over his next statement, but it had to be made. "I am going to *lead* a team down there."

Chapter Seven

As Picard had anticipated, Riker was the first to object. "Captain, I can't allow that. It's an unknown world, and it is also my duty to lead any away team."

"Normally, I'd agree," Picard answered. "But, once again, this is not a standard situation. Mr. Nayfack has informed us that this is a world colonized by human stock. Clearly conditions there will support human life. And you know as well as I do, Number One, that Starfleet regulations state that in cases where the Prime Directive has been broken, the captain of the vessel must make a personal examination of the situation and attempt to rectify it. With the communications problems that Data anticipates, I can hardly stay up here and gather all the information I need, can I?"

"Nevertheless," Riker began. "I still don't think that we can risk you on initial contact."

This wasn't going to be easy. "Excuse us for a moment, please," he said. "Will, perhaps we could continue this in my ready room?"

Riker's eyes narrowed. He was obviously puzzled by Picard's request. "As you wish."

Beverly watched the two of them leave the bridge and enter the ready room. As the door hissed shut, she turned to Nayfack. The man was standing in the space behind Ops, an unworried grin on his face. "Were you given any inoculations when you went down to the planet?" she asked him.

"Lots." He flashed his teeth at her. "The place is apparently subject to a number of diseases, some of them quite lethal."

"I thought as much." Beverly shook her head. "Most pretechnological worlds seem to cook up new diseases faster than hot meals. If there's going to be an away team, I'd better have my staff prepare some broad-spectrum shots for everyone." Tapping her communicator, she began issuing orders to the head nurse on duty.

Ro glanced around and sighed theatrically. "Typical. I perform a miracle of navigation to get us to this planet, and the captain's not even here to tell me what a genius I am."

Data stared at her. "From what I have monitored of the captain's conversations with you, Ensign," he told her, "I do not think that there was much likelihood of his making such a comment."

"It was a joke, Data."

"Ah." The android had long ago resigned himself to never being able to understand the human concepts of humor. The door to the ready room hissed open.

Picard and Riker strode back onto the bridge. Data immediately reported: "Ensign Ro has apparently performed exceptional deeds of navigation and brought us to the target world, Captain. She awaits being declared a genius." Seeing the astonished expression on the captain's face, he added: "I believe that is a joke."

"Not anymore," Ro muttered, her face turning red.

Picard wasn't even going to try and field that one. "Standard orbit, Ensign," he ordered. "Mr. Nayfack, the accuracy of your information has been exceptional to date. Perhaps you would be kind enough to address a meeting of the command staff prior to my assigning officers to an away team?"

"Of course," the agent agreed. "Do I take it that you've finally decided to trust me, then?"

Picard smiled. "As I said, you've proved your reliability this far. I am willing to take the rest on faith, at least for the moment."

"Better than nothing," Nayfack observed cheerfully.

"Much." Picard glanced around the bridge. "Mr. Riker, Mr. Data, Worf, Counselor, Doctor, Ensign—would you care to join us once more in the briefing room?" He tapped his communicator. "Picard to Engineering. Mr. La Forge, would you kindly report to the briefing room?"

"On my way, Captain," the chief engineer replied.

From their posts at the surrounding stations, the relief bridge crew moved down to take over from the personnel tapped for the meeting. The duty officer slipped into the command chair. "Orders, sir?" he asked.

"Maintain standard orbit, Mr. Van Popering," Picard told him. "I know sensors aren't much use, but try and scan the planet below. If you can get anything useful, let me know. And inform me instantly if there is any change in the tachyon background count."

"Understood, Captain."

Picard strongly hoped that there wouldn't be. By the time the ship registered any rise in beta tachyons, they would probably all be as good as dead anyway.

By the time the meeting assembled in the briefing room, Van Popering had managed one of his feats of research again. He patched through a holographic projection of the planet below them with one of the bloblike continents lit in red. There were twelve small points of light, all on or close to the coast of this continent.

"That's the best we can do, sir," he apologized. "Only one continent shows signs of intelligent life. There are just a dozen small cities and virtually no signs of industry or anything."

"Excellent work, Mr. Van Popering," Picard commended. He turned to Nayfack. "Right, what can you tell us about the planet?"

The long-haired man stepped forward. He gestured at the display. "As the sensors show, there are five large continents and a number of small chains of islands. Most of it is pretty bland stuff, filled with smaller reptilian species that must be first cousins to the dragons. These beasties themselves live only on the main continent, where all of the settlements lie. There are several chains of mountains, which is where the dragons prefer to live, along the coast here and here, and then in the central massif. The human towns—actually more like fortified villages than real towns—lie on the coast or on navigable rivers. There's some trade between the settlements, and some fighting. The towns are all ruled by dukes—local warlords, I suppose you'd call them. They're constantly making and breaking alliances."

"Do they ever fight wars?" asked Ro, with interest.

"They can't," Nayfack replied. "They couldn't put out an army because the dragons would spot a large concentration of men and attack. They seem to have developed a real love for human flesh and will often ignore easier prey if there are people around. As I said, this does discourage travel. Anyway, the chief town is here, on the coast." He pointed to the most eastern of the pinpoints of light. "It's named Diesen, and this is where the poachers have their base. They've hooked into the local duke somehow and pose as legitimate businessmen. They run their hunting preserves on the side." He gestured to where he had indicated the mountains to be. "There's a survival dome in the foothills, way off the main track, that they use for a hunting cabin. The hunters stay there, well away from the towns. It's not normally manned unless there's a hunting party on planet. Naturally, it'll be empty now, so we'd have to go to Diesen."

Picard studied the holographic projection thoughtfully. "Mr. Data, what can you tell us about thirteenth-century Germany that may throw some light on the people here?"

The android inclined his head slightly, turning his own yellow eyes onto the globe. "It was a society based on status," he explained. "The nobility ruled everyone. They had their own private armies, funded by taxation of the peasants and merchants. The main strength lay in the Teutonic knights. These were men who wore suits of armor made from forged iron and who rode war-horses of considerable strength and skill. These knights all subscribed to a concept known as *chivalry,* from the French *cheval,* meaning a horse. It was an ethical code based on honor and strength."

Worf smiled, baring his teeth. "It sounds like an excellent principle. I could like those humans."

Data shook his head slightly. "It was mostly lip service that was paid to the concept of chivalry," he explained. "Frequently the knights ignored the precepts and simply became bullies. Many took whatever they desired, knowing that there was no one who could resist them. The knights answered only to their liege lords, though they often plotted to overthrow weak or unpopular lords and take their places." He paused and then looked over to Worf. "In fact, it was a system very much like that of the Klingon homeworld."

"So it would appear," agreed Worf. The smile was still on his face. Picard knew he was imagining what the world below must be like.

"The other main force on society was that of the Catholic Church," Data continued. "The peoples of this time and area were all, in at least nominal standing, members of that church. The local bishops possessed much power and authority—and frequently their own armies, also. The church claimed spiritual authority for its practices and attempted to control the society. Theoretically, the nobility were ordained by God in their estates, so they were supposed to bow to the authority of the bishops. In fact, the nobles often meddled in the matters of the church, appointing or arranging the appointment of men loyal to themselves in the ranks of the clergy. Both factions—nobles and bishops—competed for ultimate authority.

"What this meant for the mass of the population was that they paid taxes to the lords and tithes to the church. Both were supposed to help the average person—one on the Earth, the other in heaven. In actuality, what frequently happened was that each became greedy and desired to increase their own portion of the take. Corruption was inevitable, and many in positions of power used those positions to better themselves financially at the expense of the lower members of society, who could do very little about the situation."

"It sounds dreadful," Beverly commented.

"It sounds typical," Ro said. "Power and greed are common bedmates throughout the galaxy. The strong prey on the weak."

"Go on, Data," Picard urged.

"Except when the clashes between nobles and the clergy became open hostilities," the android lectured, "little of the power struggle concerned the common man and woman. They simply worked to stay alive and to raise their children. There was a general belief in the powers of magic and witchcraft. Superstition was rampant, as were ignorance, illiteracy, and violent death. There were many diseases, exacerbated by the lack of sanitary knowledge and the prevalence of vermin."

"The perfect vacation resort," quipped Riker.

"Hardly." Data paused and inclined his head. "Ah—a joke."

Picard smiled slightly. "Precisely." He looked at the projection again. "Mr. Nayfack, the away team will obviously have to beam down to this town of Diesen. If these settlements are so small, we are bound to stand out somewhat as different, if only by our accents. Are there any people who habitually travel about the continent?"

Nayfack shrugged. "Very few. Most people don't like the idea of being eaten by a dragon." He considered for a moment. "Musicians and singers. Entertainers. Sometimes students."

"Hmmm." Picard considered the matter. "I doubt we'd make convincing students," he decided. "Since we have no idea what books we should have read. Musicians, I suppose." He smiled wistfully. "I manage to hold my own with a flute." This was the legacy of a particularly odd alien contact he had made.

Worf glared at him. "You are going with the away team, then?"

"Yes, Mr. Worf. Commander Riker has agreed to bend his interpretation of the rules a little to allow me to go."

"So," Geordi asked. "Who else will be along?"

"I have to rule you out, Mr. La Forge," Picard apologized. "Much as I'd like to have you along, your VISOR would make you far from inconspicuous."

Geordi grinned widely. "Yeah. I kinda guessed that."

"I want to take as few as possible," Picard continued. "This is not an armed raid but a swift reconnaissance mission. Once I know what the situation is, then we can discuss any plans to rectify matters. Mr. Nayfack will obviously be with me to lead me to the criminals. Data will come with me." He stared at his yellow-skinned android officer. "A little makeup will obviously be in order beforehand," he added. "We must not reveal ourselves as aliens."

"It is my place to accompany you, also," Worf growled.

Picard shook his head curtly. "Out of the question, Worf. What I said about Geordi applies doubly to you. You are not exactly able to blend into the crowd."

"Besides," Deanna said with a smile, "you don't play any musical instruments."

"Then the captain must take one or more of my officers," Worf stated. He didn't look at all happy. Then again, considering he always looked like he was having his teeth extracted by terrified amateurs at the best of times, it was rather hard to tell. "He must be protected."

"I concur," Riker stated.

Picard had to smile. "Thank you for your concern, gentlemen. I trust I shan't be getting into trouble. We are not in real danger from the natives, and, frankly, the villains we are after sound as if they're hardly going to detect and ambush us when we land. I am not anticipating anything more than a brief survey for this initial landing so that I may get an idea of the lay of the land. Any actions against the hunters will be taken by a second away team, which Commander Riker will lead." He glanced around the table. "This team will stand ready to transport down. Mr. Worf, you will detail twenty of your security team to be part of the assault force. As soon as we determine where the ringleaders are located, then they will beam down and arrest the criminals. Mr. Nayfack will be able to alert me to any potential trouble. With Data along I think that I shall need only one further member of my away team. I had in mind Ensign Ro for that task. If you both agree?"

Riker glanced at the grinning Bajoran. He knew from personal experience what she could be like when angry. "I have no objections."

"She is not a Klingon," Worf said. "Nor is she a security officer. But she is capable. I would still prefer that you take along one of my personnel."

"Agreed," Picard smiled. "But only one."

"I would suggest Lieutenant Miles," Worf said. "Then I shall be satisfied."

"And I'm grateful to be part of the team, Captain." Ro rubbed the ridges of her nose. "Except it means more cosmetic surgery. I doubt Bajoran styles of beauty apply here."

Beverly patted her arm in a kindly fashion. "It won't hurt a bit, I promise."

Her eyes glittering wickedly, Deanna asked: "And what instrument do you play?"

"I don't," Ro replied. "But wait till you hear me sing!"

Picard said firmly: "That will be the full away team. The five of us should be sufficient for a quick evaluation of the planet." He rose to his feet. "That will be all for now. Mr. Data, Ensign—if you would accompany Mr. Nayfack and myself to Stores, we'll see about getting ourselves outfitted for the journey." He turned to his Klingon officer. "Have Mr. Miles meet us there, please."

* * *

The head of Stores was Smolinske, a tall, elegant woman of indeterminate age. She looked up from her deskpad as Picard entered. Tapping the "save" command, she examined him with interest.

"What is it today, Captain?" she asked. "An Andorian wedding? A Japanese tea ceremony? A Klingon death ritual?" It was her duty to dress and outfit the away teams in the correct style under numerous conditions. She was extremely good at her job, and Picard took a perverse pleasure in trying to come up with the impossible for her. So far he hadn't even managed to make her blink. She had always delivered, no matter how bizarre the request.

"Thirteen-century Germanic garb," he told her. "Strolling minstrels. Nothing too flashy."

"Hidden communicators?" she asked.

"Yes. Probably as pieces of jewelry or something."

"Teach your grandmother to suck eggs," Smolinske sniffed. "*Cheap* jewelry, then. Don't want to tempt thieves, do we?"

"Quite correct." Picard had to smile. "And I shall require a flute and Mr. Data a violin."

"For medieval Germany?" scoffed Smolinske. "You'll have to settle for a shawm and a fiddle." She glanced at Ro. "And what will you require?"

"I'm going to be a singer," Ro said. "Something to keep the locals' interest."

The door opened, and Lieutenant Miles strode in. He was a tall, slim officer, with a mane of dark hair. Picard had met him only a few times but had been impressed with his alert manner and easygoing efficiency. If Worf had picked him to accompany the away team, then he was most likely an exceptionally good security man.

"Ah, Mr. Miles," Picard greeted him. "I trust you have no objection to playing percussion for our little group?"

"None, sir." Miles smiled. "I'm quite looking forward to our trip."

"Excellent." Picard turned back to the Stores chief. "Another outfit, with suitable instruments for Mr. Miles," he added. "A *bodhran* perhaps."

Smolinske grinned. "Sorry, Captain, that's an *Irish* drum."

"Whatever," Picard said, beaten again.

Smolinske sighed. "And you want it all yesterday, of course."

"Half an hour will be fine," Picard told her. "Meanwhile, we'll be in sickbay if you have any problems locating the right materials."

"Problems?" She sounded shocked. "It'll be ready before you are."

In sickbay Nayfack frowned slightly at Beverly. "I've already been inoculated against everything down there," he protested. "I assure you, I don't need more holes in my arm. Or chemicals in my blood."

"If this gang of yours is as efficient with their vaccines as they are with their plots," the doctor replied, "then you've probably already contracted the Black Death. It will relieve my mind to know you've been given the correct antibodies. And you *know* these hypos don't make holes."

"It feels like they do," he grumbled. But he allowed her to give him the shot. Then she moved on to the others.

Data had been given extensive makeup applications

to make his skin look human. He wore contact lenses that masked his yellow eyes and made them look brown. As an android, he didn't need the inoculation, so Beverly moved on to Picard, Miles, and then Ro.

It hadn't required much work to change her. Beverly had simply used pseudoflesh to build her nose out and cover the Bajoran ridges. Then she had induced growth in Ro's hair to give it more body, greater length, and a softer style. In the simple dress and cloak she wore, Ro looked very attractive, Riker noted.

Picard, in a jerkin and trousers of mixed off-brown colors, topped with a long cloak and a silly-looking hat, cut almost a rakish figure. He was completely unaware of it, of course. Beverly smiled fondly. Maybe she could persuade him to wear the outfit on a trip to the holodeck some day. And she'd try something like Ro's. . . . With a sigh she brought her wandering attention back to the present.

"Right, Number One," Picard said. "We're just about ready, I think. Remember—wait for us to call. Under no circumstances is anyone to try and contact us from the ship. I'd hate to try and explain that away if it should be overheard."

"Understood, Captain," Riker agreed.

Picard turned to the android officer. "Mr. Data, please remember that you are to act as human as possible while we are on the planet. I don't anticipate any problems, but the Prime Directive requires that you keep your true nature completely hidden from these people. They have no idea that such a being as yourself is even possible."

"I shall bear that in mind, Captain," agreed Data.

"Fine," said Picard, rubbing his hands together in

satisfaction. He tapped his communicator, which was disguised as the clasp that held his cloak secured. "Mr. O'Brien, are you ready to beam us down?"

"Aye, Captain," came the response. "Ready when you are."

"We're on our way. Picard out." He smiled at Nayfack, Miles, Ro, and Data. "Well, if you're all ready . . ." He gestured at the door and then led them out.

Beverly smiled to herself. Jean-Luc was obviously enjoying himself. Well, he deserved to do so. He didn't get much chance to dress up and play these sort of roles. She was rather surprised that Will Riker had allowed him to lead this team, whatever the requirements of the Prime Directive might be. As she moved to store away her hypo, Riker touched her elbow.

"Not just yet," he told her. "You'll be needing that again."

"Oh?"

"Yes. There's to be a second away team."

Beverly raised an eyebrow. "Would it be related to what the captain asked me to add to the hypospray?"

Riker grinned at her. "It would indeed. Sometimes our captain can have a very devious mind."

"Only sometimes?"

Chapter Eight

FEELING SOMEWHAT FOOLISH in his outlandish garb, Picard led his small party into Transporter Room 3. Chief O'Brien glanced up from his panel and almost managed to hide his smile before Picard could see it.

"All ready, Mr. O'Brien?" he asked.

"Well, we are having a few problems, sir," the chief replied.

"Anything that will prevent us from beaming down?" asked Picard sharply.

"Hard to say," O'Brien told him. "There's nothing wrong with the transporter itself, Captain. The graviton fluctuations don't create trouble there. It's the sensor array that's giving us grief." He tapped the panel in front of him and red lights began flashing all over the sensor panel. "Normally, I'd look for a quiet spot to set you down inside the village. But with all this going on"—he gestured at the flashing lights—"I couldn't begin to tell you whether you'd materialize in private or in a crowded room."

Picard turned to Nayfack. "This could be a problem. How did your hunters handle it?"

"They have a couple of houses in the city they rent under aliases," Nayfack replied. "Knowing when ships are due, they keep them empty at those times. It won't help us much."

"This is a problem I hadn't anticipated," Picard muttered, annoyed. To be stopped by something like this!

"If I may offer a suggestion," Data ventured, "we might beam down just outside the city proper. There is a small beach not far from the dock area. In the society we shall be visiting, few people cared for the beaches or getting wet."

"Capital idea," approved Picard. "Make it so, Mr. O'Brien. And try not to get our feet wet. We wouldn't want to be conspicuous."

"Aye, sir." O'Brien began to tap in the codes.

"Places," Picard ordered, striding onto the platform. Data, Ro, Miles, and Nayfack joined him. Seconds later there was a slight wrenching in his stomach (which Beverly assured him had to be psychosomatic) and a shimmering of his vision.

Then the five of them were standing on a stretch of sand beside the ocean. A bitter wind whirled through the rocks around them, tugging at Picard's cloak and hat and raising goose bumps on his exposed skin. He grabbed the edges of his cloak, tightening it about him to stave off as much of the cold wind as possible. Nayfack, Miles, and Ro did likewise. Data simply stared around.

"Mr. Data!" Picard snapped, trying not to let his teeth chatter. "Remember, you're supposed to be human! You should be cold, man."

"Sorry, sir." Data pulled his cloak about himself. "I shall endeavor to remember."

"Good." Picard turned to Nayfack, who didn't have to pretend to be chilled to the bone. "Perhaps you could lead us out of the wind, Mr. Nayfack?"

"My pleasure," the agent agreed. He gestured with his head, to avoid having to expose his hands to the icy blast. "This way."

The other four fell in behind him, following as he led them through the tangle of coastal rocks. They struggled on against the bitter wind. Finally, rounding a headland, they saw the town of Diesen ahead of them.

It was a natural harbor, thankfully shielded by the surrounding hills from the worst of the winds. A small river debouched into the bay, making the siting of the village obvious. It wasn't a large settlement, but there were huge walls about the landward side of the place. In the waters of the bay were moored thirty or forty small fishing vessels. With their destination in sight, they picked up their pace. A short while later they were in the town itself and sheltered from the winds almost completely.

Picard was fascinated. He loved history as an academic pursuit, but this whole place was like stepping into the past. The streets were cobblestone where they weren't dirt. The houses were small, crowded close together, and none too sturdy-looking. Most were of wood, with a dirty off-white plaster splattered over the wood. There wasn't much glass, and most houses were only two stories tall. Anything higher than that had a distinct tendency to sway slightly.

The people, by and large, were shorter than the captain. None looked in the peak of condition. Some bore obvious signs of crippling diseases, and most had pockmarked skin. When anyone smiled, Picard could see that few of them still retained all of their teeth—and that many mouths had nothing but rotted stumps. Their costumes were crude—resembling sacks tied about their waists. The men wore trousers and smocks, the women unadorned dresses.

Nobody spared the five strangers as much as a glance.

There was plenty of noise—people calling, horses clopping about dragging squeaky-wheeled carts, birds screaming and fighting in the streets over some choice morsel of trash, dogs barking and darting along the narrow paths. But worst of all was the stench.

"Gods!" cursed Ro, fanning her face. "I can't imagine how the locals stand the stench. I know I have a very sensitive nose, but this place *reeks.*"

Data was, naturally, unaffected. "It is mostly due to local concepts in sanitation," he explained. "All waste is thrown into the troughs in the center of the streets. This includes human bodily wastes."

Ro swiveled about to walk closer to the houses. "Great. No wonder it smells like we fell into a cesspit. We did."

Picard could sympathize with her. "And it's quite obvious why disease runs rampant here," he added.

Data gave him one of his stares. "If this is an analog of thirteenth-century Germany, then modern notions of disease will not occur for several hundred years.

And, given the retardation of progress on this world, perhaps not for thousands."

"I'm glad we don't have to stick around that long," Ro muttered.

"Believe me, I'm in favor of leaving here just as soon as we can." Picard turned to Nayfack. "Perhaps you'd be kind enough to tell us where we are heading?"

"Right." Nayfack pointed off in the direction they were going. "The duke's castle is up that way. In front of it is the market. He likes it close, so he can skim the profits from the merchants with less effort. The local contact for the gang is a man named Graebel. He runs a wine and spice store. He's on good terms with the duke, supplies him with the best of wines. Beer and watered-down rejects go to the local inns. As a trader, he has the duke's ear and passes along the bribes for not investigating the gang's activities."

"Logical," Data commented.

Nayfack shrugged. "They're pretty well established here by now. We have to cross the market to get to his store. It's likely to be kind of crowded there. If we get split up, we'll meet again at Graebel's place. You can't miss it: There's a large banner over the door. A rampant bear over two red stripes."

"Fine," Picard agreed. "Lead on."

The street they were following brought them into a small square. One of the buildings here was obviously an inn for travelers. Through an archway Picard could see the rear yard. A team of horses was being unharnessed from an uncomfortable-looking stagecoach. "There is obviously some intervillage travel," he commented. "Nobody would need that for getting around a town this small."

"Mostly mails and trade goods," Nayfack told him.

"Interesting," said Data. "That design is slightly in advance of its time. There is an attempt to provide springs for a smoother ride. Clearly there has been a modicum of evolution here since the colony was seeded."

"There's a little," Nayfack agreed. "Time hasn't completely stood still."

"What interests me," Miles pointed out, "is that there are plenty of other Earth creatures here." He gestured at a shaggy dog that was seated under the archway and scratching its coat ferociously, trying to dislodge fleas. "Obviously the Preservers must have brought along plenty of company for the humans they transported."

"Making them feel at home, probably," Picard mused. "I wonder if the locals know that they've been transported away from Earth? It might be intriguing to talk with a few locals—when our main task is over."

Nayfack led them through the square and into another of the narrow streets. This in turn led to the market square. This area was much more crowded and noisy but at least the smells improved.

There were dozens of booths, most of them gaudily arrayed in flags and streamers to attract attention. People flitted around the tables as they did on countless planets all over the settled galaxy. Traders bargained with potential customers while others shouted out the virtues of their wares. Picard was fascinated. There were dealers in pottery and simple metalware. There were some jewelers, but not many. There were armorers, most selling short daggers rather than swords. Some tables held brass knuckles and other nasty weapons meant to be hidden on the body. The common people were forbidden to wear actual armor, of course, that privilege being reserved for the nobility. Some stalls sold candles, the most common form of lighting. A few sold thick, pungent oils for lamps.

A great many of the stalls sold cooked food. Even in this cold climate the fresh food no doubt went bad very quickly. There were pies and pastries, breads and heavy cakes. There were sausages of all shapes and colors. There were smoked and salted meats. Birds—some plucked, most not—hung by their feet from hooks over the stalls. There were other carcasses that Picard couldn't begin to identify. There were creatures that looked very much like crabs, and others that Picard had seen illustrated only in texts on xenobiology. It was a curious mixture of familiar Earth and exotic—presumably native—life-forms.

There were stalls selling furniture and tools, along with others that offered bolts or pieces of cloth. Very few sold completed clothing. A number held pins, needles, and other implements for home sewing.

On the far side of the market square stood the grand duke's castle. From this angle the place looked to be all walls and towers. Most of the latter were flat-topped, but a couple formed spires. There were a number of men-at-arms stationed along the wall. Picard imagined that there would be more at the main gate.

It was difficult moving through the throng. Picard was getting rather irritated by the whole process when Data stopped dead in his tracks right in front of him. The pressures of the crowd shoved Picard heavily into the android's back.

"What the blazes are you doing?" snapped Picard, pushing himself away from the android.

"My apologies, Captain," Data replied. "But I would suggest that you examine the merchandise for sale on this table."

Puzzled, Picard and Ro both turned their attention to the booth Data had halted beside. It was clearly owned by a woodworker of no mean skills. There were musical pipes and carved birds in abundance. There were bowls, decorated with patterns of ferns and flowers. There were flagons and wine goblets, and there were children's tops and whips. There were footstools carved into the shapes of reclining dogs. There were small caskets and boxes with cheery faces grinning from the sides. There were carved drinking horns.

"It's very nice," Picard grumbled. "But I don't see the need to stand here and examine it."

"Captain, the next table holds some interesting pieces of silver jewelry." Data gestured. "Does none of it seem familiar?"

"No. Why—should it?"

Data inclined his head slightly. "It is very familiar to me. Last month I chanced to be perusing some books of art history. Many of the pieces in it bear striking resemblances to the pieces that we see here."

"That's hardly surprising, Data," Picard told him. "These have hardly changed designs in five hundred years or more."

"It is more than that," Data insisted. "Some of the artistry is absolutely identical. I can only surmise that some of these artifacts are being taken back to Earth and sold on the archaeological black market."

Ro admired a very ornate earring. She wished she

had some local currency with which to purchase the ring. "It's hardly surprising," she commented. "The gang *did* start out selling black market relics. They were originally archaeological plunderers. But wouldn't these show up as pretty fresh?"

Data shook his head slightly. "Given the concentrations of tachyons present in the cloud about this system, I can think of several mechanisms by which fake aging might be induced." He turned to Picard. "Captain, with your permission, I should like to look around a little before joining you at Mr. Graebel's establishment. I am intrigued to know the extent to which this little . . . I believe the word is *scam* . . . is being operated. I may be able to turn up further evidence against Mr. Nayfack's poachers."

Sighing, Picard nodded. "Very well. But don't be too long about it." As Data moved off to examine the stalls, Picard turned back to Ro. "Is it much farther, Mr. Nayfack?" Then the Captain stiffened.

There were plenty of people all about them, but there was no sign of the agent at all.

Chapter Nine

RO FOLLOWED THE CAPTAIN'S GAZE. A wry smile fluttered across her lips. "Do you think he's gotten lost?"

"If so, it's quite deliberate, Ensign." Picard's eyes glittered. Miles was about to move off into the crowd, but the captain shook his head. "Don't bother attempting to follow him at the moment," he ordered.

Ro's smile became wider. "Ah. Do I take it, Captain, that you expected something like this?"

"Of course." He snorted. "Federation security indeed! The man was a blatant imposter from the very beginning. I simply wanted to see how far he'd go in his little charade."

"What gave him away?" Of all the people she'd ever served under, Picard was the one that Ro had learned to respect. "I hardly thought you were gullible enough to believe him, to be honest."

"I take it that is meant as a compliment?" Picard

asked rhetorically. "I became convinced Nayfack was a fake simply because he knew too much about the gang's operations. I don't care how efficient he might be, the coordinates for the tunnel through the cloud would be their most closely guarded secret. The gang would never allow an outsider to discover them, no matter how inept they might be. Which meant that Mr. Nayfack was logically one of the gang, not a security agent. As for his absurd claim that the gang had a spy inside of Starfleet communications . . ." He snorted. "It was a transparent lie aimed at keeping us from reporting our findings."

Ro nodded. She had wondered as much herself. "And it explains his hasty and potentially lethal escape from the yacht," she agreed. "He *knew* that there were standing orders to blow up the ship rather than be captured. And he had no intention of dying."

"Quite." Picard gestured. "There seem to be a bunch of warehouses over to our left. Shall we make our way across?" As the trio moved, he continued. "What intrigues me is why he led us back here. I mean, it's obvious that he had to keep us from reporting in to Starfleet, but why bring a starship with the *Enterprise's* capabilities right into the cloud? If the gang has only a couple of pleasure ships at their disposal, he could hardly have imagined that they could defeat us. There has to be more to it than that."

Ro had been thinking through the captain's actions, trying to deduce his plans. "Then you think that he may have told us the truth about this Graebel being the front for the poachers?"

"Not for a second." He smiled at her. "I'll wager he's some local businessman—the first name that came to Nayfack's mind. But a short conversation with the man wouldn't hurt so that we can confirm or deny my assumption."

"You expected Nayfack to skip out on us," Ro continued. "And, logically, he's now reporting in to the *real* contact. . . ." She snapped her fingers. "The shots Dr. Crusher gave us all. You slipped a subcutaneous communicator into his."

"I knew you'd figure it out, Ensign." He beamed at her approvingly.

"And Riker—um, *Commander* Riker—let you beam down because you convinced him you'd be safe. And he's now trailing Nayfack."

"Absolutely splendid," Picard told her. "Data would be proud of your reasoning. Yes, Mr. Riker and Counselor Troi should now be following Mr. Nayfack to the real contact. As soon as they find out who that is, Mr. Worf's security team will beam down and round the criminals up. I hope the two of you are not too disappointed to be on the wild-goose chase."

"Not *too* disappointed," she replied. "It's interesting to watch you in action."

Rare praise from Ro! "Thank you," he said, accepting the compliment.

"And my task is to watch out for your safety, sir," Miles added. "Not to arrest anyone." He smiled. "Though a little action might have been fun."

Picard smiled back. "Well, let's just hope that this isn't too dull, shall we?" He stopped and pointed at a large, stone-walled building ahead of them. "Unless I'm very much mistaken, that must be Herr Graebel's establishment. The banner is just as Nayfack described it."

In the breeze the banner was snapping and twisting,

but the rampant bear and the red bars were unmistakable. The crowd thinned out as Picard, Ro, and Miles left the market proper and made their way across to the warehouse. There were no ground-floor windows—probably to deter would-be burglars—only a large, oaken door. Picard grasped the bear-head door knocker and slammed it twice. After a moment a small square in the center of the door opened up.

"Ja?"

"I wish to see Herr Graebel," he replied. "My name is Lukas. This is Rosalinde and Martel."

The suspicious eyes on the other side scanned them. After a moment the door was unbolted and swung open about two feet. "Enter."

Picard stepped inside, followed by Ro and Miles. The attendant slammed and bolted the door again before turning to them. He was a burly man, and the sword hanging at his side was hard to miss. He was obviously a guard as well as doorman. "This way, *bitte,*" he said gruffly. He swept his eyes over them again, and seemed satisfied that they bore no weapons.

"Danke," Picard agreed. He nodded for Ro to accompany him.

As Nayfack had claimed, Graebel obviously dealt in wines and spices. The room they were in was some forty feet across. Heavy racks lined the walls, and barrels filled most of the racks. Tall stone pillars provided support for the ceiling. Through the rows of barrels, they made their way to a flight of stairs leading to the second floor. The scent of spices filled the air—thyme, anise, cinnamon, and others Picard couldn't immediately identify. Lighting in the warehouse was sparse. Under his feet the earth had been packed hard, then lined with straw.

For this day and age it was clearly a wealthy establishment. In the twenty-fourth century on Earth, it would be considered a hovel.

The guard stomped up the creaking stairs. Picard, Miles, and Ro followed with a lighter tread. They emerged onto a short landing, with three doors, all closed, blocking their way. The guard rapped on the center one. "Herr Graebel—visitors."

"Come," called a voice from inside. The guard opened the door and gestured for the captain and his two companions to enter. Picard did so.

This room was much smaller than the main warehouse. It was also brighter and more comfortable. Lamps on the table and in the window alcove burned brightly, with the slight scent of oil. The room was lined with tapestries that showed various courtly scenes of knights on horseback and hunters and falconers after their prey. In the center of the room was a table and four chairs. All were well carved and probably cost a good deal of money. In the far corner was a tall chest, covered with some kind of runner. By the door was a tall desk, and on a high stool was perched Graebel.

The man was obviously well-to-do. His tunic and breeches were simple, but the material was clearly of fine workmanship. His boots were knee-length and without scuffs or marks of wear. There was a bracelet of gold about his right wrist, and a large signet ring on his right hand. He was slightly running to fat, and the veins in his nose were flushed a light purple. He obviously sampled his own wares fairly frequently. His dark hair hung to his shoulders and was neatly cut and styled. On his head—possibly to cover a bald spot—was a small cap.

As Picard studied Graebel, the merchant surveyed him. His disappointment that they were clearly not wealthy customers was hard to miss. "Herr Graebel," Picard said, bowing slightly. "My apologies for disturbing you, but I have a few questions to ask, if you have a moment?"

"Questions?" Graebel's eyes narrowed. "About what?"

"About a man named Castor Nayfack."

Graebel considered. "The name doesn't sound familiar. But"—he stood from the desk with a sigh and put down the quill pen he had been holding—"to be honest, I'll be glad of the break. Keeping records always makes my eyes ache." He looked up at the guard. "Fetch my guests and myself some wine."

Having grown up in a wine-making family, Picard was naturally intrigued at the opportunity of sampling the local wines. Since Graebel was to share a glass with them, he rather expected it would be of an interesting vintage. It would certainly enliven the process of interogating Graebel to see if he was connected to the criminals. Picard was more and more certain that he, Miles, and Ro were off chasing a red herring, but he reasoned that he might as well enjoy as much of it as he could while Riker finished off the mission. So when Graebel waved them to seats, he accepted. Ro sat beside him, and Miles by her side. Graebel eased himself into the chair facing Picard.

"So, Lukas," Graebel asked amiably. "What does this Herr Nayfack do for a living?"

"I understand that he's a hunter."

Graebel laughed and slapped his thigh. "Well, in

that case I should most likely not know him at all. Given my own weight, it is difficult to find a horse brave enough to attempt to carry me!"

Picard smiled politely. "I suspect you overstate the case, sir. I must confess, though, that I had thought that Herr Nayfack mentioned your name to me merely because you are a solid citizen of some renown in this town and he believed it would impress me."

The guard returned, bearing a silver tray. He placed this on the table, and Graebel waved him out. Grasping the pottery jar on the tray, Graebel poured a little into all four pewter goblets that were with it. He handed Ro and then Picard and Miles goblets, taking the last for himself. Miles stared at his drink without making a move to touch it.

Graebel wasn't insulted. "A suspicious one, eh?" he asked Picard. He held up his own goblet and took a good draft. "Ah, Gustaf brought the good wine." He nodded at Ro. "Is she your wife, Lukas?"

"I can speak for myself," Ro said. "Yes, we're married." She gave Picard a wicked smile. "Very happily."

Picard managed not to loose his smile. Trust Ro to stir things up! "Very," he agreed dryly.

Graebel nodded thoughtfully. "You are perhaps a little too gentle with her, Lukas. It is not a woman's place to speak out like that."

Picard was grateful that Ro kept her temper in check. "We're travelling musicians, sir," he said carefully. "Perhaps our customs are not as . . . civilized as those of this town." He took a sip of the wine. As he had expected, it was excellent. "Ah! A noble vintage, sir." He tasted a little, rolling it on his tongue. "A good body, mellow and not too sweet. There's a hint of rosemary and just a touch of apple, I fancy."

Graebel looked impressed. "You know your wines, my friend."

"My family owns a vineyard," Picard explained. "I spent my youth among the vines."

"Ah. Perhaps I know the family?"

"I doubt it," Picard replied. "I'm from Drakar." This was the name of the farthest city on the continent. "We never exported this distance."

"You've come a long way, then." Graebel smiled. "And you do not look like a vintner now."

Picard sipped his wine again. "No, I decided that while I enjoy drinking good wines, I was not cut out to produce them. I prefer to wander, I'm afraid."

"With your companions?" the merchant asked, nodding at Ro and Miles. She smiled sweetly and took a deep gulp of her wine. Picard winced. It was not the right way to savor a good vintage. Miles was cautiously sipping at his own.

"Yes, that's right. We're newly arrived in Diesen. We did meet up with this Nayfack, and he suggested we speak to you."

Graebel nodded. "Well, if you aim to stay a while, perhaps I can find you a few places where you might be able to make money with your music. Does the lady play or sing?"

"She sings," Picard replied.

"Excellent. There's a great demand for good singing." Graebel smiled widely. "It does explain her brash manner. She is no doubt used to much flattery and attention."

Nodding, Picard had to catch himself. He felt

slightly giddy. It was his own fault, really, for taking wine on an empty stomach. He should have known better. He moved to put his goblet down, to avoid the temptation of indulging in any more of the excellent drink. His hand didn't seem to want to find the table, and he sloshed some wine on the floor. "I do beg your pardon," he muttered, leaning forward to see how much he'd spilt.

He was unable to stop his body. He pitched forward, slamming onto the edge of the table, then rolling to the floor. The room was swaying about him. He felt as if he were falling backward into a long, bright tunnel. He vaguely heard Ro stumble to her feet. Her goblet fell to the floor and bounced. Miles muttered something as he staggered upright.

"You—" Picard said in a very strained voice. "Drugged . . ."

Then Ro fell down, on top of Picard.

"Steady on, Ro," he muttered. "What will the crew think?" Then he dropped into the tunnel, and everything went blank.

Graebel glanced down at his drugged guests with satisfaction. There had been a hairy moment when the leader had shown some knowledge of the wine and its contents, but thankfully he'd been too preoccupied to notice the knockout juice in with the rest. The merchant had no idea why Nayfack had sent the two men and the woman to him. Presumably they were problems he wanted removed. Well, that was Graebel's specialty. . . .

He called for the guard, then bent to examine his captives. The older man was past his prime by the looks of him, but his life as a wandering player had left him with a good, muscular body. He could get a nice price for such a slave. The younger man was perfect for the mines. And the girl . . .

Graebel considered himself a fine judge of feminine pulchritude. He turned the girl's face in his hand. Flawless skin! He pried her mouth open. Even better —she had all her own teeth, and no sour breath to spoil a kiss. An excellent specimen!

The guard and his companion arrived. Graebel gestured for them to take Lukas out. Without effort they hauled him to his feet and dragged him from the room. Graebel's gaze returned to the girl. Grasping the hem of her skirt, he pulled it up to get a good, lingering look at her legs. For a moment he was tempted to have her sent up to his bedroom before he sold her. Then, regretfully, he realized he had better not. This one was good enough for the duke himself, and His Lordship hated his inferiors playing with his toys. Much as his body protested the decision, Graebel knew he'd better not touch this girl. He'd have to make do with his wife.

With a real sigh of regret, he let the skirt fall back into place. The sacrifices he made for his clients!

Chapter Ten

"MIND IF I JOIN YOU?"

Worf glared up from his glass of body-temperature *tagaak* milk. "I wish to be alone." The scowl with which he accompanied this statement would have sent almost anyone on the ship running for a good place to hide. Guinan simply slid into the booth beside the Klingon. "I wish to be alone," he repeated, this time showing his fangs.

"I heard you the first time," Guinan replied. "And, normally, I'd love to let you sit here and sulk by yourself." She gestured around the almost-empty Ten-Forward cabin. "But you're scaring off my customers, and that's bad for business."

"I am not sulking," Worf snarled.

"You want to talk about it?" Guinan gave him one of her I'm-ready-to-listen-to-whatever-you-say looks.

Worf shook his head curtly. "Since I am not sulking, there is nothing to discuss, is there?"

Guinan looked at him quizzically. "Alexander's showing great signs of maturity nowadays," she remarked. "Sometimes more than his father. You *are* sulking. I know that look. Now—do you want to talk about it, or shall I get six or seven people over here to evict you?"

Worf stared at her, wondering if she was really serious. He felt like a good fight. When it was obvious that she was merely using verbal force, he gave in. "It is not fair!"

"Now you're sounding even more like your son. What's not fair?"

Worf gestured at the planet that hung in space outside the huge viewport. "That is not." Gripping his drink almost hard enough to crush the unbreakable glass, he said: "This is the first human world we have ever found that appeals to me. They believe in the force of arms, ritual combat, honor and glory. And, because of the Prime Directive, I am the only one on the ship forbidden to visit the planet!"

"You're not the only one," Guinan told him mildly. "Geordi can't go down, for one."

"That is not the point," he snapped. "This is a world I would give almost anything to visit! A planet where humans understand the passion for combat!"

Guinan looked at the cheery world. It reminded her that she had no home—an old wound, but one barely healed. "Most of us grow out of that kind of passion," she remarked. "The humans almost have. My race did."

"Then you do not comprehend the true meaning of

the word *passion,"* he told her. "And there is good reason to remain combat ready. Your people lost the understanding. They were destroyed by the Borg without a fight."

"With the Borg," Guinan countered, "even a fight would have been useless. You can't defeat an enemy like that with weapons."

"You cannot defeat them any other way." Worf gave her a long, hard look. "We Klingons have a proverb. 'It takes two to make peace, but only one to declare war.' As long as there is one foe ready to declare war, we must be prepared to fight for peace. It is the Klingon way. It is the way of life." He gestured at the planet below the ship again. "The humans down there understand this. I would give anything to be able to visit them."

Guinan shook her head wearily. She should have known better than to argue with Worf. She could have had a lot more fun instead banging her head against the cabin wall. "The humans have a proverb as well: 'Be careful what you wish for. It may come true.' " She rose to her feet. "Can I make a suggestion, then?"

"If you must."

"Go and see Barclay in Engineering."

"Barclay?" Worf frowned. "What about?"

Guinan patted his arm. "Just do it," she said. "Explain your problem to him. Mr. Barclay has a very good understanding of frustrations. I really think he could help you."

"I will consider it," Worf promised. He looked a little more cheerful now. Well, Guinan amended, at least less likely to rip someone's arm off and beat them to death with it.

* * *

Riker strode through the backstreets of Diesen, trying to breath through his mouth. The earlier session in the holodeck had almost prepared him for the stench of this place, at least. Checking the homing detector that Smolinske had built into the pommel of his sword, he called over his shoulder: "He seems to be heading for the docks."

Behind him, Deanna Troi tried to muster as much grace as she could while holding the hem of her skirts a couple of inches out of the noxious mud. She was dressed as a fairly wealthy woman, wearing a long blue dress with lace trim and a small cap of similar color. Smolinske had assured her that this was all the rage, and Deanna had to admit that she didn't look at all out of place in the town. But the skirt was uncomfortable and impractical, given the terrible conditions of the street, and the cap was at once too small for protection against the rain and too large to forget she was wearing it. "Did you somehow bribe Smolinske into making me wear this torturous outfit?" she asked.

Riker grinned at her. He had come out slightly better, dressed in boots, trousers, and a tunic belted at his waist. He was supposed to be her man-at-arms, protecting her as she ventured forth on a shopping expedition. It gave him an excuse to wear the sword and to keep his hand on the hilt. It also meant that he was expected to clear the way through the crowds for her—by force, if necessary. He was grateful that the locals clearly understood the system and gave way before them. "No," he replied. "It was all her own idea."

"And I thought she liked me," Deanna muttered.

"Just be thankful she didn't suggest you pose as a harlot."

Deanna gave him a frosty glare. "Well, at least then I'd have gotten some practical clothes to wear."

Riker grinned and gestured at the indicator in the pommel once more. "Our target seems to have reached his destination. Not much farther."

"I couldn't go much farther." Deanna sighed. "Why do we get all the good jobs?"

"Because the captain likes us."

"If everyone likes us so much, why do I have to wear this stupid outfit?"

Riker grinned again. "Because it would look really silly on me. Come on."

Nayfack glanced over his shoulder for the hundredth time. There was still no sign at all of the gullible Picard—or Ro, or the android. As he'd suspected, those Starfleet types were all reputation and no brains. They'd fallen right into his trap. Now all that was left for him to do was to close the jaws around the *Enterprise,* and he was home free.

The booth in the side street near the docks was hardly conspicuous. Given its nature, it hardly wanted to be. Many of the locals, when they passed it, crossed themselves to ward off evil. It was known locally and shunned by all but the desperate. Nayfack sneered at the local superstitions. For all their Christian faith, the locals believed just as firmly in the Devil and the Black Arts.

And Dr. Hagan played up to it. A little imported technology, some hocus-pocus, and a good deal of intimidation worked wonders on the stupid yokels. Hagan was good at that. The whole town was convinced he consorted with demons, but they were too terrified of his powers to report him to the local officers of the church. Because of this reputation, any slips the gang made were easily covered up as witchcraft.

There was another advantage to the role. The local duke was a fervent believer in the powers of astrology and called Hagan to the castle frequently to consult with him. Hagan had the lecherous old goat eating out of his hand.

Nayfack slipped into the small shop. The room he entered was small and dark. Shelves lined the walls, all filled with bottles. The air was heavy with the sharp stink of preservatives, barely masked by the burning incense in the lamp on the small table. The bottles contained various chemicals, drugs, and body parts of numerous animals. They came in very handy for Hagan when he was supposed to be making magic. By the rear door, on a tall lectern, was a large globe of crystal, currently covered with a velvet cloth. This was his crystal ball, in the depths of which Hagan supposedly glimpsed the future. Tiny lights rigged inside it made some of the readings rather spectacular indeed.

Entering the shop had triggered a signal in the living quarters above the store. As Nayfack's eyes adjusted to the gloom, the curtain covering the door to the stairs was flung back, and Hagan swept into the room.

Nayfack had to admit that the man was very impressive. He wore long, pure black robes and a dark cap. In his right hand he carried a cane of twisted ash, the silver head molded in the shape of a snarling wolf, the eyes twin rubies that appeared to burn in the light of the lamp. On his left hand he wore a large ring on his forefinger. It was solid silver, in the shape of a skull. The eye sockets held small glowing emeralds.

Hagan was tall and well built. His skin was pale, and the black beard he sported for his role looked appropriately sinister. His dark eyes glittered angrily as he saw who his caller was. "Nayfack! You were supposed to have left with the ship. What's wrong? Did you get drunk again and miss the launch time?"

"No." Nayfack wasn't impressed with all this mumbo-jumbo. He knew that Hagan disliked him. Hagan disliked *everyone.* Well, see how snide and superior he'd be when he knew what was going on. "The ship has been destroyed."

The dark man stared sharply at him. "What do you mean? If you're concocting another of your stupid lies, I swear you'll end up in pieces in these jars of mine. You're the most miserable excuse for a first officer that I've ever had the misfortune to work with."

"Save the threats. I'm not impressed." Nayfack was enjoying himself. It wasn't often he had a chance to humiliate Hagan like this and show their boss how smart he was. Maybe the chain of command would change as a result of Nayfack's actions. He'd love to end up giving Hagan orders for a change. "The ship's gone. When we left the cloud, we ran into a Federation starship."

"You incompetent oaf!" Hagan glared at him, then shook his staff. "If you'd been intercepted by a starship, then you'd be dead by now."

"Oh, we ran into one all right. A science ship, mapping the cloud, I gather. The *Enterprise* herself."

Nayfack was addicted to the popular press and had seen enough vids that mentioned the famous exploration vessel. It had helped him to hoodwink the captain. "O'Leary triggered the self-destruct."

Hagan glowered at him in disgust. "You lying turd," he snapped. "If he had, you'd be dead by now. So why aren't you dead?"

"Because I didn't see any point in dying. I knifed O'Leary and Tanaka and got out in the survival pod."

"You couldn't have got back here in that," Hagan observed. He was making an effort to restrain his temper.

"Of course not. I came back in the *Enterprise.*"

As he had anticipated, this news almost gave the old fake a heart attack. "You did *what?*"

"Brought the starship in here."

The magician stared at him in open hatred. "You stupid, blundering imbecile! Aside from your natural idiocy, whatever possessed you to bring the *Enterprise* here?" His hand holding the staff was twitching furiously.

"I stopped them reporting in to Starfleet," Nayfack replied. "Right now they are the only ones who know about this place outside of us."

"Wonderful!" yelled Hagan. "All we have to be worried about is a fully armed starship! That you brought here! Against explicit instructions!"

"Yes," Nayfack agreed casually. "Stupid instructions, if you ask me. All we need to do is to destroy the *Enterprise* and we're in business again. Nobody else has the slightest idea that we're here."

"Destroy a starship. Oh, yes, very likely!"

Nayfack laughed. "Come on, you know what the boss has in that Preserver vault of his. It should be a breeze to get rid of them. All you have to do is contact him and tell him. And be certain you let him know that this was *my* idea. If I hadn't convinced Captain Picard I was a Federation security agent, he'd have reported the destruction of the yacht to Starfleet. The whole cloud would have been swarming with ships, and we'd have been finished."

"They would never have found the tunnel, you jackass!" Hagan shook his staff again. "You just did this to save your own miserable hide. And if the captain hadn't believed you, then you'd no doubt have told him everything to curry his favor and get a lesser sentence."

"Never," insisted Nayfack. He wasn't stupid enough to admit that had been his secondary plan. He could have bought his freedom with information.

"Do you think that if we destroy the *Enterprise* Starfleet will just ignore it?" Hagan was beyond fury now. "They'll take this sector of space apart with microscopes! Anything that can annihilate one of their ships will be of great interest and concern to them. You've placed us in greater danger with your stupid attempt to save your own miserable life."

"I'm helping us build a better bargaining platform," Nayfack argued. "Look, we know that the stuff the boss has stashed away in that Preserver base of his can wipe out the *Enterprise.* Once we've done that, we can contact the Ferengi, the Romulans, and the Federation. Offer to sell this stuff to the highest bidder and free passage to wherever we want." He didn't bother to mention that the idea was mostly culled from his conversations with Picard's staff. "Then we could retire and live in luxury. No need to work again."

"You moron," Hagan snarled. "We'd already considered the idea of selling what we've found. But we could never trust the Romulans or the Ferengi. They'd slit our throats and steal what they could. And the Federation wouldn't deal with a bunch of outlaws for this stuff. We're safer doing things the way we are, even if it means more work." He glowered at Nayfack in disgust. "But we all know how little you like work, don't we?"

Nayfack hadn't expected Hagan to be happy, but he was getting annoyed with the other man's refusal to see what he had accomplished. "Just contact the boss and tell him what I've done," he ordered. "Let's see what he's got to say."

"I know what he'll say." Hagan twisted the head of his cane, and there was a soft click. The wooden length fell away, exposing a long, thin blade. With surprising speed, he whipped the dagger up and thrust hard. Nayfack gave an incredulous grunt of pain and shock as the stiletto rammed into his heart. "He'll say he wished he had killed you long ago." Hagan twisted, then tugged the blade free.

Nayfack fell, his face still locked in a gasp of astonishment. He was dead before his body hit the floor. Hagan knelt, fastidiously avoiding the spreading pool of blood. He wiped the blade clean on Nayfack's tunic, then replaced it in its wooden sheath.

"You were always a problem to us," he said to the corpse. "Now I have to dispose of your body. And you've left us with no other option than to destroy the *Enterprise.*" He kicked Nayfack hard. It felt good, so he repeated the action. "You utter imbecile." He turned toward the curtain at the end of the room just as the front door opened.

His first reaction as the man-at-arms entered was

one of disgust. Now he'd have to *pay* this man to get rid of the corpse. All the swordsmen in this town seemed to have empty pockets. He unclipped the pouch of coins from his belt, ready to hand it over for services rendered. His second reaction was panic.

"Nayfack!" The man-at-arms stopped, seeing the body on the floor. Behind him, a finely dressed lady stumbled against him in the doorway.

Hagan realized that Nayfack's stupidity had surpassed even the loose boundaries he had set it. This pair could only be from the *Enterprise,* trailing the dead man here—to him! The whole game was unraveling, thanks to Nayfack. With a curse Hagan dropped the purse and leapt backward. His hands grabbed the jar he had left conveniently beside the exit and threw it down onto the floor in front of the swordsman.

Riker whipped around to shield Deanna as the jar exploded. Green flames leapt up from the floor. He managed to snatch up something from the carpet before heat seared across his exposed skin. He pushed Deanna backward, into the street. As they staggered out, the whole room caught fire. The wooden walls were thoroughly dry, and probably the shop's owner had treated them. Riker had seen only the swirl of the curtain at the far end of the room. The man had made his getaway, obviously long planned.

The fire danced about the room, turning a brighter yellow and crimson as everything burst into flame.

The inhabitants of the street began yelling and piling out into the open. With buildings as close together as these were, there was a real threat of the whole street—if not the whole town—going up in flames. Riker grabbed Deanna's arm and urged her back through the growing crowd. They hurried away, casting anxious glances back over their shoulders as the building writhed in the grip of the fire.

Deanna sighed. "I think that's what they call a dead end."

"Right." Riker stopped in an empty street. Everyone in this section of the town was rushing to help beat down the fire before it spread. When he was certain he couldn't be seen, Riker tapped the communicator button in his sword hilt. "Riker to *Enterprise.* Come in, Geordi."

His only reply was a crackle of static. He tried again, with the same results.

"It's no good, Will," Deanna said. "Geordi told us there was a good chance that the graviton fluctuations might interfere with transmissions. I guess we're cut off for the moment."

"Yes." Riker slammed his fist against the nearest wall. "Damn." Then he gave her a weak smile. "Well, I hope the captain is having better luck than we are."

Chapter Eleven

"Oh, that's very soothing." Lieutenant Reg Barclay closed his eyes and dug his fingers deeper into the soil. "Yes, you're right—it's a sort of primitive pull deep in the soul, isn't it?" He opened his eyes again and smiled happily at Keiko O'Brien. "It's really therapeutic, isn't it?"

Keiko's face wrinkled in a smile. "Reg, I think you're overdoing it a bit. I know I said that working with the soil is very relaxing, but it's not *that* great."

"Oh." Barclay jerked his fingers out of the dirt, brushing them off on the pants of his uniform. His face fell back into its normal expression of vague worry, coupled with an embarrassed flush. "I guess I was kind of trying a bit hard, wasn't I? But I do so much want to experience the thrill of returning to humanity's roots, so to speak."

Keiko couldn't restrain herself, and she had to laugh this time. Her husband, Transporter Chief Miles O'Brien, had recently befriended the overenthusiastic systems analyst. He had suggested to Keiko that she introduce Barclay to the joys of gardening, while warning her that Barclay's responses were sometimes a little out of alignment with reality. Now she could see what Miles meant—Barclay was simply trying too hard to experience the emotions that she had explained to him. "Just relax," she advised him. "Don't force it. Just do it, and let the emotions come by themselves. You don't have to dive into it. In fact, it's better if you don't. One of the great pleasures of gardening is that you can simply work without too much conscious thought. It's very relaxing, even when you get tired and sweaty."

Reg swallowed and nodded. "Okay, I'll try and remember that. Don't try too hard. Just relax and let it flow. Okay, got it." He gave her another nervous grin. "What's next?"

Laughing again, Keiko led him to a tray of seedlings. She loved her work in the botanical section, and it took very little effort to relay her love to Barclay. For all of his nervousness around her—and almost everyone else—Barclay was almost pathetically eager to please. He was very bright, but he was more at ease in the rarefied atmosphere of the intellect than with human contact. He was always uncomfortable around other people but constantly attempting to make them happy. Keiko could see why Miles thought Barclay would relate well to plants. It would be less emotionally draining for him than working with people. "I'll assign this tray of Andoran glitterlings to you," she said. "They grow quickly, so you'll see results in weeks instead of months. But you have to take good care of them, because they are rather delicate."

"Oh, I will, I will," Barclay promised fervently. Leaning over the tray, he beamed down at them. "Hello, little seedlings."

Keiko smiled again and handed him a compupad. "Here are all the instructions, Reg," she told him. "Just be very careful to establish a routine and stay with it." She gestured across the large indoor garden. "I have a lot of other work to do, so I'll leave you to get on with it, okay?"

"Okay," he agreed. "And—thank you, Keiko." He watched her leave and sighed. O'Brien was one lucky guy to have married someone as pretty and personable as Keiko. He wished he had that kind of luck, but he always felt so self-conscious about women. He was so afraid of making an idiot of himself that he invariably did precisely that.

He dragged his mind back to the matter at hand. He'd been given charge of these glitterlings, and he'd be very careful to cultivate them properly. Placing the compupad on the table beside the tray, Barclay reached over and gently touched the soil's surface with the tips of his fingers. He wanted to experience the earth that his little charges called home. Closing his eyes, he attempted to empathize with the seedlings. He breathed slowly and deeply, feeling himself relax. It really was quite therapeutic when you—

"Lieutenant Barclay!"

Barclay's eyes snapped open as he heard his name snarled. Facing him across the table was Worf. Unable to prevent himself, Barclay gave a yelp of terror and leapt back a pace, stumbling against another table of seedlings. The table rocked, and he grabbed at it wildly to prevent it from collapsing and scattering the trays all over the deck. His heart pounded in his ears. What had he done now that the head of security was after him? He couldn't think.

"Are you well, Lieutenant Barclay?" inquired Worf. "You seem somewhat—tense."

"Tense?" squeaked Barclay. "Me?" He swallowed hard. "Oh, no, sir. Not me. I'm fine. Perfectly fine. Just dandy, really."

Worf's eyes narrowed suspiciously. "You are certain?"

"Oh, yes, quite certain," Barclay assured him nervously. "Never felt better in my life."

"Good." Worf dismissed the problem. "I have come to seek your help."

Barclay's jaw fell. "My help?" He was at a total loss now. "Uhh . . . I don't understand, sir. My help with what? I'm off-duty right now. . . . But if it's important, of course I could reschedule my work period and—"

Worf couldn't understand why Barclay was ranting on like this. "It is a matter of leisure, Lieutenant, not work. Guinan suggested that you may be of assistance to me."

"She did?" Barclay was still in the dark. "Oh, well, I'm sure if she said that, then she's bound to be right. I'm definitely able to help you. She's always right on the ball." He blinked several times. "Uh—with what?"

Worf looked rather uncomfortable. "I am experiencing . . . envy," he finally admitted. "I am jealous of those persons who have been allowed to beam down to the planet below us. The culture of this world fascinates me." He smiled reassuringly at Barclay, who looked as if he might faint at any second. "Do you know anything at all about Germanic knights and their code of chivalry?"

"Chivalry?" On safer ground now, Barclay stopped trembling. "Oh, yes—lots! King Arthur and the Knights of the Round Table and all that! I love it!"

Worf draped a friendly hand about Barclay's shoulders. Barclay staggered under the weight. "Excellent, Mr. Barclay. Then it appears that Guinan was correct. You can help me."

"What would you like me to do, sir?"

"I want to meet these knights in combat. . . ."

Picard groaned as he started to waken. He tried to roll over to check the chronometer he'd brought with him, but was brought up short by a sharp tug on his wrists. He groaned again as he tried to open his eyes. His head felt terrible. What on earth could have happened?

His eyes refused to respond. Instead, he tried to bring his other senses into some sort of order. He was flat out on something very scratchy. His bare skin felt as if it had been whipped. He tried to roll over again, but once again his wrists caught fast. There was something around them both that rattled as he moved. And wherever he was stank. It was obviously not his cabin.

Then his memory began to come together again. He, Miles, and Ro had been in that merchant's shop. . . . What was his name? Graebel, that was it. They had been talking, and he'd suddenly lost all his coordination. He'd spilled his—

"Wine," he groaned. "He drugged the wine after all!" Miles had been right to be suspicious. And he'd just walked right into it. How foolish could he have been? He'd *known* that Nayfack wasn't to be trusted. Why had he blindly assumed the man would send him off to an innocent merchant? Innocent men don't drug their guests. He'd been so certain that he'd outsmarted Nayfack that he'd underestimated the ingenuity of the locals.

"Is that how they got you?"

Picard tried to straighten up, to discover who had spoken. A pair of arms slipped under his shoulder, enabling him to rise into an uncomfortable sitting position. The arms steadied him, then moved away, clanking in the same manner as Picard's.

"Here," the other man said. "Drink this."

Picard felt the rim of something touch his lips. What if this, too, was drugged? But his throat was on fire, and the water that touched his lips overcame his caution. He drank. Even though it was rather bitter—and probably none too pure—Picard's throat eased a little. "Thank you," he managed to croak.

His eyes had finally decided to listen to his brain. With difficulty he managed to open them. His vision was blurred, but he blinked, and then managed to focus. He almost wished he hadn't.

He was in a cell of some kind. The prickly stuff on the floor was old straw, which clearly served as bedding—for numerous insects as well as the human inhabitants of the cell. His wrists were clanking because they were manacled together. The smell and the lack of light were due to the fact that there was only one small opening for air and light, up by the ceiling. It was much too small to allow anyone out, and almost too small to allow light and air in.

"You'll feel better in a minute. Then you'll feel utterly miserable for the rest of your life. The one comforting thought is that it isn't likely to be very long."

Picard swiveled around to study his cell-mate. The man was of average height, with a shock of dark hair. Like Picard, he was bare to the waist and chained about the wrists. He had dropped the pottery cup back into the bucket of dirty water by the door. As he moved back to join Picard, the captain saw his face was pocked. Probably from disease. The man must have been lucky—many people died.

"What's happened to me?" Picard asked. His strength was returning, but he wasn't ready to move yet.

"You've become a mine worker, friend. Just like me and the other twenty or so men in this jail."

"A mine worker?" Picard shook his head. "There must be some mistake."

"I'm sure there is. You've made it, or you wouldn't be here. Drugged wine, you say?"

"Yes. A merchant named Graebel." Picard felt like kicking himself for being so arrogantly self-assured.

"Graebel?" His companion laughed bitterly. "The biggest slaver in Diesen, and you drank wine with him? I had hoped for at least an intelligent companion, but I guess I'm in for yet another disappointment."

"I didn't know his reputation," Picard answered. "I'm not from around these parts."

"Obviously." The man extended both hands. "My name's Kirsch. Michael Kirsch."

"Lukas," Picard replied, shaking his hand. "How did they get you?"

"Heresy." Kirsch smiled. "A trumped-up charge, of course. A convenience to them. I'm a scholar, really. Came here from Bittel to study. I must have stepped on a few toes with my theories. They had me up before the magistrate, and—" He shook his wrists. "I guess this means I don't get to publish. You?"

"I'm a musician," Picard replied, sticking to his story. "My companions and I—" He broke off sharply. "Ro!"

"Pardon?"

"I had two companions," Picard told him. He tried getting to his feet, but he lacked the strength to rise. "A man and a woman. Martel and Rosalinde."

"God, you *are* naive, aren't you?" Kirsch shook his head. "Graebel must be thanking God for the profits you brought him."

Picard felt a stab of fear for Ro and Miles. "Why? What will he have done to them? Are they going to be sent to the mines as well?"

"The man, probably. The girl? Not unless she's got the looks of a horse's backside, friend. Does she?"

"No." Picard shook his head. "To be truthful, she's very attractive."

"Well, I doubt that'll last long." Kirsch sighed. "I hope she wasn't too good a friend of yours. If she's lucky, she's been sold as a prostitute."

Picard groaned. "And if she's unlucky?"

"If she's unlucky, Lukas, she's been sold to the duke."

Picard wasn't willing to bet on her being lucky. Given the fortunes this far, he was certain Ro was going to be in a great deal of danger indeed. He willed himself to ignore the fatigue and pain as he pushed himself to his feet. "I've got to get out of here," he gasped, wincing with the effort.

"Oh, you'll get out of here all right." Kirsch loaned him a supporting hand. "We all will—from here right into the mines."

"What mines?" Picard took deep, slow breaths to control the buzzing in his head and the nausea that threatened to overcome him.

"The gold mines," replied Kirsch. "In the mountains. We're working for the duke now, as penance for our sins. Mining him gold, to make the old bastard filthy rich as well as just plain filthy."

"In the mountains?" Picard shook his head. "That's where the dragons are."

"Ah! You're starting to catch on. Like I said, the rest of your life is going to be miserable. But it'll certainly be short. If the mine work doesn't kill you, the dragons surely will. That's why they always need new supplies of slaves." He shook his wrists. "Us."

Wonderful. Not only had he managed to walk right into a trap, but he was now in chains, on his way to become either another statistic in the mine fatalities or else lunch for a hungry dragon. With his cloak gone, there was no chance of communicating with the *Enterprise*. It looked as if Miles would be in this prison with him somewhere. And he'd apparently dragged Ro into an even more unpleasant fate. His only hope was that she was in a better position to get hold of her communicator and contact the ship.

Ro came awake with a start. It took a few seconds for her to recall what had happened, then she cursed herself for a fool and a failure. She'd been suspicious of Graebel and had been conned by one of the oldest tricks in the book. She'd seen him pour all their wines from one jug and, after he'd drunk, felt it safe to do so, too.

The drug had been in the goblets before he'd poured, of course. How *could* she have been so dumb? Especially when the captain was depending upon her.

Her years of living on the edge had taught her a few tricks, though. Getting caught once was dumb. Getting caught twice would be criminal. Though she was awake, she'd not moved a muscle, or altered her breathing patterns. If she was being watched, nobody would know she wasn't still drugged. It might be useful.

Ro concentrated all of her energies into her other senses. Slowing her breathing slightly, she listened for any sounds she could pick up. Straining hard, she heard nothing. She flared her nostrils. Her sensitive sense of smell detected a variety of odors—cloth and candles. Incense. Wood. But no human scents save her own.

Her skin told her other things. First, that she was in a bed. The mattress below her was certainly stuffed with some avian feathers. So was the pillow under her head. The sheets were coarse but not too hard to take. And, finally, that she was completely naked.

Wonderful. Things were looking worse by the second.

She cracked her eyelids slightly, just enough to check that her initial deductions were correct. Then she opened her eyes, still not moving the rest of her body.

She was in a large bed in a fair-size room. The walls were of stone, covered with tapestries. There was a small table, a couple of chairs, and a chest at the foot of the bed. The room was lit by a candelabra that stood on the table and by a small window—barely more than a slit—up near the ceiling. There was no way out there, even if she was dressed. At least she was alone.

Well, there was no need to fake being unconscious without an audience. She sat up and looked around.

The tapestries left her in very little doubt about her fate. They weren't technically the most adept bits of weaving she'd ever seen in her life. But she doubted that their appeal was their artistic merit. There were three of them, one on each of the walls the bed wasn't up against. All three showed naked women being used by naked men. The tapestries were obviously meant to turn someone on. They left her with a chill in her soul.

As soon as she was certain her strength had returned, she swung out of the bed and padded silently across the carpet to the door. It was large and solid-looking. She tested the latch. Not surprisingly, it didn't give. She hardly expected that the owner of this place would trust her to stay here of her own accord.

Well, first things first—clothing. She hoped that there would be some in the chest, but it was empty. Terrific.

There was a sound at the door. Ro tensed, ready to leap on whoever came in, but then forced herself to relax. She wasn't recovered sufficiently from the drug to win a fight. For now she had to hope that she could keep the owner happy without getting too close to him.

The door opened slightly, and a young woman entered. She was carrying something wrapped into a bundle. The door slammed shut behind her and was locked. That meant someone on guard outside the door.

Eyes narrowed, Ro studied the girl. She looked terrified, and she was simply dressed. A servant, obviously, not an owner. She was dark-haired and quite pretty, in a frightened sort of way. But her skin showed evidence of disease having plucked at it in places. It probably rendered her safe from the sort of fate Ro knew was in store for her.

The girl held out the bundle. "This is for you to put on," she stammered.

Ro was being allowed to wear something, anyway. It would at least stop her teeth from chattering. "Thank you."

She took the clothing and unrolled it onto the bed. It was a simple dress but obviously too short for respectable wear in this town. There was no sign of underwear. She sighed. "Beggars can't be choosers." She was aware of the girl watching her as she slipped the dress on. Whoever had picked it out had at least gotten the size almost correct. It was a little tight across the chest and loose about the hips. Then she realized that this was exactly the way it was meant to be, of course. The skirt came partway down her thighs. She wished it were longer, because her legs were freezing.

"Now what?" she asked the girl.

"You must wait here. The duke will come when he is ready." Abruptly the girl grabbed Ro's hands and squeezed them. "Be brave."

Ro realized that the girl was terrified. Well, probably because she knew what the duke was like, and Ro could only guess. Those guesses weren't too inspiring. "Uh, thanks. I think. Is there any way out of this place?"

The girl shook her head. "It is too well guarded. You have been sold to the duke for . . ." She gestured at the tapestries.

"Yes, I guessed that part." Ro shook her head. "Listen, there were two men with me. Do you know what happened to them?"

"No." The girl turned sad eyes on Ro. "Were they relatives?"

"No. My . . ." Ro bit back the next word. "Companions."

"Then they were probably sent to the mines. That is where most male slaves go."

This was getting worse by the minute. It looked as if the captain and Lieutenant Miles were up to their necks in trouble as well. "Listen, do you know what happened to my clothes?" She had to get her communicator back and contact the ship.

"You did not have any when you were brought in here. The other maids must have taken them from you when you were purchased."

"Great." Ro sighed. "What's your name?"

"Martina. I am the duchess's handmaiden."

"There's a duchess?" Ro gestured at herself and the room. "Does she know about all this?" Maybe she could start a little trouble. . . .

"Of course."

"And she allows it?"

Martina bowed her head slightly. "She is glad that she does not have to occupy this room. As am I. I am very afraid."

"If I had any sense, I probably would be, too," Ro

admitted. "What happened to the last person who was here?" Martina blanched. "Okay, forget I asked."

Someone hammered on the door. Martina looked around, pale. "I must go!" she said in an urgent whisper. "The duchess wants me. Try to stay brave." Then she ran to the door and rapped on it twice. It opened and the poor girl fled.

Ro sat down on the edge of the bed. This was not looking too encouraging. Graebel was obviously some sort of slave trader who'd sold her to the local duke for a sex toy. And the duke clearly used up toys rather quickly. . . .

Dr. Hagan normally enjoyed striding imperiously through the streets of Diesen, watching the ignorant peasants shying from contact with him and cringing in fear of his supposed powers. This time, however, he wasn't striding—he was almost running. And he wasn't enjoying himself at all. He was furious and more than a little scared. And he felt humiliated for once.

Damn that fool Nayfack! The whole carefully constructed scheme they had worked out was teetering now, threatening to crash down around their ears. The *Enterprise* might not have reported back to Starfleet yet, but they had trailed that imbecile straight to Hagan. Hagan wished that Nayfack were alive again so he could have the pleasure of murdering the man again.

Thankfully, he had planned for almost any eventuality. Those two Starfleet officers wouldn't discover anything from his burned-out store. It would be nice if they'd been burnt to death, but there really wasn't much chance of that. Still, if they beamed back up to their vessel, then they'd be finished off there once he managed to contact the boss. *He'd* settle that starship!

Hagan arrived at the docks. He had a small boat moored here as a secondary base. His reputation alone kept the locals well away from it. He hurried to where it was berthed and slipped aboard. The cabin looked innocent enough, but he'd worked hard on this craft. Bending to the deck, he pressed his hand down on the secret palm lock. The computer verified his identity, and the deck split silently apart to reveal a flight of steps. As soon as he descended them, the hatchway closed behind him.

The interior of the boat was state-of-the-art. He didn't see why he had to subject himself to the squalor that the locals considered civilization, especially since he was making more money from this operation than even he could spend. Settling into his chair, he ordered the replicator to make him a single malt scotch on the rocks. It materialized in seconds, and he swallowed a good mouthful. The burning of the liquid in his throat made him feel a little better. The alcohol hitting his stomach calmed his nerves.

Turning to the communicator, he tapped in the code for the boss. Then he waited for a response. There was no telling how long it would be before the boss would be able to drag himself away from the locals and find out what was happening, but Hagan had hit the emergency code.

Two minutes later the screen lit up. "What's wrong?" a deep voice growled. The figure on the screen was clouded. They were as affected by the graviton fluxes down here as the *Enterprise* would be in orbit. There was no escaping the problem, and

Hagan had learned to adjust. Voice contact wasn't quite as fuzzy.

"Big trouble. The starship *Enterprise* is currently orbiting the planet."

"What?" The boss leaned forward. "Explain!"

Hagan swallowed. "When the yacht left the tunnel, the starship was mapping the cloud. The yacht was destroyed, but Nayfack escaped. Thinking he was being smart, he convinced the captain he was a Federation security man and brought the ship in through the tunnel."

"The fool!" The man on the screen slammed his fist down on his desk. "I'll kill the idiot!"

"You're too late," Hagan replied. "I beat you to it. He was trailed to my home, and I was forced to destroy it to escape. Two Starfleet officers were there, but I doubt they were killed. The one good aspect of this is that Nayfack convinced the captain not to send a message to Starfleet before he entered the cloud. If we act now and destroy the *Enterprise,* we'll be safe for a while."

"Not for long." The boss thought for a moment. "All right—I'll get the starship. It'll buy us time to evacuate the planet, I suppose. As soon as Starfleet realizes they've lost the vessel, they're bound to search the area. Sooner or later they'll spot the tunnel."

"Shall I begin shutting down here?"

The other man shook his head. "Not yet. It'll take me a little while to get the defenses working. I can't go into the operations center just now. The first thing you'll have to do is to locate and terminate those two Starfleet snoopers. Then close down operations and join me here. I'll set the destruction of the *Enterprise* into motion, and we can leave. I'll bring the Preservers' map with us. Maybe we can find another world that's as rich as this one."

"Is that likely?" Hagan had never seen the map—only the person in charge had. Understandably, he kept it tightly under his control. Being the only one who could read it helped his monopoly. "This has been a very sweet money-making machine for us."

"I don't know. It's damned hard to understand the Preservers' script. But we'll have time to study it. Now—get those two interlopers."

"Understood." Hagan turned off the viewer. He then opened a small closet and took out a second cane, almost identical to the one he had been using. Only this one didn't hide a knife in the handle. Instead, there was a small but powerful phaser in the wolf's head. The Starfleet officers would be bound by their stupid Prime Directive not to bring their own weapons down to the surface. They'd be sitting ducks because he was not confined by such petty morality. All he had to do was to locate them and then cut them down.

Chapter Twelve

"RIGHT," BARCLAY SAID, giving Worf a nervous glance. "That should have done it." He stepped back from the computer panel outside Holodeck 4. "I've—ah—managed to program in what the world below is kind of like. Of course, since we've not heard from either away team, I can't be *certain* that what I've programmed is correct. It's a sort of best-guess scenario, really. And I'm not very familiar with the Germanic knight period, so I sort of transposed it to the court of King Arthur. . . ."

"I'm certain that it will be more than adequate," Worf replied.

"Well, anyway, the code of chivalry is intact," Barclay pressed on. "And it's going to be along the right lines, I'm certain—well, *almost* certain. And—"

"Mr. Barclay," said Worf emphatically.

"Yes?" Barclay croaked.

"Thank you for your efforts. I am certain that they will be most rewarding." He gestured at the door. "Shall we enter now?"

"By all means," agreed Barclay. "I mean, uh, yes." He faced the doors. "Ah—computer! Run program *Arthur Rex.*"

After the briefest of pauses, the computer replied: "Program now engaged. Enter when ready."

Worf strode toward the door, which hissed open. The Klingon marched into the holodeck, Barclay trailing nervously along behind him. As they crossed the threshold, the doors hissed closed and vanished, isolating them in the illusion that the room created.

It was as if they were standing inside a castle. Huge stone walls rose about them. Torches set in niches guttered and danced as they burned. There was the scent of roasting meat and the cheery laughter of a number of people from directly ahead. Worf glanced down at himself and found he was dressed in brightly polished metallic armor. Atop the armor he wore a tunic of white, with the red outline of a rampant lion. Under his arm Worf held a helmet, large enough to fit over his head, with a grating that could open where his eyes would be. Atop the helmet was a flowing red plume.

Barclay was dressed in green tights and leather sandals and wore a similar white tunic. His rampant lion was also in red but smaller than Worf's.

"I take it that I am one of these knights?" Worf asked.

Nodding, Barclay gestured down the hallway. "The others await us within," he explained. "I am your squire. It's my duty to keep your weapons ready and in good repair, and to ready your horse. That kind of stuff."

"Good." Worf strode down the hallway and into the room beyond.

The source of the noises and smells was instantly apparent: They were in a huge banqueting hall. Two long tables, facing each other, were crammed with all kinds of dishes. On each table sat an entire roast pig, with an apple in its mouth. Servants were cutting and tearing steaming slices from these to hand out to the feasters. There were cooked swans, large pastries, hot loaves of bread, tureens of soup and stews. There were figs, apples, pears, and a dozen different types of berries. There were smoked chickens and sausages, along with vegetables and gravies. And there were flagons of rich, red wine that further servants were slopping into goblets held up by the seated revelers.

Beyond the table a group of minstrels were vainly attempting to make their music heard over the din. The far wall was broken by an immense fireplace, within whose confines a stack of wood was burning lustily. On a spit, being turned by a young urchin, was another huge boar, crackling and spitting as it roasted.

The men at the tables were dressed similar to Worf, but the tunic each wore bore a different device. One was a blue eagle, another a rearing unicorn. There were real and fabulous animal designs, along with arrows, swords, and shields. Each man quaffed wine and tore at the meat he held with great good cheer.

At the head of the table sat a regal couple. Worf's eyes narrowed as he examined them. The man was undoubtedly the king—a circlet of gold on his thick brown hair made that abundantly clear. He wore a full beard and a wide smile, but the underlying features were clearly those of Captain Picard. The woman beside him on his left was of course the queen. She wore a silken dress that clung to her figure and flowed to the floor. On her flaming red hair was a small diadem of gold and diamonds. She bore an unmistakable resemblance to Dr. Crusher.

The king rose to his feet. "Ah! Sir Worf—come to join us at last! Welcome, welcome!" The assembled feasters all echoed the greeting. Worf caught glimpses of Commander Riker, Lieutenant O'Brien, and others in the throng. "A seat!" the king cried. "A seat for a worthy knight!" Turning to the seated soldier at his right, he said: "Make way, fellow. Sir Worf requires your seat!" The knight, laughing, picked up his stuffed plate and goblet and made his way down the table to a spare seat. The king waved at the empty chair. "Come, Sir Worf, and join us!"

"I should like that very much," growled Worf, lowering himself into the chair. Two of the servants immediately thumped a loaded plate and a filled goblet in front of him.

"Eat! Drink!" the king roared merrily. "On this feast to celebrate the birth of our Savior, all men should rejoice!" He took a deep draw of his own wine, then wiped his lips on the sleeve of his tunic. "Ah! Good wine, good food, good companions—and a beautiful wife!" He smiled happily at Queen Beverly. "What more could a man ask of life?"

"What indeed?" asked Worf, somewhat uncomfortably.

The king's eyes sparkled. "Ah, but you jest, Sir Worf. You know the true answer to that as well—if not better—than any man in this room!" Raising his cup, he howled: "What more do we need, my knights?"

The men all thundered to their feet. "A Quest!" they roared in response.

"Indeed we do," the king agreed. "And—unless I am very much mistaken—I do believe that adventure even now strides within our walls!"

Following his outflung arm, Worf saw another figure march into the room. It was similar to the men already feasting in that it wore armor. But this man's armor was of shining black, not silver. The plume of his helmet also was ebony. He carried a huge shield, and by his side swung a long sword.

The knight beside Worf slammed a fist onto the table. "The Black Knight, by my oath!" he snarled. "Has he the gall to come here and insult the king to his face?"

Worf was beginning to get the drift of this adventure. Leaping to his feet, he called out challengingly: "What are *you* doing here on this day?"

The dark figure halted and turned to examine Worf. His voice, when he spoke, was hollow and echoing. "I come to offer single combat to any knight worthy of his rank," he replied. "Or else I require his abject surrender."

"Sir, you insult me in my own court!" cried the king. "You are fortunate that I have taken an oath not to spill the blood of any man on this day of rejoicing, or I should cut off your head myself!" He gestured about the room. "But here are four score and eight goodly knights—all braver and more worthy than you. Mayhap one of them would take up the challenge you so coldly fling out."

The knights all began to call out that they would

gladly accept the honor of single combat. Worf turned to the king. "My leige lord," he said. "Allow me, I beg you!"

The king's eyes sparkled in gratitude. "Sir Worf! I knew that I could count on you. So be it!" After removing his sword, he rapped loudly on the table with the hilt. "Silence!" he cried. The knights all fell quiet and looked to their monarch. "Sir Worf has asked of me the honor of meeting the Black Knight in single combat. And I have granted his request!"

There was a great cheer from the whole hall at this. The Black Knight turned his head to study Worf. "I shall take great pleasure in cutting off his head," he announced.

"To the fields, then!" cried the king. "Let the combat begin!"

As everyone began to file out, slapping Worf heartily on the shoulders and calling out encouragement, the Klingon turned to Barclay. His teeth flashed. "You are quite correct," he growled. "I am truly enjoying this!" Then he shook his head. "If only I were really down on the planet, where the others are truly involved in adventure!"

If Data had been human, he would certainly have been feeling excited and smug by now. As he lacked emotions, though, the most that he felt was satisfaction that his time had not been wasted. On a leisurely swing through the market, he had detected two hundred and seventy-three close analogues to so-called antiques auctioned off on various worlds over the past eighteen months. Not requiring sleep like the other crewmembers of the *Enterprise,* Data had evolved a large number of pastimes to occupy his leisure hours. One of these was to zip through all the current news releases from the museums of the Federation. Several articles had dealt with the surprising rise of available —and apparently genuine—antiques dating from the medieval period of Earth. A number of conjectures had been suggested and shot down. Data was confident that he could now explain the puzzle.

The two hundred and seventy-three items he had cataloged should all stand up in a court of law, and that should be sufficient to convict the members of the gang for this profitable little scam of theirs.

It was a shame, really, that they had been practicing such a subterfuge. Data appreciated good art, and some of the craftsmanship demonstrated here in the wood carvings and metalwork was indeed highly skillful. The items that had been sold as fake antiques were actually almost worth the prices paid for them.

Data judged that he had spent sufficient time and energy on this aspect of the mission. It would be appropriate to join Captain Picard and report his discoveries. He carefully scanned the market and quickly detected the banner that bore the emblem of Graebel. Attempting to look as fully human as everyone about him, Data headed for the warehouse. The captain, Lieutenant Miles, and Ensign Ro had been gone for over three hours now. They must have discovered some lead of their own, else they would have emerged from Graebel's establishment before this. Worry was alien to Data's mind, but he did register a slight anomaly. This was not typical of the captain's behavior.

Was it possible that something had happened to the

captain? Data knew that on any alien world there was a chance of a problem. It was impossible to calculate the odds for such an event, because by its very nature it would have to be an unknown problem. But both Captain Picard and Ro were very observant for hominid life-forms and well able to take care of themselves. He had to assume the same held true for Lieutenant Miles, else Worf would not have assigned him to his duty. Still, it might be as well to be careful when meeting with this man Graebel.

Arriving at the warehouse, he rapped on the door to gain admittance.

Geordi La Forge leaned forward in the command chair. He virtually had to drag his attention away from the main viewscreen. The sight of the cloud was dazzling—quite literally. He'd been forced to shut down the input on his VISOR twice to avoid sensory overload. The forces of nature even in this bubble were staggeringly powerful. It irritated him that he couldn't come up with the mechanism to explain how such a bubble could be maintained in the heart of the nebula.

"Any signs of the communicator interference clearing up, Mr. Van Popering?" he asked. He'd been asking that question every twenty minutes since Commander Riker and Counselor Troi had beamed down to the planet.

"No, sir." Van Popering had also been giving the identical answer every twenty minutes.

"Damn," Geordi muttered. He felt so helpless, just sitting there, waiting.

"Relax, Geordi." Beverly Crusher patted him on the arm. She was seated in Deanna's position, to the left of the command chair. "They're all adults and capable of taking care of themselves."

Geordi nodded. "You're right, Doc. I know that. But if they *are* in trouble, how will we know it? And what if they want to beam back aboard?"

"They'll just have to wait. Like we will."

"Yeah." Geordi sighed. "But I've never considered patience to be a virtue. Especially when we can't even talk to them."

"The interference is bound to clear up, isn't it?"

"Oh, sure. The problem is that we've got no way of knowing *when* it'll clear."

Beverly smiled at him. "Then we'll just have to be ready when it does, won't we?"

Geordi nodded. Then he tried to sit back and force himself to relax. It didn't work.

What was happening down there?

Kirsch turned out to be quite an interesting conversationalist. In other circumstances Picard might have enjoyed their dialogue. As it was, he was constantly being brought up short while gesturing with his hands as his chains prevented his free movements. And it was difficult to forget that he was stripped to the waist and sitting in a rather odiferous dungeon. None of this seemed to worry Kirsch too much. He was clearly enjoying himself.

"Don't these chains inhibit your freedom of thought at all?" Picard asked him.

"Why should they?" asked the scholar. "After all, we live all our lives with mental shackles, don't we?" He rattled his chains. "These only serve to remind me of that."

"These," Picard pointed out, shaking his own manacles, "mean that we'll be spending the rest of our lives in the mines. Or do you have an opinion about that, too?"

Kirsch laughed. "I have an opinion about everything. In some matters, I have more than one opinion. That way, at least one of them is bound to be right."

"Is that why you're here?" Picard felt that he was beginning to understand the young man at last.

"Yes. I was stupid enough to say that I thought the accepted line on the Disappearances was foolish."

The way that Kirsch looked at him after saying this made Picard realize that this was clearly a crucial point. He only wished he knew why. "You don't agree with the—ah—official story?" he countered, stalling.

"Of course not. How could anyone with an ounce of brains?"

"Quite." Picard wished he knew what the official line was—and what the Disappearances were. He could hardly ask directly. "But what precisely led you to disagree?"

It was clearly the correct question. Kirsch grinned. "Two points, really. First of all, I could hardly believe that God would allow everyone in the world to be wiped out by the Black Death with the exception of just twelve villages. I mean, just because there were twelve tribes of Israel and twelve apostles doesn't follow that twelve villages will be left of all the world, does it? We're not even any better than the other places used to be. Besides, even if it were true, there would be ruins left, wouldn't there? The Bible mentions a good deal more than twelve villages by name, and nobody has ever come up with a viable answer as to where even one of them might have been located."

So that was how the inhabitants of this world explained their origin! Picard had to admire the logic. Discovering that they were no longer where they had once been and that almost all of their former neighbors had vanished, the locals had believed the whole world to have been wiped out by the bubonic plague. It made a sort of comforting sense, he supposed. But Kirsch had realized that the theory didn't work. "And the second reason?" he probed.

"I found a book that purported to tell of the stars. It even had sketches of what the author termed *constellations.*" The young man laughed. "And, as you know, there are no such things. But there once were. The Bible speaks of stars, and of the fall of night, so they must have existed—and perhaps still do, elsewhere."

Picard realized what Kirsch meant. Here, inside the protocloud, there could be no night. Even when the planet turned its face away from the sun, there was a second star. And when that, too, was gone, there would be the background glow from the cloud itself. This world had no night at all.

"Then," he asked slowly, "what is *your* explanation for our world being the way it is?"

"Ah! An open-minded man," Kirsch said approvingly. "I believe that we are now in the age of Revelation, friend Lukas."

"The what?"

"In the book of Revelations," the student replied, "we are told that God will create a new heaven and a new Earth. And that there will be no more night. Well, there is no more night. And if this were a new Earth, then it would explain a great deal."

"Hmmm." Picard was warming to the youth. He

may have drawn incorrect conclusions, but he was at least thinking reasonably logically through the problem. "Then you think we're in heaven?"

Kirsch laughed. "Hell, more likely! No," he added, more seriously, "Revelations tells us that in heaven there will be no more sea, and no pain or suffering." He rattled his chains. "And we've plenty of all three of those, haven't we? But I am certain that we are no longer on the Earth our forefathers knew."

Picard smiled. "I suspect that there's a great deal of truth in what you say."

"You'd better be careful, agreeing with me," Kirsch told him. "You could get into trouble."

Picard shook his manacles. "Worse than this?"

"Hardly. But—"

At that moment the cell door opened. Two men in dark clothing stepped inside. Each had a drawn sword in his hands. Neither looked as if it would bother him to use the weapons.

"Move," the first man said. "Outside."

"Where are we going?" Picard asked.

The man slapped him across the face with the back of his hand. Picard winced but kept silent. "Don't talk back," the guard snapped. "You're off to the mines, with the rest of the scum. Now—move. Say anything else, and you'll be leaving fingers behind on the floor."

An eloquent argument, Picard mused. He rose to his feet. The two guards used the points of their swords to drive him and Kirsch from the cell. Other slaves, all wearing manacles, were being forced out of adjoining cells. Together, they were herded toward the courtyard. Many of the other men looked as if they had been beaten, and some had cuts and bruises. One was missing his ears, left with terrible scar tissue instead. These men were all the dregs of their society, or simply people who had fallen afoul of the authorities. For that, they were being condemned to death in the mines. Picard had wondered why there were no beggars in the streets. Now he had his answer. If you had no job, the authorities gave you one. . . .

The men were shoved and beaten into two lines. There were at least thirty of them, and an equal number of guards. When the two ragged columns had been formed, two longer chains were run down them, passing through every man's manacles, so they were linked together. This was obviously to make it almost impossible for a single man to make a break for it. The chains were locked off on the front and rear of each line. Picard was chained next to Kirsch near the front of the first line. He caught a glimpse of Lieutenant Miles toward the end of the rear line. He didn't dare chance a word with his crew member. He could only hope that the man was holding up.

Once the chaining was finished, the guards pulled back. Another guard—obviously of higher rank from his better cut of tunic, the helmet he carried, and the cloak that flapped in the breeze—stepped forward. He was heavily bearded and had narrow, brooding eyes.

"Right," he growled, barely loud enough to be heard. "I'll say this once. Any trouble from any of you, and you'll regret it. I won't kill you, so don't think you'll get lucky. But I'll make damned certain that you'll wish you were dead. And just so you'll know that I'm not making idle threats or think that maybe underneath this tough skin I've got a soft center . . ." He uncurled a whip from under his cloak and cracked it in the air. Picard saw that it had a metal weight tied to the tip. The weight would make the blow from the weapon much nastier. The officer cracked the whip a second time, then slapped it out in a blow.

The blow whistled past Picard's ear. The man in the line behind him screamed as the metal tip lacerated his skin. Blood splattered onto Picard's back from the man's wound. It was a fight for him not to turn and look at the victim. He knew that if he did, he'd be the next example.

The officer scowled, clearly disappointed that Picard hadn't "provoked" punishment. "Now," he said, "I think we all know who's boss around here. Keep it in mind at all times." He snapped his fingers. One of the men came over at a trot, leading a horse. The officer vaulted into the saddle of the beast and curled the whip about the saddle horn. "Now, let's get moving. You've all got work to do, and the sooner we reach the mines, the sooner you can all start praying to die."

The two lines began moving, forcing Picard to go along with them. Six of the guards fell in beside the column, and the officer brought up the rear. Picard's spirits fell. Once he was outside the city walls, it would be very difficult—if not impossible—for his crew to find him. Always assuming he could survive long enough to be found.

After Martina had fled the room, Ro had been left alone for about twenty minutes. She wasn't sure whether this was to give her time to panic or to get turned on by the draperies. In fact, she did neither. Instead she sat on the bed—the floor being too cold even carpeted—and concentrated her thoughts.

She was obviously in some remote part of the castle

that they had seen earlier from the market. The duke wouldn't want his playroom too close to the main traffic of the castle. Besides, she'd heard very little outside her room. That suggested remoteness from the busier areas. If she could escape from the room, it would have to be into the castle proper, which would increase her chances of getting caught again. Besides, there was at least one guard outside the door to get past. And, finally, this room would have been selected by the duke because it would be difficult for any of his victims to leave.

Which meant that her best chance of escaping from this room would be to have someone take her out. She strongly doubted that feigning sickness would help her. Aside from the fact that it was the oldest trick in the book, she didn't think that the duke would care enough about how well she felt when he arrived. It might increase the danger to her, if anything.

Could she simply stall for time in the hopes of rescue? That didn't appeal to her for a number of reasons. For one thing, she wasn't some helpless female from an ancient holodrama that needed to be saved each episode. And waiting was simply not her style. Besides, there was no evidence that either the captain or Lieutenant Miles would be able to trace her, even if they were in a position to do so themselves. Data might be able to track her. He was, to say the least, very skillful and determined. But nobody else from the *Enterprise* knew that they'd gone to Graebel's warehouse, so a rescue party from the ship was a remote possibility.

And, to cap it all, stalling for time would mean playing the duke's rather nasty and clearly lethal games. The thought made Ro nauseated.

So, there was just one option left to her. Risky, to say the least. But what choice did she have?

There was a sound of metal clinking outside the door. The guard snapping to attention. So—the duke must be here. She jumped to her feet. Ro heard the bolts snap free, and the door swung open to admit the duke. It was immediately locked behind him. As the duke studied her, she examined him.

He was middle-aged and gray. He had a pepper-colored mustache but no beard, and his hair was shoulder-length. His other appetites were obviously as well indulged as his sexual tastes—he had a beer belly and thickly veined hands. His green robe was expensive, belted loosely at the waist, and picked out with gold leaf patterns. In his beringed right hand he carried a slopping goblet of wine that he took a long swig from, then placed on the table.

"So," he finally said, "Graebel was telling the truth for once. You *are* an attractive prize."

"I am nothing of the kind," Ro told him flatly. "I am not merchandise, to be bought and sold."

The duke flushed, annoyed. "You are what I say you are. Graebel assures me that you were his property, and I believe him."

"Because it suits you."

"Yes," he agreed. "It suits me very well. And if you know what is good for you, it will suit you just as well."

Ro snorted. "As it suited the former occupant of this room?" she asked.

The duke moved closer to her. His eyes were glittering as he looked her body over. "She wouldn't enjoy herself here," he said softly. "But you can—all you have to do is to relax. I'll do the rest."

"I'm sure you will," Ro purred back. She gave him a smile that encouraged him to step in closer. Then she exploded. She spun about in a tight circle and lashed out with her right foot. It slammed with all of her weight behind it into the duke's groin.

His breath exploded out, and his face went white. Clutching his injured area, he collapsed, wheezing, eyes popping, onto the floor.

Her foot hurt from the blow, but Ro didn't care. "You're right," she told the gasping duke. "I *am* starting to enjoy myself." She crossed to the door and rapped on it twice, as Martina had done. As she had expected, the guard thought it was his master with some request. The bolts clattered open with some alacrity.

Ro put all of her weight behind her right shoulder and rammed the door hard. It exploded outward, hurling the startled guard into the wall. Before the shaken man could move, Ro jumped onto him and smacked his head hard into the stone wall. Then she let him roll to the floor and grabbed up his sword. She felt less vulnerable now.

She found herself in a short corridor. Steps led downward into the castle proper. She hadn't been expecting the three further guards with short spears, though. For a second she considered throwing herself into battle, but it was clearly pointless. They could cut her down before she reached any of them. Carefully she allowed the sword to clatter to the floor. "The best laid plans of mice and Bajorans," she murmured to herself.

Two of the guards backed her to the wall with gestures from their spears. She was forced to stand there, the points centered on her stomach, while the third man ran into the room she had just left. A moment later he reappeared, supporting the staggering duke. Ro noted with satisfaction that the duke was walking with a distinct waddle. He was obviously hurting badly between the legs. His face was sallow, and he was still gasping.

"Take her to the dungeons," he ordered, between wheezes. "See how she likes a night there instead of in a warm bed." He glared hard at her. "Then tomorrow we'll see how cooperative she is."

"Sweet dreams," she murmured. The two guards hurried her away as the third helped the duke back to his own rooms.

Ro couldn't help feeling rather smug. So far, so good. She was out of that room, and out of immediate reach of the duke. Now all she had to worry about was escaping from the dungeons. . . .

Chapter Thirteen

OUTSIDE OF THE FEASTING HALL, a short walk had brought the holodeck knights to an oak door. This in turn led to a large field. In the center was a large ring. Seats under an awning were clearly for the king and queen, who made their way toward them. The other knights, along with various ladies and some of the servants, crowded about the sides of the large ring. Worf allowed Barclay to lead him to one of two small tents outside the ring.

Beside the tent stood an impatient horse, pure white, with a large, heavy saddle on its back. Gaily colored cloths over its sides fluttered in the breeze. Over its head was a metallic piece of armor, clearly to prevent injury. A large spike rose from the plate, making the beast look like the mythical unicorn.

"You and the Black Knight will be jousting," Barclay explained. He seemed much less nervous now that he knew Worf was enjoying his game. "You ride from opposite sides of the ring at each other."

"Good." Worf grabbed the horse's bright reins and vaulted into the saddle. The weight of his armor didn't appear to slow him down at all.

"No, wait!" Barclay cried. "You need your lance and shield."

"My what?"

"Lance." Barclay ran to the tent, then emerged a moment later with a long pole. The end was tipped with sharpened metal, and about halfway down there was a grip. "This is the weapon you use," he explained. "You use it to knock your opponent off his horse if you are able. Once that happens, you jump down. You're allowed to finish the joust using your sword, until your opponent yields or you kill him." He then handed Worf a long, thin metal shield. "Fend off his blow with this."

Worf studied the weapons. "Intriguing." Gripping the lance tightly, he lifted it over his head. "Am I allowed to throw it?"

"No!" Barclay looked quite upset at the suggestion. "Humans aren't strong enough to do that. You have to play by the rules."

"Very well," agreed Worf. He lowered the lance. "When do we commence?"

"When the king gives the word. You'll hear a fanfare."

"Good." Worf scanned the ring and saw that the Black Knight was now astride a coal-black steed at the opposite end of the field. He held a lance of jet close to his side. "I am looking forward to this combat immensely."

The king bent to speak something to his queen. She

nodded and stood, raising a small square piece of cloth.

"Am I supposed to spear that?" asked Worf. "If so, I should practice. I might accidentally injure the lady."

"No," said Barclay. "That's her signal. She'll let her handkerchief drop to start the combat."

"Ah! I understand." Worf focused on the piece of cloth, restraining the eager horse from charging. It seemed to be as excited as he was. This was definitely a human culture he could appreciate!

Then the queen released her cloth. It fluttered and fell.

Worf dug into his steed with his knees, and the animal shot forward. Worf leaned into the motion, one hand loose on the reins, the other gripping his lance. The Black Knight shot toward him on the jet-colored horse. The thunder of their hooves almost drowned out the cheer that rose from the watching knights.

Concentrating on his opponent, Worf shifted the point of his lance to target the shield the other man carried. It was a large target and offered the best chance of unseating his opponent. His own shield was held loosely over his left arm. A thrill of pure excitement jolted through him. This was living!

Then they were on each other. Worf felt a heavy blow to his shield and at the same time the shock of his lance ramming into something unyielding. With a grunt he managed to stay in the saddle, despite the force trying to throw him. He felt the lance shatter and splinter to pieces in his hand.

Then they were racing in opposite directions away from each other.

Worf took stock as he reined in his galloping horse.

His lance was broken and he cast it aside. His shield was scratched but functional. He turned his steed and faced back the way he had come. The Black Knight was whirling about. His shield was also shattered, and had been thrown aside. But his lance was intact.

The other knight raised his lance in brief salute, then charged.

Worf threw aside his own shield. Ignoring Barclay's scream of panic, he set his horse hurtling toward the Black Knight. The point of his opponent's lance was aimed directly at his heart.

At the last second Worf released his reins. As the lance thrust for him, Worf gripped the metal tip and jerked hard.

Caught by complete surprise, the Black Knight was hauled bodily from his saddle and thrown to the grass. With a loud roar of triumph Worf flung himself from his own horse and fell lightly to the grass. Drawing his sword, he strode across to where the Black Knight lay.

"Do you yield?" he snarled.

"Never!" the knight growled back. He staggered to his feet and whipped his own sword free of its scabbard. "To the death!"

"To the death!" Worf agreed happily.

Graebel shook his head firmly. "I'm sorry, Dieter," he told his guest. "I am afraid that I have seen nobody by the names of Lukas, Martel, or Rosalinde today."

Data inclined his head slightly. "They were on their way to visit you when I parted from them in the marketplace," he replied. "If they did not arrive here, then do you have any suggestions as to where they might have gone?"

The merchant shrugged. "They knew me only by

my banner, you say? Well, perhaps they confused the devices and visited a different merchant."

"That is not likely," Data responded. "Lukas was most emphatic about the design of your banner. I saw none similar that he might have mistaken for yours."

Graebel shrugged. "Then perhaps he was attacked by robbers. I regret to say that in this city not every man is as honest as you and I." He clapped his hands. "I'll tell you what. Why don't you and I share a cup of wine, and I'll send my manservant to check among the other merchants and see if anyone has heard from or seen your friends?"

"Thank you." Data nodded gravely. "I would appreciate the inquiries. As to the wine, I thank you for your offer, but I do not imbibe."

"Come, now," Graebel said. "It's rude not to drink with a man—especially when he's offering you aid and opening a rather fine vintage."

Data considered the matter. He did not require food or liquids but could eat and drink if needed. The captain had ordered him to appear to be fully human. The merchant's logic appeared somewhat flawed, but the point was clear. "Then I will accept," Data agreed.

Graebel went to the door and spoke quietly with his servant in the hall. Then he returned with a tray holding the wine and goblets. "It should be a matter of less than an hour, Dieter. And what more pleasant way to spend an hour than in the company of good wine?"

This was clearly a rhetorical question. Data could recognize such quite well now, so he did not reply. Instead, he accepted the proffered goblet of wine and took a sip. Graebel smiled and took a healthy draft from his own goblet.

"Are you a connoisseur?" he asked. "Can you tell what's in that delightful bouquet?"

Data took a further sip and set his internal sensors to work analyzing the liquid. "Aside from the obvious alcoholic content," he replied, "there are traces of apple, a small percentage of cinnamon, and a third ingredient." This one he was having trouble identifying. Finally his computer memory produced an analog in the form of an atropine variant. There was nothing to suggest that it was customarily used to flavor wines. It was extracted from the Common Hensbane, a weed found throughout Europe and most commonly used as a drug.

Ah. That would explain it. The wine had been doctored with the addition of a knockout substance. Interesting, because atropine hadn't been isolated on Earth until 1833 and—

Data was suddenly aware that Graebel was staring at him. He wondered if he had allowed his pose of being fully human to slip, thus making the merchant suspicious of his behavior. Then he realized what the problem was: A human would have been rendered unconscious by the drug. Perhaps this was what had befallen the captain and his companions. Data therefore shut down his motor responses.

Graebel yelped and leapt to his feet with surprising speed for a man of his bulk as his guest suddenly appeared to go stiff and then collapse. "Gods!" he muttered, "I've never seen the powder produce that effect before." He bent to Data's body and groped at the wrist.

He was obviously feeling for a pulse. Data's nutrient system didn't require pumping in the same manner as the heart pumped blood, so he did not possess a normal pulse. However he was able to simulate the action required by adjusting the flow of his chemical nutrients. Data made it slower than a normal human pulse, since he was supposed to be unconscious.

"That's better," Graebel muttered. Then he stood up. "Sigfrid!" he yelled. The manservant popped in through the door. "Here's another slave we can sell to the mines."

"The guards just took the latest lot out, Herr Graebel," Sigfrid replied. "They won't want to take another slave tonight. They'd have to feed him an extra day."

"Oh, wonderful," muttered Graebel. "Now I suppose *I'll* have to lock him up overnight." He sighed. "Pity. He's apparently a friend of that man Lukas we had here earlier. They might have enjoyed working on the same crew in the mines. I'm such a sentimentalist, Sigfrid, I know, to find pleasure in such a thought."

Data noted that Graebel had been lying when he claimed not to have met the captain. He had evidently been sold as a slave for some mines in the hills. Data continued to feign unconsciousness, hoping he'd overhear more useful conversation.

"What shall I do with him, then, sir?" asked the manservant.

"You'd better lock him in the cellar for the night," Graebel decided. "It's very inconvenient, but I suppose we'll have to put up with the trouble."

If they were going to lock him up, Data knew, his chances of discovering anything useful were slim. "Allow me then to relieve you of that burden," he suggested, springing to his feet.

It was hard to judge who was the more amazed, Graebel or Sigfrid. Both paled and jumped back. Data reached out and fastened a hand about each man's right wrist.

"That's not possible," squeaked Graebel. "You should be unconscious!"

"I agree." Data considered the point. Technically, he had broken the captain's orders to appear to be fully human. On the other hand, the captain's life—as well as those of Ensign Ro and Lieutenant Miles—might depend upon Data's being free and able to come to the rescue. "Fortunately I am immune to atropine. A birth defect." While not exactly true, Data hadn't told a lie. He had merely implied that he had been born, instead of constructed.

Sigfrid was straining to pull free of Data's implacable grip, without success. "He's skinny, but he's stronger than he looks, Herr Graebel," the man protested.

"I exercise frequently," Data informed him. "Now, I wish to know what you have done with Lukas and Rosalinde." Sigfrid darted a look at his master, then shook his head, too scared of Graebel's wrath to talk. "Very well." Releasing the merchant for a moment, Data tapped the manservant with sufficient force to render him unconscious. Before Graebel could seize his chance and flee, Data had a firm grip on his wrist once again. Sigfrid collapsed onto the floor.

Graebel was shaking. He was clearly expecting physical assault, and ill prepared to cope with the concept. Data knew that it would be relatively simple to make such a person talk. All he needed was the correct encouragement. Data smiled for effect. It seemed to scare the merchant. "Now, perhaps you would be kind enough to supply me with the information I seek. If you do not cooperate, I shall be forced to commence inflicting pain on you. It will not give me pleasure. I am reasonably certain that it would give you no pleasure, either."

"Now, don't be hasty, Herr Dieter!" gasped Graebel. "I'm sure we can work this out like sensible men."

"That is a distinct possibility." Data inclined his head slightly. "Another is that if you do not tell me where my friends are, then you will discover that you have a broken wrist." To emphasize his words, Data squeezed the hand he was holding very slightly.

Graebel screamed, more from fear than pain. "All right! I'll tell you." Data eased up slightly. "I sold all three to Binder, the glassmaker in the High Street."

"That is a lie," Data stated. Aside from the fact that he'd heard Graebel mention selling Lukas as a mine worker, he could tell the man was lying by his bodily responses. Somewhat like a lie detector, Data could sense the change in the electrical conductivity of the man's skin and see the narrowing of his eyes. "If you attempt to lie again, I shall be compelled to injure you. Now, where is Lukas?"

"I sold him to the mines!" Graebel yelled, shaking with fear. "He's been taken off to them already, along with Martel."

"By what route?"

"I can't be certain," the merchant said. "Honestly! But I imagine through the Portergate and out on the mountain road. Believe me, that's all I know."

Data did believe him. He had shown no signs of lying. "And Rosalinde?" he prompted.

"Her, too!"

"A lie." Data shook his head slightly. "Accept my word when I say that I do not feel pleasure from doing this." He activated the servo-motors in his hand and constricted.

"No!" Graebel screamed, falling to his knees. Data stopped applying pressure but did not loosen his grip. The merchant's hand was deadly white, all circulation in it stopped. It was as if Data's hand were a powerful tourniquet. "I sold her to the duke as a servant girl," Graebel sobbed, pawing with his other hand at Data's remorseless arm.

Data considered the matter briefly. The captain and Miles were clearly in great danger. The mines could not be a safe place for humanoid life-forms; otherwise slaves would not be needed to excavate them. And there was the possibility of meeting one of the dragons on the way to the mines. Ro, on the other hand, should be relatively safe—if somewhat overworked and perhaps abused—inside the castle. By simple arithmetic, he would be able to aid two of his companions by following the slave train, as opposed to only one if he went after Ro. He would have to attempt to find the captain and Miles first, Data decided. Then, together they would be able to rescue Ro.

The android realized that all of this time, Graebel had been clawing at him to try and break free. He moved his attention back to that problem. There was a real danger of permanent damage to the man's hand if Data held the wrist this tightly for much longer. He abruptly released his grip. Crying incoherently, Graebel collapsed into a blubbering bundle on the floor, nursing his damaged hand.

Data realized that he could not leave Graebel like

this. He would prefer to stop Graebel's little slaving racket once and for all, but the Prime Directive forbade such interference in native matters. On the other hand, if he left the man conscious, then he would undoubtedly warn the duke of Data's interest in the new servant girl. That could complicate freeing Ro.

There was an obvious solution to his troubles. Data picked up the drugged flagon and refilled it with wine. This he then proffered to the shaking, sobbing merchant. "Drink this," he ordered. "It will make me feel much better."

"No." That much was plain even between the sobs.

"If you do not drink it," Data told Graebel, "then I shall be forced to render you unconscious through more physical means. It is not simple to gauge the force of blow required. Your high percentage of body fat would dull my blow. I might only hurt you. Alternatively, I might break your bones with the force of my blow as I try to correct for your size."

Graebel grabbed the wine goblet and emptied it in a single gulp. After a few moments he fell forward, completely limp.

Data nodded in satisfaction. There should be sufficient drug to keep him oblivious for the rest of the day. That should be adequate time to free the captain and return. He tapped the communicator hidden inside the broach pinning his cloak about his body. "Data to *Enterprise.*"

Even with his sensitive hearing, Data had trouble making out Geordi's response. Static chittered and barked throughout the whole call. It was possible that the ship, with its greater communications facilities, was receiving better than his pin could. Data had to act on that assumption. "The captain, Lieutenant Miles, and Ensign Ro have been kidnapped and sold into slavery, Geordi," he reported. "I shall endeavor to rescue the captain and lieutenant first, as they are currently outside the town and potentially in the greater danger. Data out."

Gathering his cloak about him, Data left the building and strode toward the main gate. He would be able to travel much faster once he was unobserved. For now, though, he must continue to appear human.

The Black Knight grunted as he swung his sword down in a vicious arc. Worf brought his own blade up to block the blow. The two metal edges sang as they collided under the force of the blow, showering sparks. The impact strained Worf's arms, but he laughed with the pleasure of the combat.

It was time to do the unexpected.

Releasing his sword, he grabbed the surprised knight's still-upraised arm. Twisting about, he applied leverage and all of his strength. With a howl of surprise the Black Knight was thrown over Worf's shoulder, and he slammed down onto the turf. Worf dropped upon him, wresting the sword from the stunned man's fingers and then holding the point of the blade to the man's exposed neck, visible under the rim of his helm.

"Do you yield?" he demanded.

The knight's face was invisible behind the faceplate, but his exhaustion and fear were apparent in his voice. "I . . . yield," he conceded.

Worf let the sword fall and jumped to his feet as cheering broke out among the king and the other knights. Barclay hurried across the field, grinning. Then his face fell, and he yelled a wordless warning.

Spinning about, Worf fell into a crouch. The Black Knight had regained his feet and had drawn a knife from a hidden sheath. Weaponless, Worf's eyes narrowed as he watched the wicked blade close in. Then, with a roar of rage, he lashed out with his right foot. Passing beneath the startled knight's guard, it connected with his stomach. Even though he wore a chestplate, the force of the kick slammed him from his feet. Worf limped over to where he lay and glared down at him.

Barclay ran up, panting. "Are you okay?"

Worf glowered. "This man was not honorable," he complained. "He cheated."

"Well, I tried to make the program realistic," explained Barclay. "That sort of thing happened a lot, you know. The idea of chivalry was—ah—accepted and believed in. But it wasn't always practiced."

With some disappointment Worf turned away from the fallen man. "Computer," he called. "End program." The scene vanished, and the bare walls of the holodeck returned. Worf looked down at Barclay. "Thank you for your help. This has been a most entertaining diversion. But we must return to duty now." He shook his head slightly. "I had hoped that a human society based on chivalry would appeal to me. Perhaps I was mistaken."

Barclay nodded. "The problem is that although they have high ideals, people don't always live up to them. It's not the fault of the ideals. It's just human weakness."

Worf looked down at him. "The same, I must

confess, can even be the case with Klingons. It appears that the appeal of ideals is universal—as is the failure of all races to consistently attain those goals."

"I hope I didn't disappoint you," Barclay said anxiously.

"No. The program was most enjoyable." Worf strode toward the door while Barclay scurried beside him to keep up. "The cheating knight was a good reminder that our expectations and desires are not always met in the real world."

"Now what was *that* all about?" wondered Geordi aloud. "I couldn't make out a word of it in all the static."

Worf had returned to duty only five minutes earlier. Traces of a smile still lingered about his features. "I shall attempt to clean up the message," he stated, working over the communications panel. After a few moments he announced: "I've made it listenable." Then he played it back.

In the quietened—but still irritating—hiss of the static, Data's report could be heard. As he announced the loss of the captain and Ro, Worf stiffened with rage. At the end of the message the Klingon rounded on Geordi.

"Permission to lead an away team to rescue the captain," he demanded.

"Sorry, Worf," Geordi replied. "No can do. The captain gave strict orders—no further away teams unless he or Commander Riker calls for one. We'll have to trust Data to get the captain back."

"I do not like waiting and doing nothing," complained Worf.

"None of us do," Geordi told him. "But we gotta do

it, anyway. And I'm sure that Data will get him free. He's pretty darned resourceful, you know."

Worf slammed his fist down on the plasteel rail surrounding the deck. It buckled visibly. "A fight!" he snarled. "And I cannot take part!" Then he launched into a string of Klingon oaths. Geordi winced at the anger in Worf's voice and turned back to his work. He could sympathize with Worf's frustration. He, too, hated having to just sit and wait. But what else could they do?

"Are you *absolutely* sure that this is just to try and gather information?" asked Deanna with a mischievous smile plucking at her lips.

Riker halted, hand outstretched, by the tavern door. "Why?" he asked. "What other possible reason could I have for visiting a place like this?"

"You wouldn't happen to be thirsty, would you?"

"I'm hurt, Deanna. I'm really hurt." Riker clutched his heart dramatically. "Your suspicions wound me, you know that."

"I'm sure they do." Deanna shook her head. "Seriously, Will, do you really think you'll be able to pick up anything here?"

"Trust me. You *know* the best place on the ship to pick up scuttlebutt is Ten-Forward. And down here this is the local equivalent. There'll be someone here who'll sell what they know for a drink."

"But we don't have any local currency to buy them a drink," Deanna protested. Riker winked. Then he tossed her a small silver coin, which she snatched from midair. "Where did you get this?" she asked, amazed. "Did you lift someone's wallet?"

"Almost. Remember that little bag I grabbed when

we left the shop? It turned out to have been Hagan's purse. I thought it would be kind of appropriate to use his cash to buy information."

Deanna favored him with a dazzling smile. "Will Riker, sometimes you amaze me."

"Only sometimes?" He grinned and pushed open the tavern door. "Follow me."

The tavern was quite crowded. From the noise and the stench that hovered over the room, it catered to mostly working-class types. The customers were mostly fishermen, vendors, and laborers, drinking thick beers and gambling. There were one or two women, but none in clothing as fine as Deanna's. She and Will looked rather out of place in the smoke-filled room. As befitted his role, Riker pushed his way through the crowd toward the bar. The people who started to complain changed their minds when they saw his outfit and the hand on his sword. Deanna followed in his wake, not deigning to look at the peasants she was passing through.

At the bar Riker rapped for the tavern owner's attention. "Do you have a quieter room?" he asked. "Somewhere that's fit for a lady?"

The owner was a bulbous man, with an apron about his waist that was more stained than his shirt. His bald head gleamed in the light from the fireplace. "What you see is what I've got," he replied. "Who can afford two rooms in this town? I don't get many customers of your class, sir."

"Well, you wouldn't have us if the house of the man we were to have visited hadn't burnt down." Riker shook his head. "God, what a poor excuse for a town."

One of the women elbowed her way across to the bar. She was dressed plainly and was of an age with the tavern owner. She was obviously his wife. Pushing the strands of hair from her eyes, she gave a short curtsy. "I've a nice chair by the fire Your Ladyship could rest in," she offered.

"It's better than nothing, I suppose," Deanna said, pretending aloofness. "Very well."

The woman led the way to the open fireplace. After the chill of the outside air, it felt good to be close to the warmth. The only drawback was that every now and then a gust of wind would send smoke hiccuping into the room. Deanna settled into the chair, which was surprisingly cozy. It was also still warm from the previous occupant that the owner's wife must have turned out to make room for Deanna.

"Could I get you a drink, milady?" the woman offered.

"Wine," Riker told her. "And a good vintage, mind. Not the slop these beggars drink. One for me, too."

The woman curtsied and scurried away. Riker leaned on the mantel above the fire and warmed his hands. "What a town," he grumbled, loud enough to be heard by the others about the fire. They were studiously pretending not to have noticed the lady and her man-at-arms. "They seem to have a fascination with fires here." He glared at the closest bunch of men. "I don't suppose any of you know anything about the house that burned down an hour or so ago?"

The men exchanged uneasy glances. None of them wanted to reply, but they were also aware that not answering might get them the back of Riker's hand—or sword. Finally an older man cocked his head.

"The house of Dr. Hagan, you mean, sir?"

"How many houses are there that burned down?" Riker snapped. "Yes, of course I mean that house."

"If you ask me, sir," the man continued, "it went back to its true master, if you know what I mean." He looked as if he wished he could vanish into the gloom of the room somehow. It was dangerous to attract the attention of the arrogant nobles, and just as dangerous to discuss the workings of the vanished sorcerer. But the threat of the armed man's sword was immediate, while Hagan's powers were possibly avoidable.

"I *don't* know what you mean," Deanna broke in. She sensed that the man was afraid to speak—and almost as frightened *not* to speak. He needed a little extra encouragement to loosen his tongue. The woman had returned with a flagon of wine and two pewter goblets. She handed the goblets to Deanna and Riker, then poured their drinks. Deanna held up a hand. "Perhaps you'd give our friend there a little, too."

The woman blinked with surprise and glanced at the old man. Then, shrugging, she filled his hastily emptied goblet.

"Leave the bottle," Riker told her. He flipped her another of the coins. When she looked at it in shock, he realized it was probably far too much. "We'll want food later," he said.

The woman gave a deep curtsy this time. "Of course, sir." Then she skittered away, quickly, the coin disappearing down the front of her dress.

"Thank you for your kindness, milady," the old man said. He scratched at his neck. "What I meant was that old Hagan wasn't black in just his clothing. He communed with the Devil. And the Devil must have let loose the fires of hell on that house."

"Aye," one of his companions added. "Those were no ordinary flames. They refused to be put out." That made sense—it had been a chemical fire, after all, and these people wouldn't have understood such things. Water and dirt were probably all they had to extinguish the blaze.

"An evil man," the old man said. "I heard they found a body in the ruins. I hope it was his." Then he suddenly paled as a thought occurred to him. He swallowed nervously. "Was he . . . someone you knew?"

"No," Deanna said, easing his fears. "We were looking for him."

Riker tapped the hilt of his sword. "I had a message for him. The person who died in his house wasn't this Hagan. It was a companion of ours. Hagan killed him."

"He got away?" The old man made the sign of the cross. "Then he'll loose demons on the town." He was clearly frightened of the power of the supposed sorcerer.

"Not if we find him," Riker promised. "Do you have any idea where the scum might have fled?" He took a sip of his wine. It was bitter but drinkable. If this was the house's best, he was glad he wasn't drinking the *vin ordinaire*. Another coin appeared in his hand. He could afford to be generous with Hagan's money.

The eyes of the men widened. Their informant leaned forward eagerly. "He has a boat down in the docks. Never seems to go out in it. It rides low in the water, so it must be well loaded, probably with the Devil's own wares."

"Could you show me how to find it?" Riker asked.

The man eyed the coin but hesitated. He was clearly afraid to go anywhere near the boat, but he also badly wanted the money. His indecision finally resolved itself. "I won't need to get too close?"

"Just close enough to point at it."

"When?"

Riker smiled. "When you've finished your drink." He picked up the bottle and handed it across to the other men. "And perhaps your friends would like to finish the rest of this." It was snatched eagerly from his hands and shared out. Things were going well. The chances were that this boat was Hagan's bolt-hole. He'd have gone there from the shop, to warn his fellow conspirators. It might just provide them some clue as to the location of the ringleaders of the gang. By the sound of things, it no doubt contained off-world technology forbidden under the Prime Directive.

When their informant had finished his wine, he led them back into the street. Riker noticed that it was still light, though it had to be quite late in the evening by now. He wondered briefly if the town stayed open all the time. Without a true night, how did the locals adapt to sleep cycles? Perhaps as they did on the *Enterprise,* assigning times of the day to work and sleep? Riker shrugged mentally: It hardly mattered at the moment.

The old man hesitated. "You're sure I won't have to get too close?"

"Quite certain. Just lead me to Hagan."

"There's no need to go to any trouble."

Riker, Deanna, and the old man spun around. At the next intersection stood the black-garbed magician. He was leaning on his cane, staring at them with an intense, unwavering gaze. Grouped about him were four men, all with drawn swords and nasty smiles plastered on their faces.

"It looks as if you won't have to get any closer than this to his boat," Riker murmured. He flicked the old man the coin, then drew his own sword. The informant fled back into the tavern. Riker moved into the center of the street, protecting Deanna. "You want to surrender now?" he offered. "You might get a lighter sentence."

"Your consideration touches me," Hagan mocked. "But I think I'd prefer to kill you." He gave a jerk of his head and the four thugs moved forward.

Chapter Fourteen

"It looks as if I owe Worf an apology," Riker murmured. That simulation on the holodeck might prove to be useful, after all. And no matter how good these men might be with the swords, they were hardly likely to be on the level of *'tcharian* warriors. He fell into an easy stance, scanning his advancing opponents. They all looked as if they'd done this sort of thing before. Professional killers, Riker realized. He hated to kill anyone himself, but in a fight like this he might not be able to avoid it.

The first of the four men was the most impatient. He had a cold, arrogant air about him, and he obviously believed he could take Riker on without aid. He flickered his sword around in pretty patterns that looked impressive to a novice. Riker was not impressed: such playing about couldn't get anywhere near him. He held his own sword in a deceptively casual manner.

Then the man darted in, thrusting with his blade. Riker moved slightly, parrying the thrust and twisting the blade away from his chest. The assassin grinned slightly, danced back out of the range of a counter-thrust, spun his sword, and slashed downward. Riker whirled, bringing his own sword up to block the force of the blow. Sparks flew as the blades clashed. The man tried to push past Riker's guard through sheer brute force, but Riker was prepared. As the man pushed, he dropped the point of his sword so that the other's blade screeched down the length of his own. The man's own thrust had brought him in close. Riker slammed the hilt of his sword up, catching the unbalanced man in the face with the pommel. Blood welled up as the blow slashed the assassin's cheek almost to his eye. With a scream the man staggered back. Riker kicked him in the stomach to help him on his way.

Two of the remaining three men closed in from opposing sides. With their colleague no longer blocking them, they nodded to each other and attacked at the same time. Riker fell back a pace, whipping his sword in wide arcs to prevent their advancing. The man on the left thrust, forcing Riker to parry the blow with his own blade. The man on the right then plunged in before Riker could turn to fend him off.

Deanna jumped in, throwing the silly hat she'd been wearing directly into his face. The attacker threw up his hand, blocking Riker from his view. Riker stabbed out quickly with his sword, slashing across the swordsman's arm. The man screamed, dropping his weapon and clutching at his injured arm.

Riker jerked his attention back to the other attacker, who had regained his balance and slashed his sword around in a lethal scything motion. Ducking, Riker felt the blade whip over his shoulder. The man managed to twist his hand as he swung, and the tip of the blade sliced through Riker's cloak and shirt. A sharp pain lanced through his back as the sword cut into his skin. Fighting down the pain, Riker thrust with his sword at the other man. It struck home in the top of the man's thigh. The man howled with pain, staggering aside, unable to stand on his injured leg.

Straightening, Riker fought down the urge to scream himself. Pain lanced through his entire back from the wound he'd received. His vision blurred for a moment as the final assassin moved in. The man had been smart, waiting for his fellows to tire or wound Riker. He was still fresh, while his intended victim was trying to ignore his pain. Breathing heavily, Riker tried to move to keep himself covered. This was going to be very tricky.

Hagan had been holding back, hoping that his hired thugs would be able to finish off the two Starfleet officers. It was becoming clear that this now might not happen. It was a good job that he'd brought his phaser cane, then. . . . He flicked on the *arm* button, and then raised his staff. It was dangerous to use an open display of power like this, of course, but he had little option left now.

Deanna saw the movement out of the corner of her eye. She wasn't sure what Hagan was up to, but he was clearly readying a weapon of some sort. Stooping, she picked up a fist-size stone from the filthy street and hurled it as accurately as she could and with all of the strength that she could muster.

It hit the fingers that Hagan had wound tightly around his staff. With a cry of pain the sorcerer's grip loosened, and the weapon fell into the stinking mud. There was a hiss of steam as the filthy water leaked into the power cell, then a burst of bright light as the power pack built into the staff discharged.

Then she heard noises approaching, the jingle of metal, and the cries of angry men. Riker heard the same but didn't dare drop his guard to see what was happening. It was clear that more people were heading for the area of the fight. Crouched slightly forward, he waited for the last man to make a move.

To his surprise, the assassin backed away. Puzzled, Riker glanced quickly over his shoulder. A group of six or eight armed men were running toward them. Since his opponent looked as if he was making ready to run, Riker assumed the men would back him up for some reason. As a result, he was unprepared when three of the men ran past him and two more grabbed his arms, preventing him from fighting. The last of his attackers hastily dropped his sword and allowed two of the men to grab him. The other man collared Hagan, who had been trying to recover his staff without electrocuting himself.

Riker looked around, causing his back another jolt of pain. Another man had Deanna gently but firmly by the elbow. Two more stood at attention as a man on horseback rode up. The horse was spooked by the scent of the blood, but the rider calmed it enough to survey the scene.

"You know that there is a public ordinance forbidding street brawling," the man snapped. He was lean and dark, with a pointed, neat beard and angry eyes. "What do you think you were doing?"

"These men attacked my man-at-arms and myself," Deanna said before Hagan could speak. "I believe they were after our money. My man was merely defending himself from their unprovoked attack."

"That's not true!" retorted Hagan. "These two people attacked me in my home and burnt it to the ground. My men and I were attempting to arrest them when they started this brawl."

"Four against one?" Riker laughed. "I'd hardly be the one to provoke such a fight, would I?"

The man on horseback held up his hand. "Enough." He glanced at the three injured men. "You seem to have acquitted yourself pretty well nonetheless," he observed dryly. "But all of you will come with me for the duke's judgment in this matter." He glared at the injured men. "Can you three walk?"

The man Riker had wounded in the groin shook his head slightly. He was pale from the loss of blood and had a wad of cloth pressed against his leg. The other two managed to stumble across to join the squad of soldiers.

The rider sighed and pointed to Hagan. "He's your man. Help him."

"Me?" The sorcerer drew himself up to his full height, glowering. "I am not a serving man. Don't you know who I am?"

"To be frank, I don't much care. And either you help the man or I'll have him killed on the spot for resisting arrest. Take your pick."

Hagan looked for a moment as if he was still going to refuse. Then he saw the looks on the faces of his other men and realized that they would not back his story if he didn't help their wounded friend out. "Very well," he snapped with bad grace. He took the injured man's free arm—ignoring the man's whimper of pain—and slung it over his shoulders.

The guard captain signaled for them to start moving. Deanna fell in beside Riker. Her face mirrored the pain in his own.

"Now what?" he called to the rider.

The man gave him an amused stare. "The duke will have to decide which of you is telling the truth," he replied. "Not that it will make a great deal of difference, really. He distrusts arguments like yours and prefers to get at the facts himself." He smiled nastily. "That generally involves the torture of one or all of the people involved." He glanced over at Deanna. "I rather suspect that he enjoys that part of the trial. It's generally the longest."

Wonderful. They were on their way to a trial by fury. Riker sighed. The one consolation he had was that matters could hardly get worse.

An hour outside of the city the band of slaves was in the hill country. The march continued, following an ill-defined pathway. It was not a difficult journey, except for the fact that the slaves were given no water. Picard's mouth was getting very dry. The eternal sunshine didn't help. In the hills, the cold winds died down, and they were all starting to work up a sweat from the march.

He was tired, too, from the activities of the day. Aside from his drug-induced coma, he'd been without sleep for almost twenty-six hours now. His body was getting more and more urgent in its demands for rest. Picard shut the cries out of his mind for the moment, but there was no telling how much longer he would be able to bear up without a few hours sleep to recover.

The guards watched the men with only a fraction of their attention. None of the slaves could make a break for it, linked together as they were by their chains. The guards all possessed canteens, which they resorted to at frequent intervals.

To take his mind off his aches and pains, Picard said to Kirsch: "Tell me about the dragons. Are they really as dangerous as people say?"

"Hard to be certain," Kirsch muttered back. "Few people survive encounters with them. Once they're on your track, they're implacable. Sometimes they've been killed, though. A few knights make a living by slaying dragons. Most just get themselves killed. The odd thing is that until a few years ago, there really weren't many dragons in these parts."

"Oh?" Picard felt his suspicions stirring. "But now there are?"

"More than there used to be, anyway. They're carnivores, generally preying on the herds of deer that live in the mountains. There's not much down by the shores for them to eat. That's why they go for people, I expect—we're about all the food they can catch down here."

"Interesting. And do you have a theory to explain why they've starting coming down to the plains?"

Kirsch managed a thin grin. "I have a theory for everything, remember? I have a couple in this case. Maybe the herds of deer are dying out, and the dragons need more prey, so they're venturing further afield. Or maybe the dragons have overbred themselves, and some younger dragons have been forced to leave their normal territory."

Picard nodded. Privately, though, he had a theory of his own: The hunters he had come here for were somehow forcing the dragons down toward the towns, in order to make their own hunts simpler. The gang didn't seem to be too bothered about people losing their lives. If this theory was true, then it might solve both of his problems at once. Removing the gang from this planet would stop them from interfering with the dragons. The dragons would return to the hills, where they could live out their natural lives. And the people of the towns would have the pressures of the dragon attacks taken from them.

It was nice and neat—too neat, Picard suspected, for it to work so simply. There had been dragons that attacked humans before the gang came. That danger would continue. It wouldn't be as bad as it currently was, however. Maybe with the removal of at least some of the dragon attacks the local humans would be more inclined to travel and link together. That way it would be possible for them to progress. Or would they simply stay as they had for a thousand years?

With the rest of the slaves, he trudged along wearily.

Ro surveyed her latest accommodations. The cell was stone, like the rest of the castle. There were no windows, which explained the stink. The only ventilation was a small grille in the thick oak door. And that led only into the corridor linking the cells together. As she had been pushed in here, she had seen that there were at least a dozen similar tiny rooms. Some were occupied, a few more had open doors. This duke seemed to have plenty of enemies—at least in the short term. She suspected that few of them lived very long lives.

If she lay down on the floor—which was unlikely in the extreme, given its filthy state—she could have touched both opposing walls. It was only about six feet across and eight tall. There were exactly two points of interest in it. The first was the heavy iron ring set in the wall opposite the door. She had been chained by the right wrist to this with a small padlock. The other was a small hole in the floor in the corner. It was quite clear that this was the toilet facility for the room.

Hardly luxury accommodations. At the same time it wasn't the worst place she'd been in. The Cardassians who had persecuted her and murdered her father had been much more imaginative in their own cells.

Ro had been mercifully left alone here. This was clearly supposed to be a punishment—leaving her in the near-darkness to reflect on her attitude and her possible fate. In fact, Ro was more than happy with this turn of events. In the available light she examined the padlock. A simple enough device, operated by tumblers inside the lock. They had to be triggered and twisted in a set pattern by a key—which, naturally, she had not been given. Still, there were ways around that. . . .

The tight-fitting dress now proved to be useful after all. It was so obvious that she was hiding nothing that Ro hadn't been searched. She had, in fact, taken a length of wire from the chest in the duke's bedroom. It was clearly intended for some of his games, but Ro had other plans for it. She fished the wire out of the top of her dress—she had threaded it around the neckline, where it had not been seen. Ro carefully bent the wire in the middle and then inserted it into the keyhole of the padlock. She'd not had much practice at escaping from jails these past few years, but it was like swimming. Once learned, the skill never left you. Concentrating carefully, she began probing for the shape of the tumblers.

Barclay was back on duty. He paused and stared at the readings on the Engineering board. Puzzled, he tapped the CONFIRM pattern. The same information presented itself again for his scrutiny. Smoothing back his thinning hair with his hand, Barclay turned to stare at the massive engine core. It looked fine, but if these readings were correct, then appearances were definitely deceptive. He started the computer running a swift diagnostic, then tapped his communicator. "Engine room to bridge."

A second later Geordi's voice replied: "La Forge. What is it, Lieutenant?"

"Uh . . . I'm getting some strange readings, sir," Barclay replied nervously. "According to my panel here, we're got field disruptions inside the engine pods."

"What?" Geordi's voice suddenly became very alert. "Are you sure about that?"

"No," replied Barclay. "That's why I'm running a computer verification. I just don't see how we could have developed any kind of imbalance in there. Every readout says the equipment is functioning perfectly. Ah, and the computer diagnostic confirms that. But the readings are still showing a microscopic field disruption in both the matter and antimatter pods."

Geordi was definitely sounding worried now. "Are you reading any kind of tachyon dampening?"

Barclay caught the meaning of that question. "None," he replied. "The . . . the shields are still holding out the residual effects of the protocloud." He forced his emotions down and concentrated on simply reporting the facts. "This has got to be some new kind of phenomenon that wasn't operating a few minutes ago, sir."

"Get me some answers, Mr. Barclay," Geordi snapped. "And fast. What's causing that imbalance?"

"I'll let you know as soon as I find out," Barclay promised. He turned to the assistant engineer. "Hinner! Get me a number seventeen probe, and fast!" He ran across to the protective equipment locker and started to pull on one of the shield suits. This was going to be very tricky . . . and possibly very, very dangerous.

He tried hard not to think about that aspect of it at all. If there was any other way, he'd avoid what he had in mind. But the only alternative was to wait and see if the ship blew itself apart.

Beverly frowned as she saw the strain on Geordi's face. "What's wrong?"

"Barclay's detected some minute field disruption in the matter and antimatter pods." He jumped to his feet and ran to the Engineering panel on the bridge. "And it's real, all right."

"What does that mean?" asked Beverly, joining him. "I'm a doctor, remember, not a fusion engineer."

"It means," Geordi told her, "that the containment fields that hold the antimatter and matter apart are warping slightly. If the warping increases, the fields could break down. And when the antimatter and matter mix . . ."

That much she understood only too well. "Boom. No more *Enterprise*. . . ."

Chapter Fifteen

THE PATHWAY INTO THE MOUNTAINS led through a narrow ravine. The party of slaves moved on, driven by an occasional crack of the whip from the captain. Picard could see no reason for anyone to be punished, so it was clearly sheer sadism on the part of the rider.

Picard struggled on. He was too tired to even try to plan an escape. It was all he could manage simply to place one foot in front of the other and keep going. He had no desire to feel the whip lacerate his back. Behind him, Kirsch seemed to be just as tired and just as determined not to drop.

The eternal daylight didn't help at all. If there had been a chance of nightfall, then the guards might have allowed them to rest. Still, in the mines the men would have no daylight at all. This might be their last glimpse of the world they had known. Picard could believe that no one survived long in the mines. Given these primitive conditions and the lack of care that the guards showed, mining had to be as good as a death penalty on this world.

Would he be able to escape? Picard had to be honest and admit his chances didn't look good. His only real hope at the moment seemed to be to try to stay alive and hope for rescue.

There was a deep booming roar from ahead of them in the valley. Picard glanced up, wondering what could have made the noise. The captain's horse whinnied in panic, rearing and pawing the air. The rider cursed, trying to steady the beast. Terrified, it bucked, throwing him heavily to the ground.

The slaves began turning back, jerking on the chains. The walking guards spun on their heels and broke into desperate sprints.

As the slaves surged back, Picard was dragged along. He saw why they were panicking as he was whirled around by his chains. A huge creature was emerging from the rocks ahead.

The monster was huge, some sixty feet long and about eighteen tall. Its body was green and brown mottled, with leathery, armorlike skin. The head was long and pointed. It gave another of the deep, booming roars, and Picard caught a glimpse of large, serrated teeth and a gaping maw. Behind the large eyes that centered on the fleeing men, a bony ridge ran across the dragon's head and down its back. The immense legs were all equipped with large claws. The long, sinuous tail ended in twin spikes.

The men were all panicking, unable to work together as this monster pursued them. Miles stumbled and fell. He was trampled as the other slaves rushed on, but he dragged down several more men. The line collapsed into a thrashing mass of arms and legs. Picard didn't get a chance to see if Miles was in need of help. He felt his feet knocked from under him, and he fell heavily to the rocky ground. A pain lanced through his left shoulder, then someone fell across his legs, trapping him. He tried to pull himself free, but the terrified slaves were not cooperating. Screaming and trying to drag themselves out of the writhing throng, they only created more problems.

The dragon paused for a second. The fallen rider was struggling to rise, but his right leg was twisted grotesquely from the fall. He barely had time to scream before the dragon's jaws closed on him. Picard heard the crunching of bones clearly, even at this distance. The dragon threw back its head, gulping in blood and intestines before shaking the corpse free. Blood and spittle dribbled from its mouth as it advanced on the chained slaves.

There was simply no way to free himself. Picard stared upward as the dragon slithered toward the trapped men.

Then there was a shadow falling over him. "It appears that I have arrived at a fortuitous moment," Data murmured.

"I'll say," Picard croaked. "Get these men free, quickly."

Data glanced at the chains. Despite his earlier orders to appear fully human, there was only one way for him to obey the captain's command. Gripping two of the links in the chain, he exerted as much strength as he could with his arms. The chains shattered, and the captain pulled his hands free.

The broken chains dangling from either wrist, Picard pulled himself from the mass of men. "Help them!" he ordered Data. Data moved quickly toward the chained men. Picard ran the other way, slanting toward the side of the valley. He waved his hands over his head. "Over here!" he yelled loudly. "You stupid dinosaurian—this way!"

The dragon heard and saw him. Unused to prey running toward him, the monster paused a second and reared its head back for a better view of the tiny creature. It obviously decided that Picard was no threat. The great head lunged forward.

Picard threw himself flat as the dragon struck. The gaping jaws crashed together where he had been standing, and he was sprayed with spittle from the impact. Rolling forward, he managed to regain his feet and rushed under the belly of the huge creature. The head jerked around as the dragon searched for the missing morsel. Spotting Picard running for his life, the dragon whipped its tail and slammed it down.

It barely missed as Picard flung himself back against the rocks. He was close to the body of the rider now. He tried not to notice the shredded flesh where the teeth had torn, or the stench of blood. He pulled the soldier's sword from its scabbard and turned to face the dragon once again. The three feet of cold steel in his grip wasn't much of a weapon against the monster, but he felt better having something he could use.

Data, meanwhile, had snapped the chains binding Kirsch. The astonished man staggered free. He was clearly tempted to run for his life. But he managed to control his fear and began dragging the other freed slaves to their feet. Most of them didn't have Kirsch's problem—they fled for their lives without a backward glance. Data found Miles, alive but barely conscious, at the bottom of the heap.

"Thank you for your assistance," Data said to Kirsch.

"What kind of a man are you?" the scholar whispered.

"I think you had better reserve your questions for a more auspicious time," Data replied. Having freed the slaves, he turned his attention to helping the captain. When the rider had been thrown from his horse, he had dropped his whip. It lay in the pathway now, beside the dragon. As the creature advanced on the captain, Data ran forward and snatched up the whip.

Picard stood his ground. On the periphery of his vision, he could see the slaves running for their lives. Well, they and he were free of the chains and the mines. All they had to do was to survive the attack of this behemoth. The dragon closed in on him, striking out with one huge claw.

He threw himself to one side, hacking out with the sword as he fell. The talons whistled over his head, and he felt a shudder in his arm as the sword struck the tough skin. He couldn't tell if he'd cut the creature or not. He slammed into a wall of rock—the side of the valley—that left him momentarily stunned.

The dragon roared again and stomped down at the tiny creature that had caused it pain. It barely missed crushing Picard. Flattened against the wall of the valley, Picard fought to regain his breath and senses. The dragon's head shot down toward him, and Picard found himself watching huge, saw-edged teeth heading directly for his body.

There was a crack of a whip, and then the dragon screamed in pure agony. Picard vaguely saw the metal-tipped whip lacerate the creature's eye. Ichor splattered out, and the dragon reared back. Then Kirsch was beside him, his arm about Picard, helping him to move. Wearily Picard allowed the scholar to lead him away. Covering their retreat, Data inflicted blow after blow with the whip he wielded. Each strike brought a fresh welt to the creature's hide. In a matter of moments it looked as if it had developed red stripes down the length of its body.

"I do not wish to continue hurting you," Data said to it. "If you would withdraw . . ."

Screaming and roaring, the dragon refused to give in. It kept lunging at Data with its head. One eye was useless, and there was a great cut down its neck and jaw. Picard was bone-weary, but he couldn't allow Data to face that monster alone. He shook off Kirsch's support and surveyed the area. The fight had brought them close to the valley wall. Fallen rocks would provide him some footing. . . . Ignoring his wounds and pain the best he could, Picard started climbing the rocks.

The dragon was not stopping its attack. It was either too hungry or too stupid to realize that its chosen prey were not the easiest targets. Hissing and howling, it jerked its head forward, lunging for Data. The android—unaffected by fatigue that a human would have felt—danced aside to avoid being injured. As the dragon reared up to strike at Data again, Picard seized his opportunity.

Gripping the sword in both hands, he leapt from the rocks directly at the creature's neck. The exposed skin here was not as tough as the hide on the rest of the body. Picard felt the blade puncture the skin, and his weight behind the thrust buried it deeply in the monster's neck. The force of the blow shook his grip from the hilt. He fell awkwardly. The dragon's rising paw slammed into his back, throwing him to one side. He hit the ground and all the breath was battered from his body.

The dragon was badly hurt by the sword-thrust. Data snapped the whip, opening a huge wound in the creature's leg. The monster screamed again in pain as the shattered leg gave way. It fell forward. As it hit the ground, the sword was driven deeply into the dragon's neck. It gave a shudder, and then nothing.

Picard felt strong arms helping him up. He concentrated hard, willing his aching body to ignore the pains and cuts. His back felt almost broken, and he knew he was bleeding in a score of places. But he was still alive. The yellow blotches finally stopped dancing across his vision, and he could begin to make out the carnage.

The dragon was dead. Blood was still flowing from its neck and trickling from the gashes the whip had opened. "This is extremely regrettable," Data said, looking at the dragon's corpse. There were several fallen human bodies, also. Kirsch was still alive, though, and helped Picard to his feet. Data, curling the whip, walked from the fallen monster to join them.

"Are you injured?" the android asked.

"Yes." Picard winced at the pain as he moved. "But it's bearable. I'm certainly in better shape than those poor devils." He took several deep breaths. "It's good to see you again, Data—*Dieter.*"

"And you, also, Lukas."

Kirsch was staring at Data in astonishment—and not a little fear. Picard followed the man's gaze and groaned. In the fight some of Data's makeup had smudged. His yellow-tinged skin was quite visible in patches on his arms.

"What manner of man are you?" Kirsch asked in a whisper.

"I am French," Data said evenly.

Picard shook his head. That was not going to work here. Well, he'd worry about that later. Data had been exposed, that much was certain. At the moment only Kirsch had seen this. Maybe the situation could be salvaged. Right now Picard needed information very badly. "Do you know what happened to Ro?"

"I was reliably informed that she has been purchased by the grand duke," Data replied.

"Terrific." Picard turned to Kirsch. "Does that mean she'll have been taken to the castle?"

Kirsch jerked his attention away from Data's skin. "Uh—yes. The duke has a room there that he keeps pretty girls in. That's where she'll be."

"Right." Picard glanced at Miles. Data had made him comfortable. It looked as if the security officer had broken his arm in the fall. Other than making him as comfortable as possible, there was little else they could do right now. Picard sighed. He didn't like what he was going to say next, but there wasn't much choice. "Data, contact the ship. We're going to need to get back to town as fast as possible."

Data looked at Kirsch but didn't object to the order. He tapped the brooch holding his cloak in place. "Data to *Enterprise*. Mr. O'Brien?" There was only the hissing of static. "It appears that we are cut off, Captain."

"Oh, that's just wonderful." Picard sat down heavily on a rock. "I really don't feel like a walk back into town." He looked up at his android officer. "By the way, Mr. Data—where did you learn to use a whip like that?"

"If you remember, I had mentioned studying the history of art. I was quite intrigued by the twentieth-century art form known as *motion pictures.* The whip was the favored weapon of one of the fictitious action heroes of that time, one Indiana Jones." Data cocked his head to one side slightly. "His adventures were most farfetched but quite imaginative." He stared at the fallen dragon. "Curiously, that creature bears a striking resemblance to giant dinosaurs that appeared in several of the lower quality monster movies, particularly the works of Irwin Allen and Roger Corman. In fact—"

"Mr. Data." Picard sighed. "This is not the time or place for a dissertation on twentieth-century motion pictures."

"No, sir." Data blinked several times, a sign that he was concentrating. "If I might make a suggestion, sir?"

"Go ahead," Picard said with a wave of his hand. "I could use a few suggestions right now."

"I suggest that I attempt to capture the fallen man's horse. You could then ride it on the return trip to Diesen."

Picard managed a smile. "An excellent idea, Mr. Data." Picard liked the idea of riding back rather than walking. He also had a great fondness and admiration for a good steed. And they could construct a makeshift travois to carry Miles. "Make it so."

Data nodded. He turned and started off back down the trail in the direction the horse and other slaves had taken. Picard, left alone with Kirsch and the bodies of the fallen, shook his head. "And what do you make of all this, friend Michael?"

The scholar still looked shocked. "What manner of men are you?" he repeated. "Your companion Dieter calls you *Captain.* And he is certainly not a man such as we are, is he? How could he have found us here? And he fights with such strength. And his yellow skin . . ."

Picard stood up, wincing at the pain in his back. "No, Dieter isn't very much like us." He moved over to the dead rider. He tried to ignore the terrible wounds as he unstrapped the scabbard from the dead man and fastened it around his own waist. "I've a feeling I may need this when we return to Diesen," he explained. He crossed to the fallen dragon. It was hard work, but he managed to pry the sword loose from the wound. "I wish it hadn't come to this."

Kirsch obviously wasn't sure whether Picard was referring to the dragon's death or the exposure of Data's nonhuman nature. "You are going after your other companion?" he asked. "The lady Rosalinde?"

"Yes," Picard replied. "You're free to do whatever you wish, now."

"Then I wish to accompany you, Lukas."

"Back to Diesen?" Picard raised an eyebrow. "Won't they just arrest you again?"

"Only if they see me." Kirsch shook his head. "Lukas, I'm a student. Everything about the world fascinates me. But nothing as much as you and your friends. I'm willing to risk being caught if I can get some answers from you."

Picard winced. He was caught on the horns of a

dilemma here. He could hardly tell Kirsch nothing—yet, neither could he break the Prime Directive and explain everything. Besides—how could he possibly elucidate twenty-fourth-century concepts to a man who effectively belonged a millennium in his past? "Michael," he said, gently, "I'm afraid I may not be allowed to tell you all that you wish to know. But I am the captain of a ship whose mission is to explore. Dieter and Rosalinde are members of my crew. I have an obligation to save her."

"Perfectly understandable, friend Lukas." Kirsch nodded. "You are honor-bound to her. But—what *is* Dieter?"

"He's . . ." Picard struggled to find the right words. "He only looks like a human being. He's actually an artificial construct. That is why he doesn't tire, and how he managed to track us down." Data must have followed their tracks, he knew, and managed to do so on the run. Data would not have needed to rest and would have had little problem in catching up with the slow-moving slave chain.

"Ah! A homunculus!" Kirsch grinned. "I had heard that some magicians have the power to animate the unliving. Are *you* such a wizard, Lukas? Can you make the inanimate animate and command obedience from such a one?"

Picard snorted. "I did not create Dieter. And he obeys me only because it is his choice, not because he is forced to do so."

"Whatever you say," agreed the scholar amiably.

Glancing at him sharply, Picard wondered if he had already said too much. Kirsch was no fool simply because he was ignorant of science. But just how much of this could he follow? And was this a breach of the Prime Directive?

The door to Ro's cell creaked open. Keeping her eyes almost shut, Ro feigned sleep while watching the guard enter. He was armed with a short pike, which he used to prod her with, none too gently.

"Come on, wake up," he growled. "The duke doesn't want you to rest."

Ro had no intention of resting. She grabbed the end of the pike, exploding to her feet. The manacle—which she had unfastened and then loosely draped about her wrist to make it look as if she were still a captive—clattered free. Before the startled guard could react, he was jerked forward. Ro chopped down hard on his neck, and he fell to the floor. He didn't get up.

Feeling very pleased with herself, Ro started for the door of the cell. Then she paused. She was freezing in the short dress, and her feet were still bare. She poked the guard with the pike to be certain he was out cold. Then she stripped off his trousers and boots. They were both a little too big, but the man's belt helped keep the pants up, and she tore rags from his dirty tunic to stuff in the toes of the boots. Feeling a lot warmer, she closed the door behind her. The keys were still in the lock. Ro couldn't help grinning.

Time to start a little interference play here. She locked the cell, then went to the closest locked cell. Peering inside it, she saw it was a virtual duplicate of her own cramped quarters. This one held a heavily bearded man, who looked terribly thin and exhausted. "Heads up," she called softly. When he started at her, she tossed him the keys. "See if you can do something with these, friend."

He stared at her in astonishment. Then he began to wheeze. After a second, Ro realized that he was trying to laugh. With surprising agility, he pounced on the keys and began feverishly trying them one at a time in his manacles. Ro nodded, then slipped away. He'd free himself, then perhaps a few of the others. If they escaped, all well and good. If they didn't, they would be returned to their cells. In either event, it was bound to cause some confusion among the guards. And any confusion was bound to help her.

Once the prisoners were free, they'd head for the nearest exit. Naturally, the guards would assume she'd joined them. Just as naturally, she had absolutely no intention of doing that. The best course of action at the moment was to do the unexpected.

Ro knew the last place they would think of looking for escaped prisoners was deeper in the dungeons. She turned and made her way down the corridor.

Chapter Sixteen

GEORDI CAUGHT HIMSELF—and not for the first time—rapping his fingers on the arm of the command chair. He forced himself to stop. "Mr. Van Popering—"

"Nothing yet, sir."

Sighing, Geordi glanced around and saw Beverly looking at him with sympathy. "I hate waiting," he told her.

"We all do, Geordi," she replied. "I'm worried, too. This interference with the communications isn't helping at all, but—"

The communicator beeped. Geordi jumped, then realized it was the internal system. "Bridge."

"Barclay here," came the response. "I'm entering the core approach now."

"Be careful, Reg."

"Believe me," came the fervent reply, "I'm gonna be *very* careful indeed."

As Hinner paid out the safety rope, Barclay eased himself into the maintenance tubeway that led to the main core. The protective suit he was wearing would shield him from the radiation inside the tube, as well as allow him to breath in the argon atmosphere. The suit was designed to regulate his body temperature as well, but Barclay was sweating. It was nothing to do with heat—the sheen was a result of fear. Barclay knew only too well what would happen if the field disruptions caused even the slightest rupture in the containment fields. It was nothing more than his own too-vivid imagination, but if even a particle of antimatter escaped, the resulting explosion would vaporize the tube and him with it—and then start a chain reaction that would annihilate the *Enterprise* nanoseconds later.

Shutting images of impending destruction from his mind, Barclay eased forward, the Jeffreys probe in his right hand. The shunt he was looking for was only twenty feet inside the tube, but it seemed to take forever to crawl the distance. Finally, his heart beating wildly, Barclay made it to the panel. Placing the probe carefully beside him, he set to work unfastening the panel. It took just seconds, and then swung open. As he reached for the probe, Barclay stared in horror.

It was juddering in place, rattling on the metal tubing. There was some kind of vibration inside the tubeway. . . .

"Geordi!" he called frantically. "I'm getting vibration in the core approach!"

"Get out of there, Reg!" Geordi commanded.

"But the readings—"

"That's an order, Mr. Barclay."

He wished he could obey it. Being trapped inside the core tubing was a nightmare Barclay didn't even want to think about. But without the probe readings, they wouldn't be able to tell what was happening in the containment fields. "Sorry, Geordi," he muttered. "I'm getting communications interference. Didn't hear what you said." He plugged the probe into the panel and tapped in the activation codes. He could feel the vibrations of the tube now, conducted through the suit. His teeth began rattling, and not entirely from the fear that was twisting at his stomach.

"Reg, get out of there!"

He ignored Geordi's insistent calls and began to transmit the readings back to the main panel in engineering. "Geordi, shut up a moment, will you?" he snapped. "I'm getting the weirdest signals down here." The tube creaked. He prayed it wasn't the onset of structural failure. "The field distortions aren't an internal problem. There's some kind of external force being exerted upon us that's causing the stressing." He began to run the second-level diagnostic. "According to the probe, we're being subjected to polarized gravitic interference."

Geordi was silent for a very long two seconds. Finally he said: "Reg, you know that's a theoretical impossibility."

"Tell me about it." Barclay saw the CONFIRM configuration. "But the computer insists that's the case."

"Okay. Now get outta there!"

"I hear you," Barclay confirmed. As fast as he

could, he detached the probe. He couldn't afford to make a mistake, but the tube was clattering about him now. The interference was affecting the containment fields, and the stresses were being conducted down the approach paths—this tube being the main one. He fastened the panel and started crawling backward. Hinner was taking up the slack on the rope.

There was a horrible sound of shearing metal as the stresses on the tubeway exceeded its tolerances. A jagged edge of metal tore free barely two feet from his faceplate. Then the tube twisted, and he felt a terrible pain in his leg. Clenching his teeth to bottle up the scream that wanted to escape, Barclay glanced back. The tube wall had ruptured, trapping his ankle.

The shaking became worse, and he knew that he was barely moments away from a containment field breakdown and the utter destruction of the *Enterprise*. . . .

"What's wrong, Geordi?" Beverly asked, her face pale.

"We're under some kind of attack," he snapped. "Worf, red alert. Shields to maximum."

"Confirmed." The klaxon began to howl.

Leaping to his feet, Geordi ran to the Ops panel, pushing Van Popering aside. His fingers flew over the panel. "Damn! Reg was right."

"What is it?" Beverly was at his shoulder, staring at the readings without understanding them.

"There's some kind of device outside the ship that's generating phased gravity waves."

"Isn't that a theoretical impossibility?"

"Yeah." His fingers tapped again, bringing up a

whole mess of flashing red lights. "But I'll worry about that later. Right now we're in real serious trouble."

Worf called out from his own board: "Engine overload. Fifteen seconds to core integrity breach."

Beverly didn't need to be told what that meant.

Geordi snapped: "Reassign the shields to Ops. Now!" His fingers flew faster than Beverly could follow. "I'm attempting to rephase their settings."

The ship was starting to shake as the internal gravity compensators began to break down. Beverly clutched at the railing behind her, helpless to do anything but watch. She didn't even have the time to become terrified.

"Eight seconds," Worf reported. "Core temperature rising."

"Got it!" Geordi grinned and slammed home the final commands. He looked up at the screen. The picture was broken up by interference, but they could all see the small metallic sphere sail past them. "Worf—phasers!"

"On line," the Klingon reported. "Firing . . . now."

The screen compensated for the brightness of the beam that lashed out from the ship toward the sphere. The interference in the picture cleared a little, but it was still like watching events through a snowstorm. The phasers seemed to slow down, and then the beam actually *bent*. . . .

"Just as I thought," Geordi whispered as the beam faded from sight.

"Target unharmed," Worf reported. "Shall I try again?"

"No." Geordi breathed out loudly. "It was just an experiment. You can't destroy that thing."

Beverly glared at him. "Are we out of danger?" she snapped.

"Not hardly." He stood up, indicating Van Popering to resume his post. "That device has made its pass, but it'll be back, count on that. It's on our orbital path."

"But what is it?"

Geordi chewed on his lip for a moment. "Best way I can think of to describe it is a kind of gravity bomb," he finally said. "It's a small device that somehow creates a point of gravity waves. When we do calculations about gravity, we pretend that the whole force is concentrated at the center of a sphere. It's not really true, but it's good enough for math. Well, in this case, it *is* true. That small sphere was somehow putting out the gravitational pull of a medium-size star. It acts like a tiny black hole, passing close to the ship. It's as if we were only a few light-minutes away from the core of a sun. That's what caused the fluctuation in the containment fields."

"And what did you do to stop it?"

"Well, it's using polarized gravity waves." He shook his head. "Man, we're facing so many theoretical impossibilities here. Anyway, it's kind of like polarized light—the gravitic equivalent of a laser beam, or phaser, only using gravity instead of light. I rephased the shields to act like a pair of sunglasses. I aligned the field phase of the shields with the beam and then twisted it to reflect the gravity waves."

"Then what's the problem?" she asked, puzzled. "Can't you do that again next time if the thing returns?"

"Maybe. But you saw how close I cut it this time. If

there's more than one of those devices out there, we could be in serious trouble."

Worf glanced up from his board. "Is there any way to detect their approach?" he asked.

"You mean apart from their almost causing our engines to blow?" Geordi scratched the back of his neck. "Yeah. I think we can get the sensors recalibrated to read them. They must be generating pinpoint gravitic fields that we could detect as they warp space about the bombs."

"That should give us an edge," Beverly said.

"Right." Geordi managed a watery smile. "Kind of like walking through a mine field on tiptoe. Those devices are pretty small, and we won't be able to detect them until they're almost on top of us."

Worf considered this. "Why don't we simply go to a higher orbit?" he suggested. "We could stay away from those devices."

"I don't know about that," Geordi answered. "According to O'Brien, we're at about the limits of his equipment right now. We won't be able to track and beam up the landing parties if we go farther out. Not that the transporters will work until I get the gravity residue cleaned out."

"Nor will we be able to beam them up if we are destroyed," countered Worf.

"I think we'd better wait to see if we're attacked again before we consider moving out of orbit," Geordi decided.

The communicator whistled. "Hinner to bridge."

"Now what?" Geordi wondered. "I'm beginning to dislike command. Go ahead, Ensign."

"Sir," Hinner reported, "it's Lieutenant Barclay. He's still inside the access tubeway, and I can't get a response from him. The tube's partially collapsed about him. I think he's trapped in there."

Ro was somewhat puzzled by the passageway that she had just entered. There hadn't been any cells for quite a distance, and yet the tunnel kept on going. There didn't seem to be much reason for it. It must have taken the locals months to dig it out, and yet it was without any obvious purpose.

Which meant it had to have some hidden reason for its existence. But what?

Ro came to a slow halt and stared at the wall that blocked her path. The tunnel simply ended here. This place was making very little sense at all. One thing that was clear, though, was that she wouldn't be getting out this way. She didn't want to stay here, either, with no place to retreat if she was discovered. Reluctantly she set off back up the passageway again.

There was the sound of footsteps just as she drew level with the first empty cell. Quickly she ducked inside and waited. As she listened, her bewilderment increased. The steps were coming from the dead-end passageway, not toward it. She peered through the grating on the door of the cell. Someone was indeed coming up the passageway. The flickering torches on the wall weren't the best of lighting, but she could make out that the man was tall, heavyset, and bearded. He wore a large cloak that was edged with some kind of whitish fur. Around his neck was a heavy-looking piece of metallic jewelry that was probably some kind of badge of office. Without concern, he strode past the cell Ro hid in and on toward the main part of the dungeons. In a few moments the sound of his steps had faded.

Ro pulled open the cell door again, deep in thought. He had been in the passageway without an exit, yet she hadn't seen him. Which meant that there had to be some sort of secret passageway or door down there. And if that man had been able to enter the dungeons via that pathway, then perhaps she could escape using it. Assuming, of course, that she could find it.

She moved slowly down the passageway, her hands resting gently on the walls, as she strove to discover any hidden exit.

Engineering was a mess. Broken equipment lay about on the floor and tables where it had fallen. This close to the core, the gravitic stresses had caused more damage than anywhere else in the ship. Beverly stepped over broken glass and shattered electronic components as she made her way to the tube where Barclay was trapped.

Most of the engineering staff was working on re-aligning the fields. The distortion produced by the gravity bomb may have been nullified, but the warp engines couldn't be brought on line until they had been recallibrated and reset. If the bomb came back, or another one arrived, this scene would be repeated —assuming, of course, that they could stave off the ultimate effects and survive such an attack.

Only Hinner and one of the other ensigns stood by the access shaft where Barclay was trapped. As Beverly had requested, they had a spare shielded suit ready for her. Geordi had attempted to argue her out of going into the tube, but she had adamantly refused to allow one of the engineers to try and rescue Barclay. If his suit was torn or its field unstable, they could kill him trying to get him out. She had won the argument.

She suspected that if Jean-Luc had been present, though, he'd have forbidden her to attempt this crazy rescue.

She tried to keep her mind off the dangers as she suited up. It didn't work. Though the argon in the tube was inert, it could kill Barclay by simple suffocation. If his suit had ripped, he'd be dead by now.

"No signs of movement?" she asked Hinner.

He shook his head. "He's been in the same position since I called the bridge." As he finished fastening her clamps and activating the suit's field, the other ensign handed her a cutting phaser. She snapped it onto her belt, slinging the medical kit over her shoulder. "You'll have to cut the plate that's on his foot," Hinner explained. "That should free him. But if the suit's torn . . ." He didn't have to fill her in on the consequences.

"I'm not likely to cut through anything vital, am I?" she asked. "The last thing anyone needs right now is my ignorance of engineering to result in a severed power coupling." She tried to keep her voice light, but it wasn't very convincing.

"No. I've rerouted the systems at that point and put in blocks." Hinner slapped her gently on the arm. "Good luck."

"Right." Beverly flashed him a nervous smile, then pulled herself into the airlock. It was a tight fit, despite the fact that she was slim. Maybe it was because of constricting entry ports like this that she never saw any overweight engineers. The hatch closed behind her, and she was shut in the tiny lock. She tapped the argon feed controls by the second hatchway. After a few seconds the green light came on. She pushed at the hatch, which gave way reluctantly. It was easy to see why there was a problem. The door had buckled slightly and wasn't a firm fit any longer.

The narrow tubeway stretched ahead of her. Claustrophobia wasn't something engineers worried about, clearly. One of the lights built into the tube flickered unsteadily, but there was sufficient illumination to show her what lay ahead.

Barclay was visible about ten feet from her. The safety line had been sliced through by the tubing where it had ruptured. The walls looked as if they had been pinched together by some giant fingers.

"Reg!" she called. "Can you hear me?" There was a chance that he was conscious but unable to move and that his communicator was inoperative. If he was awake, he ought to be able to hear her as she began to make her way into the tube. There was no response, however. Fighting back the fear that he might already be dead, she crawled toward him carefully. She had to check the passageway for any debris—it would only take a small piece of sharp metal to tear her suit and let out her precious air.

Then she had reached the fallen section of the tubing. She looked it over carefully. Part of the wall had ruptured, buckled and then collapsed, trapping Barclay's foot. Amazingly, his suit looked as if it was still uncompromised. The metal had formed a kind of clamp about his ankle. Beverly didn't need her medical equipment to show her that the bones had broken. Barclay must have passed out from the pain.

The first thing she had to do was to ease the pressure on the ankle. That meant cutting the panel away from Barclay's foot. It was going to take a precise and steady hand. If she cut too close to his ankle, she might damage his suit herself. If she cut too far away, the section might be too heavy for her to move.

Gently she brought the cutting laser into position and triggered the beam. It hissed slightly in the argon atmosphere, but it was designed not to cause an electrical discharge. Of course, if Hinner had accidentally left any of the power lines running through the wall here live, then she could trigger a massive discharge by severing it. The result would be like sitting inside a fluorescent tube as it arced. She'd probably not be aware of the problem before she was dead.

She had to stop thinking things like that! The engineers knew what they were doing. She was in no danger of being fried to death. . . . The beam slowly cut through the shattered panel. She fought to keep her hands steady, to have the beam cut gently but precisely. Sweat was pouring off her forehead. She wished there was some provision inside the faceplate to wipe her brow. There wasn't, of course.

The job seemed endless. Her eyes ached from the strain, and she had to keep blinking them. The phaser light left greenish after-images on the inside of her eyelids. Finally the last segment of the panel snapped free. Before she could move, it started to slide off Barclay's foot. Instinctively she reached out to catch it—probably the stupidest thing she could have done. The sharp edge slashed across the finger of her suit, slicing through the thin material.

The INTEGRITY COMPROMISED light inside the faceplate began to flash. She was absurdly annoyed at it—she *knew* she'd torn the suit. Quickly she reached for her medical kit and pulled out the skin spray. It was the work only of a few seconds to spray the artificial skin over the tear. It hardened almost instantly, and the light stopped flashing.

Beverly breathed again. There hadn't been any real need to hold her breath for those agonizing seconds, but instincts refused to listen to reason. That had been close, but she was out of danger. But had the shifting metal plate ruptured Barclay's suit?

The plate lay to one side of the tube. She could see no visible rips in his suit, but that didn't mean much. She crawled forward again, hauling herself carefully over his broken ankle. As soon as she could reach out and touch his belt, she extended the electronic probe in her glove. It interfaced with his output line, and she scanned his vital signs.

Thank God! He was alive and breathing. The suit wasn't torn.

She wished she dared stop to give him a painkiller. But there was no time to waste. If one of the gravity bombs came near the ship again, this tubing would collapse about them. She had to have the pair of them out into engineering before that could happen.

Beverly wormed her way backward until she was off Barclay once again. Then she clutched his uninjured ankle in her left hand. Bracing herself against the sides of the tube, she started to tug. He moved slightly. She tugged again, and he jerked toward her a couple of inches.

Ten feet to go . . . This was going to take a while. She only hoped that she would have that time.

Chapter Seventeen

RIKER TRIED not to look discouraged as he, Deanna, Hagan, and the assassins were escorted into the castle. It was a formidable establishment, made from huge blocks of stone. There was no moat, at least, but the only entrance was a large gatehouse that was well manned. A portcullis was winched upward as the guards signaled their approach. The bottom of the portcullis was like razor-sharp teeth. If that came down while anyone was under it, he'd be ripped in half. As soon as the party had entered the castle, the portcullis was lowered behind them.

Getting out again wouldn't be easy without approval from the duke. Riker wished he had faith that they would be set free. From the attitude of the guard captain, however, this didn't look too likely.

Once through the gateway, they were in the courtyard. It was some fifty feet across and lined with straw.

To the right of the entrance were the stables. The stench of horse manure made it impossible to miss. To the left were entrances to the walls and barracks. By one building several guards were working with long, lean hounds of some kind, presumably used for hunting. Directly ahead of them was the castle proper. There was no entrance on the ground floor—a defensive tactic that made storming the castle much more difficult. The approach was up a flight of steps that doubled back on itself. Directly above this was an overhang. The floor of the overhang had several holes in it, most likely for the venting of burning oil or arrows. Unwelcome guests and door-to-door salesmen would get short shrift here.

The guard captain swung down from his horse. One of the men in the yard ran out to take the animal back to the stables. The captain led the group up the steps and in through the main entrance.

Immediately ahead of them as they stepped inside was a short corridor. One door, slightly ajar, led to a flight of steps curving upward. A second door was closed. Directly ahead of them was a set of double doors. Men-at-arms stood to attention outside them. The guard captain strode toward these. The men instantly grabbed the huge iron handles and swung the doors open. The guards with Riker and the group gestured them forward.

They emerged into what had to be the great hall of the castle. The ceiling was some fifteen feet high, and the room about four times as long and wide as that. A huge fireplace at the far end of the room was filled with a blazing fire that hissed, crackled, and smoked. Above the large mantel was a large painted coat of arms, obviously belonging to the grand duke. To the right of the fire was a raised dias, and upon it stood two high-back chairs. There were two small stools to one side, but nothing else to sit upon in the room.

Elaborate tapestries lined two walls. They were predominantly green, showing a unicorn at play on the first wall, and the same creature with its head in a maiden's lap on the adjacent wall. The final two walls were bare of decoration but held elaborate candelabra. Between the mass of candles on this and the blazing fire, the room was quite well lit.

The guards ushered them, none too gently, before the chairs. The captain then strode across to one of the courtiers that stood lazily to one side of the room. After a whispered conversation, the courtier nodded and slipped out through a side door. The captain marched back to join them.

"I've sent for the duke," he said to both Riker and Hagan. "You can try to convince him of your sincerity."

"I'm not worried," lied Riker. "I've done nothing wrong."

The captain laughed. "Neither have a lot of people who rest in the dungeons below us at this moment," he replied. "You'll have to be a little more . . . persuasive than that." He seemed to realize that Riker wasn't following his meaning. "Look, friend, I don't much care which of you is telling the truth. If either of you is," he added shrewdly. "But let me give you some advice while you can still take it. The duke has two real pleasures in his life—collecting gold and indulging in a spot of torture. If you can't help him with the one, then you'll certainly suffer with the other. You get my meaning?"

"Yes." Riker was starting to wish he hadn't been

quite as generous as he had been back at the tavern. He had no real idea whether the amount left in his stolen purse was a bribe or an insult.

"Smart man." The captain cast an appreciative eye over Deanna. "Of course, he might just decide to take the lady here in lieu of better offers, so you've got one bargaining chip that your enemy there doesn't."

"She's not for trade," Riker said, flushing angrily.

The captain shrugged. "Suit yourself. I'm just being friendly."

"Thanks," Riker said dryly.

Hagan glowered at the guard captain. "Why are you being so generous to my foe?" he snapped. "When I win my case, it won't go well for you."

The captain shrugged. "I don't like your face," he said frankly. "And this foe of yours was well on his way to beating you. I happen to admire a good fighter."

"You've picked the wrong side," Hagan told him.

"I've picked no sides. I'm just handing out free advice." The captain leaned forward, glowering into the sorcerer's dark eyes. "And I don't like being threatened by men who won't lift a sword."

"There are other ways to kill than with a sword, Captain."

"And I'm sure you probably know most of them." Before the man could say any more, the door close to the fire opened and two men walked into the room.

The first was obviously the duke. He was overweight and overdressed and carrying a silver goblet slopping wine on the floor. His mood appeared to be as unpleasant as his face. Riker could tell that the man had been ravaged by disease, and he appeared to be walking very carefully, as if nursing an injury. He flopped into the larger of the two high-back chairs.

The second man was dressed very well, with a fur-edged cloak and a large medallion of office about his neck. He settled with more grace onto one of the stools. His eyes met those of Hagan for a moment, clearly in recognition. There was a sinking feeling in the pit of Riker's stomach as he saw the smile that toyed at the edges of the fortune-teller's mouth.

"All right," said the duke sullenly. "What's this about, Volker? Do you think I've got nothing better to do with my time than to listen to the whines of peasants?"

"A street brawl, my lord," the captain replied.

"Well, why didn't you just deal with it yourself?" the duke snapped. "Execute the lot of them and set the crowd an example."

"With respect, sir, the last time we did that, things grew rather ugly." Volker nodded at Riker and Hagan. "Besides, they looked to me like men of some wealth, my lord, and I thought you'd prefer to question them yourself."

Showing a little interest at last, the duke studied the prisoners. His eyes lingered on Deanna before he finally stared at Hagan. "Well—what do you have to say?" he demanded.

"My lord," the magician said, bowing low, "I ask you to grant me justice. This man"—he indicated Riker—"set upon me and my men in the street. And for no reason."

"That's not the song you sang before," said Volker gently.

Hagan shot him a filthy look. "I do not wish to

inflict my problems on such a busy man as the duke," he explained gravely.

"At least you show some sense," the duke growled. Turning to Riker, he said: "And what's your version of all this?"

Riker bowed as low as Hagan had. "My lord, this man and his thugs set upon my lady and me without warning."

"And did he have a reason for his actions?"

"Yes." Riker nodded. "I was about to expose him as a scoundrel, a liar, and a fraud. He wanted to silence me."

"That's a damned lie!" protested Hagan. The duke glared at him, and he subsided.

"If you speak again without my permission," the ruler threatened, "I'll pull your tongue out by its roots and make you eat it." Then he lounged back in his chair and took a hefty swallow of his wine. "So far, neither of you sounds at all convincing. I'm considering having you all thrown into the dungeons for irritating me."

"My lord," purred the man on the stool. "Allow me to speak, if you please."

"What is it, Randolph?" The duke obviously didn't appreciate this interruption while he was trying to shake down his victims.

"This man I know." Randolph gestured at Hagan. "He's a businessman from the town with impeccable credentials."

"How impeccable?"

Randolph smiled. "A hundred gold pieces."

The duke raised an eyebrow. "Impeccable indeed. And the other man?"

"I've no idea. He doesn't look like a local to me."

Randolph stared down at Deanna. "And the lady—if she *is* a lady—is also a stranger."

"I see." The duke sat a little straighter in his seat. "In which case, it's clear that these two scoundrels from out of town attacked one of our local merchants of fine repute and tried to rob him. Isn't it?"

"Quite clear," agreed Randolph.

"Well, we can't stand for that." The duke made a gesture, and Riker's arms were gripped by two of the guards. A third seized hold of Deanna. "I think we'd better make an example of this pair. Toss them in the dungeons for now. I'll consider what to do with them later." He stared at Riker. "Something lingering for you, I fancy. With boiling oil in it. And as for you"—his eyes fastened hungrily on Deanna—"perhaps I shall temper your fate with . . . mercy. Off with them!"

"Do you call that justice?" snarled Riker.

"I call *everything* I dispense justice," the duke said evenly.

"Quiet," Volker added, slapping Riker across the face. He gave an almost imperceptible shake of the head. Riker quieted down and allowed the guards to lead him out of the room. When the doors closed behind them, Volker sighed. "You were trying hard to get yourself killed there," he said. "Arguing with the duke isn't very smart. Now—I'm sorry for you, but it's down to the cells with you now."

Deanna stared at him curiously. "You don't seem like such a bad person," she said candidly. "Why do you work for that swine?"

"Because it's a lot safer than working against him," Volker snorted.

"Is safety everything?" she persisted.

"Without it, nothing else is worth very much," he replied. "I'm sorry for the both of you. You seem decent enough. But that Hagan clearly knows Randolph, and Randolph's the duke's adviser. You can't beat that."

"I suppose not." Riker let the guards lead him to the closed doorway. He saw that it was locked. Volker nodded, and one of the guards used a large key to unlock the door. As he reached to open it, the door exploded outward, hurling him aside.

Several howling maniacs poured out of the doorway and threw themselves onto the guards.

Picard managed to doze astride the horse. Kirsch sat behind him, arms about the captain to prevent his falling from the saddle, and guided the beast as it trotted gently back toward Diesen. Miles, still unconscious, was tied to the rough travois they had lashed together. Data kept up an easy lope beside the animal. Kirsch couldn't help marveling at how relaxed the homunculus appeared to be.

"I do not burn energy in the way that your body does," Data explained to him. "I have a small power pack built into me that keeps a constant level of power, whatever my requirements."

"Are there many more wonders like you wherever you and Lukas come from?" asked Kirsch, amazed.

"There are indeed many things you would find astonishing," Data replied. "But they are not like me. Please do not ask me any more questions on this matter. I am forbidden to answer any further."

"Ah! A magical geas!"

"No." Data shook his nead slightly. "It is merely a rule that I have agreed to uphold because I believe it to be the wisest course of action. Merely revealing myself as a non-human being has stretched to the limits the information I may impart to you."

Kirsch considered this. "I don't see what harm it has done to tell me."

"Nor do I, at this moment," Data agreed. "But we rarely get to see all of the consequences of our actions immediately."

"You and Lukas do hold some strange beliefs." Kirsch sighed. "I know that there must be much more that you could tell me, if only you would."

"This is true. But we believe that it is better for you to discover these things for yourself, rather than to be given them."

Kirsch grinned. "Ah! My father would no doubt agree with you there."

"Indeed?"

"Yes. He's quite wealthy, but wouldn't give me money to support my studies. He believes that a person values money more if he earns it than if he's given it."

Data nodded. "The principle is somewhat similar. You value knowledge more when you discover it for yourself rather than if it is handed to you."

The student laughed. "Ah, I've caught you out there, my friend! If that is indeed the case, then surely we should teach our children nothing and let them discover all about the world for themselves—if they live long enough!"

"We are talking of different kinds of learning," Data replied. "Teaching your children what you know is one thing; teaching your people what I know would be something very different." Before Kirsch could question this, Data added: "If I could explain what I mean by that, I would. But I am constrained from doing so. Please accept that what I know is of a very different order from what you know."

Kirsch thought it over and then nodded. "You know magic, being a creature of magic. I am a student of the sciences, and therefore untrained in magical lore."

Data allowed this statement to go unchallenged. It was, after all, merely an example of Clarke's Law in action: Any sufficiently advanced technology will appear to be magic to outsiders. It was best to allow Kirsch to discover his own answers—however incorrect they might turn out to be.

The access tube was groaning and moving slightly about Beverly as she dragged Barclay's unconscious form inch by inch backward. It was clearly in imminent danger of collapse. If one of the panels fractured, the sharp edge could cut her suit open, at the very least. She'd be dead before anyone could reach her. And if the tube shattered around her, she could be torn to pieces by the wreckage. She tried to force all the images of chunks of razor-sharp metal falling on her from her mind. It was by no means easy. She concentrated on moving Barclay and crawling backward, focusing her energies and thoughts only on the task at hand.

She was sweating badly, and there was a terrible itch at the base of her spine. In the suit scratching was impossible. Besides, it had to be pyschosomatic. To be honest, it had to be *fear*. Crawling down an access tube that was filled with gas and ready to break apart any second was playing havoc with her courage. She glanced over her shoulder. Just a few more feet . . . Her sweat was clouding up the inside of her helmet's faceplate. The suit was doing its best to clear the moisture from the suit, but it couldn't handle this amount. Taking a deep breath, Beverly tried to calm down.

A section of the wall beside her ruptured with a hiss of escaping gas. She flung herself aside as the metal curled and slashed at her as if it were alive. Sparks danced across the exposed gap, and one of the neurone net crystals shattered. The tiny slivers showered across her suit. If one of those hit her with any force . . . Involuntarily she closed her eyes. She had to will them open again.

The sparking died away, and there was no further movement. Beverly swallowed, realizing how close to death she had been. Her hands were clamped tightly about Barclay's ankle, and she carefully unclenched one. Gently she brushed the shards of shattered crystal off her suit and away from the section of the tube she'd have to drag Barclay across. It was painstaking, nerve-racking work. If one shard was left, it could well rupture their suits as they slid over it. But she had to hurry in case any more of the tube ruptured while they were still inside it.

Finally she was satisfied, and she began her weary journey once again. To her relief, after a few more feet, her foot slapped against the outside of the airlock door. Bracing herself carefully, she got a grip of Barclay's belt and pulled him toward her. She'd have to get him into the airlock and then wait for the cycle to complete and the technicians outside to remove Barclay before she could get to safety herself. She loathed the idea, but there was not room for two in the tiny airlock. As gently as she could, she managed to push Barclay into the small chamber. As she did so, she saw his face through the helmet's plexiglass. It was white and strained, but he was breathing. A faint spider-web crack in the glass showed just how close he'd come to death. If the plastic had suffered a little more impact, it would have broken completely.

The small airlock seemed to take forever to flush out the argon and then flood with the air mixture that the ship used. Waiting inside the tube, the door to the airlock closed on Barclay, Beverly could hear the access shaft creaking and groaning. She wondered if it was going to come apart about her.

Then there was the sound of a thump from the lock, and scraping noises. That had to be Hinner taking the unconscious Barclay out of the tube. Then the outer door closed again. Twisting around, Beverly tapped in the commands on the keypad to begin the cycle again. After another eternity the inner door swung creakily open. The joint was getting worse, she noted. The tube was still suffering stress forces. She wriggled into the airlock and closed the door. Then she used the keypad to order the argon flushed.

A red light flashed. "The inner door must be fully closed before airlock procedures may commence," the computer announced.

"Damn!" Beverly pulled at the hatch, but it appeared to be fully closed. Then she saw that there was a gap along the upper part of the seal. The hatch had warped too much to close properly. Now what?

She was about to signal Hinner when Geordi's voice sounded over the ship's communications broadcast. "Bridge to all decks: Prepare for action." The red alert siren began to howl.

Beverly started to worry seriously now: There was

another gravity bomb attack under way, and she was stuck inside of the malfunctioning access tube. . . .

Then the airlock door behind her exploded outward. Beverly fell backward, into waiting arms. Hinner lowered her to the deck as the second ensign slammed the door closed and latched it again before too much argon could leak out.

"I gathered you were having problems, Doctor," Hinner said seriously.

She gave him a thankful smile as she unsealed her helmet. "Bless you," she murmured. Then she turned to Barclay, who was on a portable null-gee stretcher. "I'll get the rest of the suit back to you later," she promised. "Right now I'm taking Mr. Barclay down to sick bay." Without waiting for a reply, she powered up the stretcher and pushed it before her.

The ship shuddered about her. The attack had begun again.

Chapter Eighteen

THE MOB RUSHING UP from the dungeons was in no way organized or efficient. But they were determined never to be taken back down again. Even though they were weak from the treatment they had received while incarcerated, they fought like demons to get free.

Volker and his guards had been taken by surprise. They had never considered the possibility of a mass escape before, even one as disorganized as this. Two of the guards were clubbed to the ground before they could react, and the one stunned by the door in his face was beaten to the ground. Three of the escapees ripped the swords from the fallen guards' hands and leapt for the other men.

It was an uneven fight from the start. Beaten, malnourished, and exhausted, the prisoners didn't stand a chance against the well-armed guards. But that didn't stop them from trying. They rushed the main doors, bearing the struggling guards back with the press of their bodies. The guards hacked at them without heed for their lack of weapons. There was a stench of blood and screams as the fighting intensified.

Volker had no option but to call in the other men from the courtyard. He flung open the door, calling down for help. The startled guards leapt to their feet and rushed to help their beleaguered colleagues. The prisoners fought as well as they could, but it was an impossible battle. They were cut down and mercilessly murdered. Volker took no pleasure in the slaughter, but his men were more than eager to commit the butchery.

Finally quiet settled again. One of the prisoners, badly wounded, cried out. A guard viciously hacked down with his sword, half-severing the man's head and silencing him. Volker turned away in disgust. He was a soldier, not a butcher. Standing by the entrance to the fortress proper, he gazed around at the dead escapees. There were a half-dozen bodies of his guards in with them. But there was no sign of . . .

"Where are Riker and the girl?" he snapped.

The guards looked about, puzzled. "They didn't escape, Captain," one offered.

"I know that. Then where *are* they?" Volker glared at the men. "Right, you three"—he indicated the men with a gesture—"into the dungeons. Search down there. You four, up the stairs. You two, with me." He crossed to the great hall's doors and pulled one open. Riker and the girl must have taken one or more of the three alternative ways out.

He had made the correct decision. Inside the great hall he saw Riker immediately.

He had the duke's head in a grip that left the duke blue in the face. Riker glanced around and smiled tightly. "If I increase the pressure," he said calmly, "then you'll be left without a leader. Come on over here, Volker, with your men, and lay down your weapons."

The duke choked and gestured feebly with one hand. It was clear that he was ordering Volker to do as he had been told. For a moment Volker considered refusing the order and daring Riker to do his worst. If he killed the duke, he'd have no hostage. Then he'd be dead meat. And Volker would not have that sadistic fool ordering him about. On the other hand, Riker didn't look like a man who would kill in cold blood. And if he let the duke live, Volker would certainly pay if he had refused the duke's orders.

With a sigh Volker obeyed. He indicated to his two men to join him and walked toward the dais.

Riker wasn't certain how far he could push his luck. When the prisoners had jumped the guards, he had quickly realized that he now had a chance for escape. Taking a hostage seemed to be the best plan, and the best hostage was the top man. He and Deanna had managed to surprise the duke as he was counting Randolph's bribe. Hagan had tried to stop Riker, but he was little match for a trained Starfleet officer. At the moment he was still on the floor, moaning softly from the swift chop to the kidneys he'd suffered.

Deanna stood beside Riker, ready to grab one of the swords when the guards laid their weapons down. She was sensing so many different feelings from all around her that she missed the important one until it was too late. Amid the fear and pain and concern, she suddenly felt an overwhelming anger. She started to cry out as Randolph flung himself onto Riker and jabbed him in the arm.

Riker collapsed soundlessly, his mouth open in shock. Deanna saw the needle embedded in his arm and realized that they had found the next link in Hagan's gang—Randolph. It made sense that their leader would be close to the local ruler, to ensure that the gang's activities went smoothly and undetected. Before she could go to Will's rescue, the two guards grabbed her. One twisted her hair in his hand and savagely tugged her to the ground. He viciously jerked her head back and raised his sword to strike at her neck.

"No!" ordered Volker. "These two attacked the duke. I'm sure he'll want to dispense their fate personally."

The guard nodded. Deanna felt the tearing pain in her scalp ease slightly, and the sword was lowered.

Volker crossed to where Riker lay on the floor. Randolph palmed the needle he had used to fell the attacker and smiled unctuously up at the guard captain. "Perhaps you'd do well to keep a better eye on your prisoners," he suggested. "Or you may discover yourself joining them in the dungeon, Volker."

Flushing, the captain gestured for the other guard to help the shaken Riker to his feet. The drug Randolph had used was wearing off already. Volker had seen the needle the duke's adviser had used. Poison-tipped, probably, and meant for his last line of self-defense. Randolph must want these prisoners out of the way very badly indeed to have used the needle. Perhaps it would do him some good to question Riker later. He disliked and distrusted Randolph. The man was a toad, flattering and bribing the duke, and all the time playing his own little games. The man had come from nowhere a few years ago, and it might be high time he vanished the way he had come.

Volker bent to examine the duke. The marks of Riker's fingers still burned whitely in the corpulent flesh of the duke's neck. The duke was breathing but was still unable to speak. This just wasn't his day, Volker reflected. First he was kicked in the privates by his latest would-be plaything, and now he was attacked and throttled by one of his prisoners.

Turning to his guards, Volker ordered: "Take this pair down to the cells. Then get that mess outside cleaned up." He offered the duke a supporting hand. "I'll see that our lord gets to his lady wife so she can minister to him." He shot Randolph a glare. "Meanwhile, perhaps you'd stay out of trouble and take that friend of yours away."

Randolph glared at the departing guards as they obeyed their instructions. As soon as he was alone with Hagan, he whirled around angrily. "That Volker is beginning to annoy me," he growled. "Almost as much as you are. I told you to have those Starfleet officers killed, not brought here!"

Hagan shrugged. "What difference does it really make? Once they're in the duke's cells, they're as good as dead. The only way they could escape is if the *Enterprise* can rescue them. And I assume you've taken care to see that won't happen?"

"Oh, yes." Randolph smiled nastily. "The good ship *Enterprise* is facing . . . technical difficulties." He glanced up at the ceiling. "It's a shame we can't watch, but the gravity mines have been activated. I think we can happily wipe the *Enterprise* off as a problem. . . ."

Geordi stared at the main screen on the bridge. Above the image of the planet were three computer-enhanced dots, plotting the positions of the approaching weapons. "Here we go again," he muttered to himself. The recalibration of the sensors had worked well enough to detect the approaching gravity distortions. They couldn't be absolutely certain of the mines' positions, thanks to all the sensor interference, but at least the ship was braced for this attack. The small devices were using their gravity-generating powers to maneuver, so it would be difficult to outrun them at less than warp speed. This close to the mines, using the warp engines was out of the question.

"Target one: fifteen hundred kilometers and closing," reported Worf. "Phasers are powered up."

"There's no point in using them," Geordi replied. "You saw what happened last time. The point gravity well acts like a black hole, Worf, sucking all the light energy in."

Worf scowled. "What about photon torpedoes?"

"Same problem. The gravitic waves they generate are powerful enough to bend any form of electromagnetic energy. A photon torpedo would simply be deflected around the device."

The Klingon officer considered this. "Then we are helpless against them?"

"All we can try to do is dodge them." Geordi shook his head. "The problem there is that they don't need to actually hit us. A close pass is good enough. Their gravitic effects could tear the containment fields apart at a distance of a few hundred kilometers."

Van Popering didn't take his eyes from the Ops panel. "With the current sensor problems," he said softly, "I can't guarantee a reading that's accurate to more than a hundred kilometers."

"So," Worf said in the silence that followed, "what we must do is thread our path between these gravity mines, allowing none of them closer than a few hundred kilometers—with an error of up to thirty percent in our instruments—and trusting that the Engineering staff—with both yourself and Lieutenant Barclay absent—can keep the containment fields in perfect balance?"

Geordi nodded, his face glum. "That's about the size of it, yeah."

"Excellent." Worf's face broke into his first real smile in days. "A challenge worthy of us!"

Geordi stared at him, and then shook his head. "Well, I'm glad at least one of us is happy." He glanced at the screen again, which was showing the mines approaching. "Heads up, everybody. Worf, red alert. Here they come. . . ."

Beverly groaned as the klaxon howled again. She didn't look up from her instruments. "Turn that damned thing off," she snapped at Nurse Ogawa. Then she returned to the delicate task of knitting together the bones in Barclay's ankle.

She knew instinctively that he would be only the first of today's casualties.

All three shifts in engineering were assembled in the huge two-story main engineering room. Every panel had at least two people stationed at it. Fingers twitched above the controls as everyone waited for the first sign that the field alignments had begun to slip. They knew that the safety of the ship depended on their reactions. As the klaxon howled, their concentration deepened.

Hinner licked his lips and watched the readouts trailing across his screen. One figure outside of the normal parameters was all that was needed to begin the chain reaction in the core itself that could rip the ship apart in seconds. . . .

"Steady," cautioned Geordi. His VISOR was focused on the screen, but he could read the nervousness in the female navigation officer. "Easy does it, Mancini."

"Aye, sir."

"Range: four hundred kilometers and closing," Worf barked. "Target two at six hundred kilometers, mark seven oh nine."

Geordi could only pray that his calculations weren't in error at this point. "Okay, Mancini," he said. "Ready on my mark—half impulse on a heading of three-four-two point five."

"Laid in and ready," she replied.

"Okay." Geordi watched the changing image on the screen, barely heeding Worf as he intoned figures. His command, when it came, was mostly calculation, and partly a gut feeling for the ship. "Engage!"

The *Enterprise* whined as it shifted to the new heading. Red lights instantly began blinking as it executed the maneuver. He muted the reports of damage incoming from all decks, concentrating on the engineering reports.

On the screen the three signals broke up as the ship passed them. The gravity compensators howled in protest, and the deck began shaking. Geordi gripped the arms of the command chair, wondering if there would be any warning if the containment fields ruptured. Or would they be dead before it could be reported?

Then the lights started to die down. "Fields holding," Engineering reported in. "Minor systems damage. Fire crews to station."

Geordi let out his breath in a huge sigh. They had made it once again. Then he started listening to the damage reports from the numerous decks. It was bad—tidal forces that had managed to penetrate the shields had ripped out part of the floor on Deck 17, injuring four crew members. One of the shuttles had been thrown against the cranes in Bay 2. On Deck 8—

"Sir!" Van Popering said urgently. "I can't be certain, but long-range scanners are picking up another five of those devices. They're closing fast."

Geordi sighed. It was definitely not one of his better days.

Some of the feeling was finally returning to Riker's legs as the two guards supporting him dragged him down the stairs in the passage toward the dungeon. Whatever Randolph had jabbed him with was wearing off. He felt like a fool for not having anticipated such an attack, but he had been convinced that Volker was the one to watch. The guard captain had been the only one armed. Though Volker had behaved pretty decently, it was after all his duty to protect his duke. And Randolph had seemed to be no more than a court fop.

And now it was obvious that he was one of the hunters—most likely the head of the ring.

Great. Well, at least he knew who to arrest—if they managed to get out of this dungeon in one piece.

The third guard poked Deanna with the short pike he carried. Deanna glowered at him but picked up her pace. She'd been walking slowly, hoping to give Will the time to recover a little. Through her empathic abilities she could feel his strength returning. Once they were locked in the cells down here, their escape would be much more difficult.

The steps gave way to a short, narrow corridor which then debouched into the main guardroom and the maze of passages and cells beyond. It was dark, damp, and noisome down there. There was a table and several chairs but no signs of further guards. As Deanna entered the room, she was suddenly aware that there was another person with them.

In a whirl of motion Ro kicked the guard escorting Deanna under the chin. His head jerked back as he was rendered unconscious. Deanna continued the turn she had started to make. Ro caught the falling pike as she brought her foot down again. The two guards holding Riker were startled by the unexpected attack. As they started to let go of their burden, Riker concentrated all of his strength into his arms. Instead of falling when he was released, he gripped the necks of the guards as tightly as he could.

They struggled to break free, or to bring their swords up to stab him. Before they could achieve either, Ro had slammed the butt of her pike into the face of the first while Deanna punched the second as hard as she could in his stomach. She winced with the pain to her fist, but the man lost all interest in the fight. Ro used the length of the pike to club the two men unconscious.

Riker allowed them to drop, then fell heavily against the wall. He managed to retain his footing, though. "I'm okay," he insisted as Deanna ignored his protests and led him to one of the chairs. Ro dragged the three unconscious guards into one of the cells and slammed the door on them. "What are you doing here, Ensign?" he demanded of Ro.

"Tidying up," she replied dryly.

"Where's Captain Picard?" Riker asked.

"I gather he and Lieutenant Miles have been sold as mine slaves, Commander," the Bajoran answered. "Look, I hate to sound critical, but can't this wait? They're bound to realize that these fellows aren't coming back out pretty soon." She glanced at Deanna. "You want to help me with this? I was just about to block off the entrance when they brought you down."

"Lucky for us then that you didn't finish." Deanna took one end of the table when Ro took the other. "Thanks for the rescue."

"You're welcome." Together, they heaved the table upright. It blocked most of the passageway into the guardroom. "I've managed to get one of the doors off its hinges," Ro explained. "We can add to the barricade with it."

"Not that I don't appreciate what you're doing, Ensign," Riker said, struggling to his feet, "but do you have a good reason for this? I mean, it looks as if we're simply making a jail cell for ourselves down here."

"I think there's another way out." Ro and Deanna started to move the freed door into position as she spoke. "I saw a man down here emerge from an empty corridor. I'm buying us time so that we can have a good hunt down there. There's got to be a secret doorway or something. Isn't that a feature of all old castles?"

"Certainly in bad fiction," Riker replied. "And, it appears, in real life." He set to work with them. As he moved, the feeling returned slowly to his body as the drug completely wore off. He and Ro managed to dehinge two more cell doors to increase the strength of the barricade. Finally, satisfied it would hold for a while, he allowed Ro to lead them down to the dead-end passageway. "Now," he insisted, "what's happened to the captain?"

Chapter Nineteen

PICARD REINED IN the borrowed horse as the small party approached the gates of Diesen. "I think we'd better lose this steed here," he said, rather reluctantly, because it was a fine animal. "One of the guards at the gate might recognize it. We can finish the journey on foot now."

Kirsch dismounted first. Picard followed, then fussed the animal before dropping the reins. Data and Kirsch removed the still-unconscious form of Miles from the travois. Picard unlashed the rig to free the horse, then slapped its flank. He watched it canter off back the way they had come. Turning back to Data and Kirsch, he said: "He'll be back soon. He deserves a good feed and a rubbing down. I only wish I could provide them." Rubbing his hands together, he gestured toward the gates. "Come on, don't dawdle. We've got a job to do."

Kirsch helped Picard to support Miles. "Is he always like this?" he asked Data.

"Inevitably," the android replied. He had repaired the damage to his makeup so as not to cause alarm in the city.

Picard led them past the lazing guards on duty as if they were not there. It was always best to look as if you owned the place when there was a possibility you might be stopped for questioning. It bred uncertainty in the enemy's mind. These guards didn't look as if they'd stop anyone.

On the way to the castle Data produced a tunic for Picard. "You would look less conspicuous if you covered your chest, Captain," he explained. Picard took the garment without comment and pulled it on over his head while Data helped Kirsch with Miles. He didn't bother to ask where Data had procured it; the android must have stolen it from a house as they were passing.

They made it back to Graebel's warehouse without any problems. Nobody seemed to find the sight of the three of them helping an unconscious companion to be anything at all out of the ordinary. Kirsch stared at the door, puzzled. "I thought we were going to the castle to rescue your companion?"

"That we are," Picard agreed. "But we'll need an excuse to gain entry. And this . . . gentleman . . . owes me a little assistance." He made Kirsch stand in front of the door, then rapped hard. He and Data gently laid Miles against the wall and then positioned themselves flat against the walls, out of sight of the spy-hole in the door. "Ask for Herr Graebel."

When Sigfrid answered the door, Kirsch did as he'd been instructed. Sigfrid, seeing nothing suspicious, unbolted the door and opened it. Picard rammed it with his shoulder. Sigfrid was thrown back, and Data moved to catch him before he could hit anything and make any sound that might alert Graebel.

As the guard opened his mouth to yell, Data grabbed him firmly by the throat. "I would suggest you reconsider that action," he suggested. Sigfrid clamped his mouth closed.

Picard moved swiftly to the stairs, then up them three at a time. He slammed open the door to Graebel's office. The startled merchant jerked up from his seat, his face paling. Picard pushed him back into it.

"Herr Graebel," he said cheerily. "It's so nice to see you again. Are you as happy to see me as I am to see you?"

The wine merchant's skin was ashen, and his plump body shook. "How . . . how . . ."

"I think the bottom fell out of the slave market," Picard told him. "Never mind. I'm sure you're very eager to make amends to me, aren't you?"

"What . . . what do you mean?" Graebel's eyes opened even wider as Data walked into the room and deposited the unconscious Sigfrid on the floor. "You again?"

"Yes," Data replied. "It is a small world, is it not?"

"You're just in time, Dieter," Picard told him. "Herr Graebel has had a change of heart. He's decided to repent of his wicked ways and become a model citizen."

Data gave the captain a blank stare. "Are you referring to the same Herr Graebel?" he asked.

"Yes. He's going to donate a few casks of his finest wine to the duke for a small party tonight." He smiled at Graebel, who quivered. "Don't worry, we'll provide the delivery service to save you work."

Kirsch laughed. "Ah! A ruse to gain entry to the castle!"

"From what you've told me of this duke," Picard replied, "he'll certainly not turn away a shipment of wine—especially one that's a gift from such a reputable merchant as Herr Graebel." He turned to his second officer. "Dieter, Herr Graebel will show you his stables. Have him hitch up a cart. Michael and I will select a few good barrels of wine to take with us."

"And if I refuse?" demanded Graebel.

Picard shook his head gently. "You won't refuse, Herr Graebel. Because if you do I shall have Dieter hold your head in a barrel of wine until you drown." This was a complete lie but spoken with such conviction that Graebel didn't question Picard's sincerity for a second. He gulped, then nodded swiftly several times. "Fine." Picard smiled. "I do so prefer a willing worker."

By the time Picard had selected several of the larger casks from the warehouse floor, Data reappeared from the yard, Graebel staggering along before him.

"The cart you requested is prepared, Captain," Data reported. "Shall I load these barrels?"

"If you would be so kind." Picard rested a hand on the merchant's shoulder as Data picked up the first cask without any obvious effort. Graebel's eyes bulged. "Herr Graebel," Picard said in a friendly manner, "I think it's time that you retired from the business world."

The trader paled. "What . . . what do you mean?" His voice was very squeaky, and it was clear that he was terrified he was about to be murdered.

Ignoring the question for a moment, Picard turned to Kirsch. "How are you at tying knots?"

Kirsch smiled nastily at the merchant. "Around wrists or necks?"

"I think the wrists and ankles should suffice."

"Shame." Kirsch laid a hand on Graebel's shoulder. "Come on upstairs, friend. If you're very good, I'll do as Lukas suggests. Otherwise—" He held up a fist and jerked, as if tugging on a rope. Graebel accompanied him upstairs very quietly.

As soon as Data had the cart loaded, Picard opened the main door to the warehouse. The market was less crowded than it had been, but there were still plenty of people around. Standing by the open door, Picard yelled out: "My friends! Your attention, if you please!"

Heads turned to stare at him. The babble of the shoppers and merchants close by died down.

"Herr Graebel has decided to retire from his trade as a wine merchant," Picard called out, loudly and clearly. "In appreciation for your support and custom, he invites one and all to come and have a drink on him." Gripping the closest wine barrel, Picard pulled it from the shop. With a small ax that lay inside the door, he staved in the lid. "Come, and enjoy!" He entered the warehouse and brought out an armload of goblets. A few of the more adventurous—or thirsty—shoppers were drifting over to the warehouse. Others, knowing Graebel's reputation, cautiously stayed where they were. Picard plunged a goblet into the barrel and took a deep draft. Then he wiped his hand on his sleeve. "Believe me, the wine is perfectly fine!"

That action proved the sincerity of the offer. The drifting of people became a stampede. "There's plenty more inside," Picard called over the din as everyone tried to help themselves. "Take what you will, there'll be no charge!" Then he joined Data and Kirsch at the cart.

The three of them watched the crowd rushing into the warehouse. Several men pulled barrels from the floor and staved in their lids. Others found goblets that they shared around. In moments the room was overrun by men and women grabbing whatever they could.

Picard smiled. "That, I think, should teach Herr Graebel a lesson or two."

"It should beggar him," said Kirsch, approvingly. "They'll drink up all his profits in no time."

Data handed the reins of the cart to the captain and then sprang down to open the gates. As they drove out into the street, they could see that other people from the market were rushing over to avail themselves of Graebel's apparent generosity. Data lifted the recumbent Lieutenant Miles and carefully laid him in the back of the cart, covering him with a small woollen blanket he had procured. Picard flicked the reins, and they started off toward the castle.

Volker had not expected the duke to be in a very good mood, but he had barely been ready for the verbal attack he had received. The duke's wife had been completely unable to calm him as he lay on his bed, ranting and screaming at his captain of the guard. Volker, his face flushed in a mixture of embarrassment and anger, simply had to stand at attention and take the assault.

"Your stupid, ill-trained men have inflicted outrageous physical and emotional abuse on me this day!"

the duke screamed. His throat, apparently, had recovered from Riker's attack long before his pride. "Two different people have been allowed to injure me. Why am I paying you that this should happen to me?"

"Both perpetrators are in the dungeons, my lord," Volker said, striving for calm. "We shall do with them whatever you desire."

"Are you absolutely certain that they are down there?" the duke screamed. "Or did the girl make her escape in that mass assault on your fools?"

"All of the prisoners who tried to escape were killed," replied Volker. "The girl was not among them. Therefore she is still in the cells. And my men took the other two down themselves."

"Your men couldn't take sheep to a slaughterhouse!" The duke lay back on his bed, coughing with the strain. "I want the guards down there doubled. If any of those prisoners escape, I'll take the revenge I aim to inflict on them out on your hide, Volker. You'll pray for me to kill you if they aren't there when I want them."

"They will be there," promised Volker. He glared darkly at the duke. What an insufferable, obnoxious buffoon! All he cared about was inflicting pain on others and pleasure on himself. But one of these days he would push Volker too far. . . .

There was a nervous rap on the door, and one of the guardsmen entered. "My apologies, my lord," he said, shaking. "But we need Captain Volker in the dungeons immediately."

Volker could hardly believe his ears. "What?"

"There's been . . . trouble, sir," the wretched guard stammered. "The two prisoners have broken free of the guards and barricaded themselves in the guardroom."

Wincing with pain, Volker heard the duke's howl of fury. "I'll be right down," he informed the guard, who fled without a backward glance. Volker turned back to face the duke, who looked as if he were about to suffer a heart attack. If he *had* a heart, he might have done, Volker mused. Aloud, he snapped: "There is no other way out of that room, my lord. We only have to break down their barrier to have them again."

"If you can hold them!" The duke—his injuries somehow forgotten—leapt to his feet. "I'm coming down with you, Volker. If you foul up this recapture, I'm going to pull out your guts with my own fingers and stuff them down your stupid throat!" He snatched up his sword and stormed from the chamber. Volker, his face blazing redly, followed him out.

"Wine for the duke's table," Picard told the guard on duty at the castle gate. "A gift from the merchant Graebel."

The guard nodded. "Buying himself out of trouble again?" he asked. "All right, take it over to the storerooms."

Picard nodded. He flicked the reins and the horse trotted forward. Glancing up at the portcullis, Picard was glad that gaining entrance had proved to be so simple. It would have been difficult to get in any other way.

In the back of the cart, Miles groaned. He had finally wakened but seemed stunned and confused. With his broken arm and dazed wits, Miles would be a liability in the event of trouble. Just inside the entrance gate was a small building that appeared to be a chapel that some owner had tacked on to the building. It looked empty.

"Data," Picard suggested, "I think it would be best for Mr. Miles to wait here for us. He'll look as if he's praying for healing if anyone finds him."

Nodding, Data helped the injured lieutenant into the chapel, then closed the door behind him. He rejoined the captain on the cart, and they surveyed the courtyard ahead of them.

Picard saw a puzzling sight: several of the guards dragging the bodies of recently slain people into piles. The corpses were all of filthy and emaciated men. His puzzled stare made Kirsch snort.

"It looks as if the duke's cleaning out the dungeons," he said. "They're a bunch of the prisoners he keeps down there. Kept, I should say."

"Data, is Ro among them?" Picard tried to keep the worry out of his voice. It was never easy to lose an officer under his command.

"No, sir."

"Thank goodness." Picard moved the cart over to one side of the yard. "Any idea where the stores might be?" he asked Kirsch. "We'd better make ourselves busy for the moment."

Before the scholar could reply, one of the guards came over. "You there," he snapped. "Off that cart. We're commandeering it for these bodies."

"But this cart belongs to Herr Graebel," Picard protested. "I really can't—"

The guard pulled out his sword. Grinning, he asked: "Do you want to argue the point?"

Picard scurried down, followed by Data and

Kirsch. "No, of course not." He held up his hands placatingly. "But perhaps your captain would be kind enough to give me a receipt? It would be more than my job's worth to go back without the cart. Herr Graebel would think *I'd* stolen it."

"I imagine he would." The guard nodded. "All right, go and talk to the captain. He'll decide whether to give you a note for your master."

"Thank you," Picard said. He jerked his head for Data and Kirsch to follow and hurried across the yard toward the main entrance. "That was a stroke of luck."

"It seems to me that you're making your own good fortune," Kirsch muttered. "And this piece will get us into the castle."

"I hope we'll get some news about Ro when we do."

Picard led them up to the main door. The guard on duty heard his story and then allowed them to enter. Once inside, they were pushed to the side by other guards. As they watched, more guards were pouring down a flight of stairs. There was the sound of much banging from the end of that passageway.

"What's going on?" Picard asked one of the guards, speaking loudly to be heard over all of the noise.

"Three prisoners have barricaded themselves in the cellar," the man replied. "Captain Volker and the duke have just gone down to lead the assault."

Picard dragged Kirsch and Data toward the far doors. "I'd be willing to wager anything that Ro's somehow behind this," he said, smiling slightly. "She can cause more trouble than any six normal people."

"Your suggestion seems quite plausible to me," agreed Data. "But does it assist us in any way?"

"It doesn't look too good to me," Kirsch said. "There must be half the garrison between us and her. How are you going to rescue her now?"

Picard didn't like to admit that he was completely out of ideas. Kirsch was correct in his assessment. Getting to Ro would not be simple. As he considered his options, the doors to the main hall opened and two men emerged. One wore black robes, the other a fur-lined robe of office.

Data gently touched Picard's arm. "Captain," he murmured, "those men are not locals."

Picard frowned and stared at the figures. He could see nothing about them that differentiated them from the others, but he knew that Data must have his reasons for what he had said. "Explain."

"They do not have the same appearance as the local people, Captain," Data said softly. "There is a distinct trace of the hygiene chamber about them. They are wearing synthetic materials carefully crafted to look like local garb while being much more comfortable. Also, their body language is subtly different. They are more arrogant and self-assured."

"Two members of the gang?"

"I am certain of it, Captain."

Glancing around, Picard saw that everyone's attention was on the guards at the head of the stairs. "Then I think we had better have a talk with those two gentlemen," he suggested. He drifted across the anteroom, trying hard to appear inconspicuous. Data and Kirsch followed him. Neither of the two men looked up from their conversation until Picard grabbed the arm of the robed man. Before the man could say anything, Picard held his sword against the small of his back.

"Quietly," he suggested. The man clamped his mouth shut. The black-robed figure stared at Data, who had apparently materialized from nowhere to fasten an iron grip on his arm. "It's a bit too crowded out here," Picard murmured. "Shall we find somewhere a little more private where we can talk?"

Kirsch caught on and opened one of the doors to the main hall behind them. Picard and Data led their prisoners through and then Kirsch closed the door behind them. The brief kidnapping had passed completely unnoticed by the guards.

"Who are you?" demanded Randolph. He tried to sound merely angry, but fear made his voice tremble. He and Hagan had been planning their escape from this world, and now this had to happen. "If it's for money—"

"That's not the reason," Picard said coldly. "I'm Captain Jean-Luc Picard of the *Enterprise.* And I believe that you're two of the men my officers and I have been seeking."

Randolph paled. "The *Enterprise?"* he croaked. "You mean . . . it's still there?"

"What are you talking about?" Picard didn't like the sound of that one bit. "Why wouldn't it be still there?"

"Shut up, you fool," Hagan hissed. "Don't tell them anything!"

Picard glanced at Data. "Try your communicator," he ordered. For the moment he was willing to allow Kirsch to see anything. He could be dealt with later. "I want to know what's happening to my ship."

Data tapped his brooch. "Away team to *Enterprise.* Come in, Geordi."

There was a howl of static, and then Geordi's faint reply. "Signal . . . poor," the voice crackled. "Can this wait? We're under attack right now."

Picard slammed Randolph against the nearest wall. "Start talking," he ordered. "What's happening to my ship?"

Chapter Twenty

"I'M GETTING a very strange feeling about this place."

Riker paused and looked at Deanna. She had an odd expression on her face. It was partly puzzlement and partly something else. "How strange?" he asked her.

"*Very* strange." Deanna ran her fingers along the wall of the corridor. "I feel as if . . . as if there are mice skittering about in the back of my mind. It's making my brain itch, Will. I've never felt anything quite like it." She blinked hard, bringing herself back into focus with the passageway. "It must be something to do with the Preservers. It's like nothing I've ever felt before."

"Is there a tunnel or something here?" asked Ro practically. "Some way out for us?"

Deanna concentrated. "No. I don't get a feeling of a way out. More like . . . a way *in.*"

"Just what we need," Ro muttered. "We're in it right up to our necks already. I was rather hoping for a back exit or something."

"There's much more here than you imagine," Deanna told her. "I get a tremendous feeling of power. There's a huge amount of untapped potential here. Stored mental energy. Records. All kinds of things." She grabbed Riker's hands, elated as a child at Christmas. "I feel very strongly that there's something here that's not quite dead."

"Us, I hope," Ro said.

"Besides us. There's . . . No, it's not one of the Preservers." Deanna face was almost glowing. "It's a sort of afterimage of them. A sensation that one or more of them left a part of their being here. It's like a shard of glass, or a splinter of wood. It's not everything they are, but it's a part of everything they are. Will, we're on the verge of finding them. I know it!"

Ro jerked her finger back down the passageway. "And *they're* on the verge of finding us. Can't you hurry this up?"

"Shut up, Ensign," Riker snapped. "Deanna—where is this . . . this splinter? Can you reach out and touch it?"

"It's very close." Deanna closed her eyes, concentrating. "It's so near, and yet . . ." She was moving with her eyes shut, yet with confidence. She walked down the corridor, toward the wall at the end.

Ro looked back over her shoulder. The noise from the guardroom had increased. There was the sound of wood shattering, then the sound of human voices. "Uh—I think they're through," she announced.

Deanna didn't seem at all bothered by this. Instead, she kept on walking, her eyes closed. As she came closer to the wall at the end of the corridor, she laughed. Ro lunged for her, but Riker held her back.

"She's going to get one hell of a bump," Ro warned.

"I don't think so." Riker eased his grip. He was as tense as Ro, but for very different reasons. "Watch."

With no sign of slowing down, Deanna walked directly up to the wall—then *into* it. She simply walked through it as if it wasn't there. Ro's eyes went wide.

"Come on." Riker grabbed her arm and jerked her after him. She winced, expecting to be slammed into stones, but there was nothing in her way.

Volker smiled grimly as the barricade crashed down. The room beyond was empty. "They must be farther in," he said. "Let's go."

The duke stomped after Volker and his men as they ran through the guardroom, then into the cells beyond. His men slammed open each unlocked door as they passed, but there was no sign of the missing prisoners. Volker picked up the pace. Astonishingly, the duke managed to keep up with him.

They came to the long corridor that abruptly ended in a wall. Ahead, they saw Riker and the other woman, Ro. Hands joined, they simply walked into the far wall as if it were not there. Volker skidded to a halt, staring at the sight in shock.

The duke grabbed his arm. "It's a trick of some kind," he snapped. "A secret passage. Have your men find the key."

"We'll see about it." Volker walked down the passageway. There was neither sign nor sound of the missing prisoners now. He had seen them walk into the wall with his own eyes. No door, or anything. They simply walked into the wall itself. He stopped a foot away from the stones. Were they, somehow, nothing more than an illusion? A trick of some kind?

Raising his sword, Volker rapped on the stones with the pommel. He expected to meet nothing there but air and smoke. Instead, the sword rang as it struck solid stone.

It was impossible! He had seen them with his own eyes walk through this wall as if there was nothing here. He slammed himself against the wall, but it refused to give way. Stone met his flesh, and he fell back, his skin tingling with pain.

"It's witchcraft," he whispered. "It can be nothing else. I *saw* them walk into this wall—but it is solid. Solid!" He slammed his hands against the stones in fury. "They must be witches!"

The duke hastily made the sign of the cross. The guards fell back a few paces, muttering to themselves. Volker struck at the wall with his sword but produced only sparks from his blade.

"It isn't possible!" he cried. "What is happening here?"

"You were right, Captain Volker," the duke said, his voice quivering. "It must be magic. There is no other explanation. Is there?" He turned terrified eyes onto his captain of the guard. Volker merely shook his head, struck dumb.

"It must be Preserver technology," Ro said, awe-struck, as they walked straight through the wall. "There's no other explanation, is there?" She had somehow sensed the stones as she had passed through them. They had seemed to be less real, somehow, than the projections on one of the ship's holodecks. At the same time they were also more real. It was as if she had somehow become out of phase with the wall, occupying the same space without overlapping the structure of the stones. What scared her the most was the feeling that her mind could *almost* grasp how it was done.

Behind the wall there was only brightness. She could just about make out Deanna, who had turned back and was holding out her hands. Ro gripped one tightly. Riker took Deanna's other hand.

"It's all right," Deanna said happily. "We're fine now."

Ro glanced down, then wished she hadn't. There was nothing there but a shaft. She could feel nothing at all beneath her stolen boots. "I wish I could believe that," she said softly.

The nothingness beneath them seemed to fade away, and they fell down the shaft.

The duke whirled around on Volker, his face white. "It seems that you are unable to keep *any* of your prisoners confined," he snapped. He was angry, but there was also fear in his voice. "That's three more of them gone—and the ones I particularly wanted to see suffer."

Volker gestured at the wall in front of them. "Do you want to try and tell me how in the name of heaven I was to have expected or prevented them from walking through a solid wall?"

The duke wasn't to be sidetracked by trivialities like logic. "They were your prisoners! I told you that if you couldn't hold them, you'd suffer for it. As God is my witness, I'll see you suffer!" He turned to the guards, who were cringing farther down the corridor. "You—

come here! I want Captain Volker arrested and thrown into some cell that even he can't get out of!" None of the guards moved. The duke's fear was being channelled into anger now. There was nothing he could do against people who could walk through walls, but there was plenty he could do with a fool who had failed him. "Cowards!" he screamed at them. Spinning back to face Volker, he demanded: "Is this how you train your men? They're not men, they're dogs!"

Coldly Volker glared at his lord. "They're good enough men when things go well. It's your fault we're in this stupid mess. Your lechery led to the first girl being here, and your venality to the rest."

"How dare you speak to me like that!" thundered the duke. "I'll have you whipped for this!" He held out his hand. "Give me your sword."

"If you insist." Volker drew his sword, then in a single swift motion thrust it with all of his strength into the duke's massive stomach. The duke gave a stunned cry, his eyes glazing. "Rot in hell," Volker snarled and twisted the weapon. Blood and bile surged about the wound. As the duke sagged, Volker withdrew the sword and stepped back.

The dying man fell to his knees, clutching at his stomach. Blood bubbled around his gloved fingers, staining the expensive fabric and splattering onto the cold stones. He stared up at his assassin, and then his eyes bulged. He fell forward, twitching slightly, and then was still.

Volker turned to his men. None had dared make a move. "I think the duke's had a slight accident, but a fatal one," he said. "Do any of you have a problem with that?" The men all hastily shook their heads.

"Good." Volker strode down the passageway to join them. "Then it's time we set to work to clean up this mess the old reprobate left us. You three, find me some masons." He glanced back down the tunnel. "We'll brick this place up. If Riker and the others want to stay here, we'll make absolutely certain that they never get out again. You two, find Randolph. Tell him nothing of the duke, but ask him to come to the main hall. It's time he paid a few long-standing debts, I think." He couldn't afford to let the duke's adviser live. Unlike the soldiers, who would follow anyone who led them well, Randolph might cause problems. There was also the matter of what to do with the duchess. Would it be better for her to have an accident as well, or should he perhaps consider marrying her to consolidate his position?

Problems, problems, problems . . .

The shaft that Ro, Riker, and Deanna were dropping down was quite extensive. There was nothing to see, and Ro's initial panic stopped when it became obvious they were in the grips of a tractor beam of some kind. It held her gently, yet allowed her to move about.

"It looks as if the Preservers have opened the door for us to come inside," Riker murmured. Deanna still had an expression of bliss on her face, so Ro assumed he was directing his remarks to her.

"But can we trust them to open it when we want to leave again?" she asked.

"We've no reason to think that they may be hostile, Ensign," Riker said.

"We've no reason to assume that they're benign,

either," Ro countered. "In fact, what we do know of them could be taken either way."

Riker frowned. "They preserve societies that would otherwise have died out. That suggests they value life."

"They preserve societies that perhaps *should* have died out," argued Ro. "That Amerind world the old *Enterprise* discovered hadn't evolved at all in hundreds of years. Neither has this planet. Maybe these Preservers are deliberately retarding their progress for their own reasons. Let's face it, putting humans on a world populated by dragons isn't the nicest possible gesture, is it?"

"A human culture that already believed in the existence of dragons," Riker pointed out. "And I think you may be judging their actions too harshly."

"Possibly I am," Ro agreed. "But we don't know." She nodded at Deanna. "She's obviously entranced by them. I figure I'd better balance that by being a little more suspicious than normal."

Riker grinned. "And I can be middle of the road?"

Ro returned his smile. "I thought you'd like being caught between two women, Commander."

Before Riker could come up with a rejoinder for this, their fall ended. There was no slowing—they simply stopped in the air. There was no feeling of inertia or motion sickness. Ahead of them stretched a short tunnel, lined with glowing metallic panels.

"We're here," said Deanna, stepping forward. Ro shrugged and then followed. Riker kept pace with her as they walked down the passageway and emerged into the room beyond.

* * *

Randolph was shaking with fear. Picard had a handful of his clothing and held him pressed against the cold stone wall.

"What is happening to my ship?" Picard repeated angrily.

"Gravity mines," Randolph gasped. As he spoke, he triggered the release for the small pouch under his shirtsleeve that held the tranquilizer needle. It slid out into his palm. Quickly he brought his hand around to stab Picard with it.

Metallic fingers closed about his wrist and squeezed. Randolph screamed, and the needle fell from his nerveless fingers to clatter on the floor. Data kept his grip on the man's wrist as he stooped to pick up the needle. "Drugged," he explained to Picard, holding it up. He seemed to be unaware that he was crushing Randolph's wrist.

"Prompt action, Mr. Data." Picard glared at the howling prisoner again. "Answer me, damn you."

"He's breaking my wrist!" Randolph screamed.

Letting go of the man's clothing, Picard turned to face the trembling Hagan. "Mr. Data, if he doesn't begin talking within the next ten seconds, snap his wrist. Then we can talk to his friend here."

"Gravity mines," said Randolph hastily. "They're a Preserver weapon, to protect this planet. I triggered them a short while ago and set them after the *Enterprise.*"

"That's much better," Picard said approvingly. "Now—how do we stop them?"

"I don't know."

"Mr. Data—"

"I swear it!" Randolph screamed. "I don't know! I

found the instructions on a panel in their control room. It's difficult script to translate. It took me months to decipher as much as I did. I only bothered with how to set the mines, not with how to turn them off again."

Picard considered this. The man *could* be lying, but he doubted it. He was plainly terrified and incompetent. A petty crook, way out of his tiny little league when he'd stumbled across something of this magnitude. It was all too believable that he would not have bothered to find out how to stop the attack once it had begun. "I'll accept what you say for now," he decided. "Now—where is this Preserver control room?"

"It's under the castle." Randolph stared at his wrist. "Tell him to let me go. Please! I'll tell you anything you want to know."

"You'll talk first," Picard replied. "And how do we get into the room?"

"Via the dungeons."

Picard shook his head. "Come, you can do better than that. Do you seriously expect us to walk into a cell and accept that there's a control room on the other side of it? I wasn't born yesterday, you know."

"It's not a cell, it's just a corridor." Randolph licked his lips nervously. "It looks as if you come to a dead end, but if you know there's a door there, you can walk into it. But you've got to believe it, or you just walk into solid stone. They must have made it like that to hide it from the natives."

"From the dungeons?" mused Picard. That was where all of the guards were milling about. It would be impossible to get into the Preservers' control area while every Tom, Dick, and Harry in the castle was in the dungeons. He'd need to lure them out first. But he couldn't plan that while guarding these two crooks. He tapped Data's communicator. "Picard to O'Brien."

The static didn't seem as bad as it had before. "O'Brien here, sir."

"Mr. O'Brien, are you able to transport up to the ship at the moment?"

"Aye, sir. I've rigged a gravity compensator, and the ship's shields are timed to the mines' gravity pulses. But I don't have any readings for you on my board. Just Mr. Data at your current position."

"Can you beam up two people?"

O'Brien paused. "I could if they were wearing communicators to lock on to."

Picard smiled. "Send me four communicators down, if you would."

"Aye, sir."

Picard smiled at Kirsch, who was completely amazed by everything and clearly understood none of what was happening. He jumped when four golden badges suddenly shimmered into existence on the floor.

"Magic," he whispered.

"Not quite." Picard bent down and picked up the devices. He attached one to his tunic, then turned to Randolph.

"What are you doing?" he yelped.

"I'm going to have you and your friend there beamed aboard the *Enterprise* so I don't have to worry about you." He clipped the communicator onto the struggling man.

"But it's going to be blown up any moment!"

"That seems only fair to me. *You* began the attack. Now you can sweat it out with my people." He clipped the second communicator onto Hagan's robes. "If there's anything that you can tell me to help me stop the attack, now would be a good time."

"I told you I can't stop it!" Randolph was on the verge of tears. "Picard, I beg of you—don't do this! It's murder!"

"No," Picard replied. "It's justice. If you wipe out my crew and ship, you'll die with it. You had better pray, then, that I can somehow stop the attack." He triggered his own communicator. "Do you read me, Mr. O'Brien?"

"Loud and almost clearly, Captain."

"Beam up the other two communicators that I've activated, together with their wearers. And have a security team escort them to cells."

"Aye, sir. Energizing!"

As his voice died away, columns of light surrounded the screaming, hysterical Randolph and the slightly more dignified Hagan. Kirsch's jaw fell open when the light shimmered and vanished, and the men were gone, also.

"Are they . . . dead?" he asked, awe-stricken.

"No, Michael," Picard replied gently. "They're now on my ship. They've committed some serious crimes while they were here, and we are going to punish them for their actions. Assuming my ship survives the attack that Randolph triggered."

At that moment the doors to the hall burst open, and several guards rushed in, weapons at the ready. They looked wildly around before dashing across to the three men. In seconds Picard was held by two soldiers, and a sword at his throat.

"Where is Randolph?" the leader of the men asked. "He was in here."

"Gone," Picard replied. "He will not be back."

"Damnation." The guard spat on the floor. "He must have gotten wind of the duke's death somehow. That black magician of his, no doubt." He thought for a moment. "Well, if we don't have their heads to take to the captain, we have yours." He nodded to his men. "Kill them."

Chapter Twenty-one

THERE WAS no doubt at all about the alien nature of this room. Riker's neck was aching from all the craning he'd done as he'd stared around the place. It was massive. It looked as if the Preservers had taken a gigantic natural cavern below the surface of this world and then turned it into a huge room by spraying glowing metal all over.

The floor was perfectly level, stretching several hundred feet in all directions from the entrance where they stood. The ceiling of the room was almost as high overhead. Stalactites hung down, each of them perfect, but of glittering metal instead of stone. The rocks in the walls and roof stood out clearly. The room had a warmth and light throughout it. Most caves Riker had ever ventured into were cool and damp, and more than a little fusty. The air here was perfectly balanced. Though there was no sound of machinery, he knew that there had to be an air purifier at work somewhere.

Around the walls and at regular intervals across the floor of the metal cavern were banks of machineries. He couldn't begin to guess at their purposes. Lights glittered and danced across them. The strange, spidery raised script of the Preservers adorned every piece of machinery. Riker—like all Starfleet academy students—had seen the examples from *Miramanee* a hundred times. It was the same style, and just as obscure here as it had been there. The only thing that Riker could recall about it was that it was somehow based on a system of musical tonalities.

It was weird, watching all of this activity taking place without a single being anywhere. What could it all be for? Was it somehow monitoring the world above them and recording information for the Preservers? Was it, even now, linked to similar machines on other worlds? Was it possible that the Preservers themselves could somewhere be watching them?

Deanna stepped into the room, her face a radiant mask. The sound of her footfalls echoed about the vast cathedral to science. "This is where they once stood," she breathed. "They were here, and a portion of them resides here still."

"You mean the machines that they left?" asked Riker gently. He followed her out onto the floor.

"No." Deanna looked at him with hungry eyes. "I can feel a part of them resting here. A fragment of their minds. It's not easy even for me, Will, but I can almost get through to them. It's hard to get their attention." She shook her head. "We're like insects to them. They see us, but they don't quite understand us."

Riker shuddered. "Is *that* what all this is?" he asked her, appalled. "Is it like some giant ant farm to them? Is that what the people on the surface are to them?"

"No, not like that," she replied. "It's much more complex than that." A tear trickled out of her eye. "I can't quite grasp it. I can't . . ." She shivered. "Will, we're not supposed to be here. This world should be left alone. That's why it was placed here—to protect it from us."

"They know about us?" snapped Riker.

"Not specifically. They only know that what they are doing is very delicate. It's like an artist at work, much more than a scientific experiment. I get the definite impression that what they are doing is more like painting a masterpiece than studying an experiment. But we're the wrong colors. We may be damaging to the picture."

Ro frowned. "Do they want us to leave? Or are we a mistake to be erased?"

Deanna shook her head. "I can't tell. It's a kind of stray thought. Not focused. It's just there. The Preservers don't see us, exactly. They're like gardeners, who've discovered a mold growing on a prized plant. They don't see the individual cells, just the blight itself."

"I don't like the sound of that," Ro said to Riker. "It suggests we're in for a dose of weed killer."

"I don't like it, either." Riker gripped Deanna by the shoulders. "Deanna. *Imzadi.* Listen to me. Can you speak to them at all? Can you give them a message?"

Deanna struggled to focus on him. "No. They can't hear me. My mind is too quiet, too small for them to hear. I can only understand them because there's just a tiny fraction of their substance here. If there were more, I'd be overwhelmed. I simply feel some of what is going through this small part of their minds."

"Are they planning to do anything about us?" Riker demanded. "Are we in danger here?"

"Danger?" Deanna sounded as if she were far away. "Yes, I feel something about danger." Then she suddenly snapped back to full awareness. "Will—it's the *Enterprise!* There's some kind of attack under way against the ship!"

The deck under Geordi was shaking like a dog with fleas. Both Ops and navigation had red lights flickering all over them. Van Popering struggled to maintain his position. Jenny Mancini had somehow braced herself in her seat and was carrying out course corrections as needed to keep the *Enterprise* in motion.

"Shields down to forty percent," Worf read out. His feet wide apart, he stood unmoving at his board. "Forward shield number four is failing."

Geordi tried to ignore this bad news. "Change to heading two one four mark seven," he called. "Keep us moving, Mancini."

"Course laid in," she responded through gritted teeth. "And engaged."

The deck shuddered again. Geordi could hear the strains the movement produced. He was itching to call engineering to discover how well the containment fields were holding up through all of this stress. But he knew that the last distraction they needed right now was him demanding a report.

Besides—the fields either held or collapsed. There was nothing he could do even if he had warning of the latter. He gripped the arms of the command chair and held on for dear life as the gravitational fluxes tore at the ship.

"Fields down to thirty-five percent," Worf intoned. "Forward shield four is down. Three and five are straining to compensate. They will both burn out in fifteen seconds."

One shield down was bad enough. Three shields would lose them almost a fifth of their cover. The remaining shields would never be able to maintain the phase guarding against the polarized gravity waves. Geordi listened helplessly as Worf counted down to disaster.

And then—

"We're through!" Van Popering yelled. It was a breach of bridge etiquette, but Geordi couldn't fault him for it. The juddering in the decks fell away.

"Shields have held," Worf reported. "We need an immediate repair team on shield four."

"Okay." Geordi tapped the communications panel. "La Forge to Engineering. What's it like down there?"

"You don't want to know," came the reply. "But the fields held. It's getting closer to disruption every time, though. I can't guarantee we'll survive another attack. The engines are overheating as it is, and I've lost five technicians to burns and other injuries."

"Can you get a repair team onto forward shield four?" Geordi asked.

"I've nobody left to spare. There's a hundred repairs we should be doing right here, but there's no one to do them."

"Okay. Do your best." Geordi flicked off the intercom. "Damn. There's nobody to do the repairs."

"Without shield four," Worf pointed out, "we place

too great a strain on three and five. If there is another attack, they will not hold."

Geordi didn't need to be told; he knew it better than anyone here. But if there were no techs to spare, he couldn't make one sprout up out of thin air. Now what could he do?

Barclay groaned as he levered himself to his feet. His broken ankle was in a brace to complete the strengthening. Dr. Crusher had warned him not to move for two days, or it wouldn't set correctly. He hated to ignore her instructions, but if things went on like this, the *Enterprise* didn't have two hours left, let alone two days. Trying to ignore the pain, he limped out of the ward, hoping he wouldn't be spotted. There were, after all, over fifty other patients in here, and Crusher and her staff were working like lunatics to attend to them all.

Naturally, she glanced up just in time to see him. "Reg!" she yelled, irritated. "I told you to stay off that foot."

"Right," he agreed, wincing in pain. "And I will, later. Right now I've got too much to do." Dr. Crusher finished using the hypospray on the technician on the diagnostic bed. The technician had blisters that were already suppurating from the scalds she had received repairing a fractured coolant line. "I'm not arguing," Beverly snapped.

"Then don't." Barclay hobbled up to her. "Geordi's got more than he can handle on the bridge. And there's nobody to spare to repair forward shield four. If that fails us, then you may as well kiss this life good-bye. I'm the only one who can possibly get it up again, so I'm going. See ya." He was past her and out the door with an amazing speed considering his condition.

Beverly swore under her breath. She was tempted to go after him and sedate him—except this girl needed her help. And, damn it, he was right: If that shield failed, all of this was pointless, anyway.

"Stop!"

The blade at Picard's throat eased away slightly. He could feel a slight trickle where it had penetrated his skin, but he was safe from immediate execution, it appeared.

Volker marched into the main hall, his face clouded with anger. "What are you doing?" he demanded.

The guard's leader glanced at him uncertainly. "We were just executing these three—"

"Nobody told you to execute anyone!" snarled Volker. "Release them immediately."

Picard straightened up, shaking the guard's hands from him. "Thank you, sir," he said. "I appreciate the assistance."

"You may not," replied Volker. "I can still have them kill you. Now—who in Hades are you, what are you doing here, and where is Randolph?"

"My name is Lukas," Picard replied. "This is Dieter, and that is Michael Kirsch, a scholar."

Volker studied Kirsch. "Didn't the duke send you into slavery?" he asked. "I recall something about heresy."

Kirsch managed a wan smile. "You have an exceptional memory, Captain. Fortunately, Lukas and Dieter saved me when the slave train was attacked by a dragon. They slew the beast."

"Really?" Volker snorted in disbelief. "Then they're more exceptional than they appear to be. They don't look capable of slaying a fly, let alone a dragon."

"They are not what they seem to be," Kirsch assured him. "Lukas is a sorcerer of mighty powers, and Dieter is his homunculus."

Volker threw himself into the duke's chair and looked at Picard. "You appear to have made a singular impression on the heretic here. Is what he says true?"

Picard was caught in a serious dilemma here. He was forbidden to tell these people the truth, and yet it was quite plain that he would be murdered casually if he didn't have some kind of story to offer them. "The truth?" he repeated, stalling for time. Then an idea came to him. "In a sense, I suppose what he says is quite correct, yes."

Volker looked slightly amused. "Would you care to perhaps demonstrate some magic for me? Or is it a private act?"

"If I may have a minute to confer with my—ah, Dieter?" Picard requested. When Volker nodded, he took the android aside a few paces. "Data," he said in a low voice. "I think I have a way to get out of this without breaching the Prime Directive. These people sincerely believe in the power of magic, don't they?"

Data nodded. "It is ingrained within their culture, Captain."

"Then if we explain everything in terms of magic, we will only be conforming to their cultural norms, won't we?"

"Indeed, Captain."

"I'm glad that you agree." Turning back to the Guard Captain, Picard said: "Kirsch does indeed speak the truth about us, sir. I am a powerful magician."

"But powerless against cold steel, I'll wager. My man almost killed you moments ago."

"It only appeared that way, Captain," Picard replied. "But—we are reasonable men, you and I. I could prattle on all day, and it would prove nothing. Let me instead offer you proof for your eyes and mind."

"Now we seem to be getting somewhere." Volker settled back, wondering what trickery this smooth-talking humbug was going to trump up.

Picard turned back to Data and said: "Open your chest access panel."

Data raised an eyebrow. Then he reached up and pulled at his tunic. It tore across his chest, revealing his golden skin below. The guards gasped but stood firm. Data then unclipped his panel, swinging it down. It revealed the circuitry, hydraulics, and motors within.

Volker leapt to his feet and hastily made the sign of the cross. "What witchery is this?" he whispered.

"As Kirsch said, my companion is not a human but an animation," Picard answered. "You can see here that he has no human heart beating in his chest. He is powered by my magic."

Volker stared suspiciously at Data. "And you control him? Is he safe?"

"He won't hurt you," Picard assured him. "But I wouldn't get too close to him. The—ah—magic might affect you. It renders the inanimate living, and I wouldn't want to take a chance that it would render the living inanimate."

"Very well." Volker moved warily back to the seat.

"For the moment I will accept your claims. But why are you here? And what have you done with Randolph?"

"I came here specifically to find him and his accomplices," Picard answered. "They have broken our laws and tried to interfere in your village life. They caused corruption and greed, seeking to influence the grand duke with their evil ways. I have sent them magically back to my ship, which is moored a good distance out to sea. We come from . . . another continent and must return there. We will punish Randolph for what he has done here."

Volker considered the matter. "Very well," he agreed. "You can do what you want with him, as long as he never returns here again." It didn't matter what happened to the man, as long as he didn't interfere with Volker's own plans. "Meanwhile, the duke is dead. I am going to appoint myself in his place, I think."

"My condolences on your loss," Picard said dryly. "And congratulations on your promotion."

"Thank you." Volker took his seat again. "Now, if you're quite finished here, I assume you're going to be off in a puff of smoke?"

"Not quite yet, if it pleases you."

The new duke scowled. "It doesn't, really, but if you're as powerful as you claim, I don't suppose that'll stop you. So what more do you want?"

"Before I could bind him," Picard replied, "the fiend Randolph cast a spell and began a magical attack on my vessel. I must remove that spell so that we can leave. He spoke of a magical place below the castle."

Things were starting to fall into place for Volker now. "Ah! Now I begin to understand some of what I have witnessed this day. You and your allies are fighting a sorcerous warfare with Randolph. And you sent other magicians here before you, didn't you?"

"They are here?"

"I saw them walk through a wall in the dungeons with another prisoner, a slave named Rosalinde."

"And Ro as well!" Picard beamed. "Excellent. If you don't mind?" He tapped his communicator. "Picard to Riker. Come in, Will."

Volker jumped as Riker's voice replied from thin air. The terrified guards drew away from Data, Picard, and Kirsch. Even Kirsch looked scared.

"Captain! It's good to hear from you."

"You, too, Number One. Where are you?"

Riker looked around. "In the Preservers' chamber," he replied. "It's astonishing, Captain. Deanna and Ro are with me."

"So I gathered." Picard's voice was grim. "I've spoken with Geordi. The *Enterprise* is currently under attack by some form of gravity mines. Apparently the poachers set them into motion from that control room you're in but never learned how to stop them. Do you think you can manage that part?"

"With respect, Captain, I doubt it. This place is way beyond anything I've ever experienced."

"That's not very good news, Number One."

"Sorry, Captain, but it's all I can offer."

There was a pause, and then: "Understood. Look around. I'll be in touch. Picard out."

"Talk about tall orders," Ro said. She crossed to the nearest panel. "It'll take us weeks just to figure the language out, let alone how to work the place."

"And we don't even know which of these machines

is controlling the attack," agreed Riker. "Well, you heard the captain—let's look around."

"What are we looking for?" asked Ro.

"I'll let you know when I know." Riker moved out to scan whatever he could.

The bridge was quite a mess. Geordi shook his head. The captain wasn't going to be too happy when he returned. He liked a clean and tidy ship. Still, maybe he'd settle for just having any ship at all. If he still had one when he came back. . . .

"Sir!" Van Popering looked up from his panel, his face pale. "I'm getting readings. There are five more of those mines heading for us. Estimated time to contact—eighteen minutes."

"Oh, damn." Geordi stared at the main screen as the computer began to detail their positions. "Now we're really in for it. . . ."

Chapter Twenty-two

PICARD DIDN'T LIKE playing the role that fate seemed to have assigned to him, but he had very little choice in the matter. If these people believed in magic, then he'd have to do a little magic for them. Thankfully they were accepting his conversations with Riker and Geordi as being some kind of sorcery that was only to be expected.

"Geordi," he asked, "what's the situation up there?"

"I'd not hesitate to describe it as grave, Captain. We're in bad shape to stand up to another attack, and we're going to get one in seventeen minutes."

"Understood, Mr. La Forge. I'll see what we can do down here." Picard glanced at Data. "Data, do you think you could turn off the Preservers' machines if you were to join Commander Riker?"

"It is hardly likely, sir," Data replied. "The language of the Preservers is based on musical notes and a symbolic form of representation. It is not a logical language. I have scanned all known translations of Preserver script, and that amounts to barely three hundred words. Few of them are technical terms."

Picard had been afraid of something like that. "Then perhaps if we beamed this Randolph fellow down, he could point out which machine at least he started the attack from. Perhaps you and Will together could turn it off."

"With all due respect, Lukas," Kirsch interrupted, "but I'd hardly say Randolph was to be trusted. He would probably lie about which spell he cast."

"True." And there was no guarantee that in the few minutes Data and Riker would have that they wouldn't make matters worse instead of better. With a sigh he turned to face his android officer. "It looks as if we're going to have to destroy the Preservers' control center to stop those mines."

"I concur."

"If we do," Picard asked, "will it affect this planet in any way? Is it possible that the Preservers somehow created this bubble and put this planet here?"

"No, Captain," Data replied. "This bubble—as you call it—exists in a stable area of the cloud. I am certain than destroying the Preservers machinery will in no way jeopardize the existence of this planet."

"I hate doing it," Picard complained. "It goes against the grain. Still, we have very little option right now. Unless you think you could get down there and turn off the machine?"

Data shook his head. "The odds are not favorable. Commander Riker did inform us that there are over a hundred machines. I would need approximately one hour and thirty seven minutes to examine them all. There is thus only an approximate fifteen percent chance that I would be able to locate the correct mechanism. And as I remarked, there is no guarantee that I should be able to translate the instructions to turn it off."

"Then we can rule it out." Picard considered. "What about using the ship's phasers to take out the control area?"

"Again, there is a low probability of success," Data replied. "Given the poor state of our sensor ability at this point in time, there is a very real chance that we would wipe out a large section of the city—and still a finite probability that we would miss the target entirely."

Picard sighed. "There go photon torpedoes as well. Then it would have to be a bomb, I suppose."

"I agree. A small, low-yield matter-antimatter device would suffice. It would need to be placed by hand." Data gave him a hard look. "The resulting explosion is bound to cause serious damage—if not total destruction—to this castle."

"I was rather afraid it might." Picard tapped his communicator again. "Mr. La Forge, I will need an explosive device to destroy the Preservers' equipment. Mr. Data will give you the technical requirements."

"Destroy the place?" Geordi's voice was filled with disappointment. "Captain, isn't there any other way?"

"Don't I wish that there were! But we've little choice if we're to save the *Enterprise*, Geordi." Picard moved back to where Volker sat. "I'm afraid that I have bad news for you."

"Oh?" Volker stared back at him. "There's going to be a plague of locusts, perhaps? Or it's going to rain snakes?"

"Nothing like that." Picard gave him a thin smile. "The magic that Randolph worked here was so terrible that I'm afraid I have to destroy the entire place. You must get all of your men out of here—now. Do not stop to take anything with you, because in fifteen minutes this place will be consumed in fire and brimstone."

Jumping to his feet, Volker cried: "You must be insane! I've only just taken this castle. Do you think I'm going to abandon it simply on the word of a self-claimed magician?"

"My lord," Kirsch said placatingly. "Lukas would not lie to you. He knows you would kill him if he did. Instead, I beseech you, recall the story of Lot and the destruction of Sodom and Gomorrah. They were consumed in fire and brimstone, and only those who fled were spared."

"I'm not going," said Volker stubbornly. "It's my castle, and I won't give it up."

Cursing the man's vanity and greed, Picard tapped his communicator again. "Mr. Worf, *you* are to bring the explosive device down to the planet. Get a costume from Smolinske and beam down with the device to my location as quickly as possible."

"Yes, Captain!" Worf could not keep the excitement from his voice. This was the opportunity he had been waiting for!

"Picard to Smolinske."

"Go ahead, Captain."

"I want you to whip up an outfit for Mr. Worf," he ordered. "Fast. He's beaming down now."

"Worf?" she repeated. "You've got to be kidding, right?"

"This isn't a joke, Smolinske," Picard snapped. "I want him here as a demon from hell, or something equally magical and terrifying. You've got that?"

"Will do."

Picard turned back to Volker. "I'm going to prove to you that what I have told you is true," he said. "In return, I want you to begin evacuation of the castle. Get everyone out of the rooms and either have them assemble here or in the courtyard."

Volker scowled. "Very well, Lukas. I will do that. But if you do not convince me, then I shall kill you for making me look a fool."

"I'll take that chance."

Volker nodded. "Good. I'm beginning to like you, Lukas. You have courage, at any rate." He addressed the guards: "Right—get moving. I want everyone inside the castle to gather in the courtyard, and I want it done *now.* Warn everyone that anyone who delays by as much as a minute will be killed. *Move!"*

They moved like lightning.

Picard handed the spare communicator to Kirsch. "Michael, please place this on Miles once you are outside. It is the only way he'll be able to return to my ship."

"I shall," Kirsch promised. He paused, as if about to say more. Then he simply turned and dashed for the door, in the wake of the others.

Worf strode into Stores, a happy smile on his face. "I am to beam down to the planet," he announced loudly. "Is my costume prepared?"

Smolinske nodded. "On the table there."

Staring hard at the small pile of clothing Worf frowned. "Surely there is some mistake?" he demanded. "I thought I was to wear a suit of armor and go accoutred as a warrior!"

"I don't know what you're thinking about," Smolinske told him, "but I do know what my orders are. That's your costume. If you've got any complaints, tell the captain, not me."

Worf was stunned. All his hopes had been dashed. Not only would he not be descending to the planet as a warrior, but he was apparently expected to wear . . .

No! It was too much for a Klingon's pride! He glowered at Smolinske. "I am not happy. We shall have words about this when my mission is over. That is a promise."

Riker still couldn't get over his awe of this place. The Preservers built on a vast scale. The room was simply overwhelming. Deanna was walking around it in a daze again. Ro was searching it for anything loose that she could take when they had to leave.

"Picard to Riker."

Hitting his communicator, Riker acknowledged the call. "We've not found any obvious computer that's guiding the attack, I'm afraid," he reported.

"All right, Will. You've done your best. I want the three of you to return to the ship now."

"But, Captain—"

"That's an order, Mr. Riker." Picard's voice was firm. "Get out of there. I have enough problems without having to worry about you making it out on time."

"Acknowledged." Riker stared at Deanna, who was still lost in her mental probing. Crossing to her, he touched her arm gently. "We have to leave."

That brought her out of it. There was pain in her eyes, and tears on the verge of flowing. "No!" she cried. "Not now. I'm getting there, I know I am, Will. A little longer, and I'm sure I can make them notice us."

"We don't have that time." Riker caught Ro's eye and motioned her to join him. "It's time to go."

"Good." She marched briskly over. "I'm getting very sick of this planet. And these clothes."

Riker triggered his communicator, keeping a tight grip on Deanna's arm. She sometimes acted unpredictably when lost in her Betazoid nature. "Mr. O'Brien, three to beam up."

"Aye, sir."

Tears rolled down Deanna's face uncontrollably. "Good-bye," she whispered. Would she ever find this kind of mind again? The destruction of the vault would not kill it, because it wasn't exactly alive. It was only a fragment of a greater mind that was very much alive elsewhere. She only wished she knew where that might be.

Then the transporter grabbed her, breaking her contact with the Preserver fragment.

Five minutes to go . . . Picard was getting very tense. The castle personnel were almost all outside now. Only Volker, two guards, and Kirsch remained with him and Data. Kirsch had returned after pinning the communicator to Miles. Picard had instantly ordered the injured lieutenant beamed directly up into sickbay.

What the blazes was keeping Worf? He slapped his communicator. "Worf!" he barked. "Where are you?"

"Just entering Transporter Room Three, Captain. I have the device."

"Beam down immediately."

"Aye, sir." Worf sounded very angry. "I am going to kill her for this," he muttered.

Picard had no idea why Worf was so annoyed, but he frankly didn't care. Turning to Volker, he said: "I am going to call down from the heavens the spirit who will destroy this place. This is a very powerful being, whose name you must not utter." Throwing his arms into the air dramatically, he cried out: *"'By the pricking of my thumbs, something wicked this way comes!'"*

Data twitched slightly. *"Macbeth,* Act Four, Scene One," he murmured. The captain's devotion to Shakespeare was well known aboard the ship—but the Bard was naturally unknown here.

There was the familiar glow of the transporter beam, and then the irate figure of Worf appeared. At his feet was a small canister. On his face was a glower of rage so potent that Kirsch, Volker, and the guards all howled and jumped back.

"What manner of creature is this?" Volker gasped.

I was wondering that myself, Picard thought. Now he could see why Worf was so annoyed.

Smolinske had indeed given him an outfit that suggested magic. He was dressed as a genie—long, baggy green trousers, a short darker-green jacket over his bare chest, and an imposing bright yellow turban piled on his head. His feet were encased in bottle-green slippers with toes that curled upward. Worf looked both imposing and ridiculous at the same time. The only thing that prevented Picard from cracking a smile was the furious glare that Worf cast about the room, as if daring anyone to laugh at him. For once, Picard envied Data his lack of emotion.

"Leave!" Worf yelled at the top of his voice. The castle walls didn't quite shake with the force of the blast. "Now!"

As Picard had expected, there was absolutely no argument from Volker. He, Kirsch, and the final few guards turned on their heels and ran for their lives as if the demons from hell were on their tails. Picard couldn't blame them.

"Excellent work, Mr. Worf," he said when the locals were gone.

"I feel very foolish," Worf growled.

"Nonsense. You look very . . ." Picard coughed, and hit his communicator. "Mr. O'Brien, beam Mr. Worf and the device into the Preservers' control room. Then beam the three of us back aboard the ship."

There was a slight pause. "That's kind of tricky, sir," the transporter chief responded. "I may have to cut this rather close."

"Do your best," Picard instructed.

There was the familiar tingle in the air as Worf and the bomb shimmered into nothingness. Picard stood where he was, waiting. It seemed like an eternity before the beam focused in again, and he felt the slight wrenching in his stomach. Then he and Data were on the pad in Transporter Room 3. O'Brien gave them a relieved smile and reset the controls.

As Picard stepped down, Worf materialized on the platform. Then the deck beneath their feet shuddered, flinging them off-balance across the room.

"That's the problem I was referring to," O'Brien explained. "The gravity mines are closing in and the ship's feeling the strain.

"Well done, Chief," Picard said. "Gentlemen?" He set off down the corridor to the closest turbolift, with Data and Worf close on his heels. He didn't look too closely at all of the damage on the way. Bulkheads had ruptured, panels collapsed. There were pools of fluids gathering. In the lift he barked: "Bridge!" The doors whined loudly as they closed.

The ride was bumpy and noisy, but they made it. The second the doors opened, Picard led the dash for their posts. Riker, Deanna, and Ro—still in their costumes—were already at their posts. The counselor looked shaken, and everyone else on the bridge looked very grim.

As Picard took the command chair, he saw the computer simulations on the main screen. They had cut their arrival far too fine. The mines had arrived.

As the *Enterprise* shook again, Worf called out: "Ten seconds to device detonation! Shields at twenty-four percent power. Forward shield number four still off-line."

Picard gripped the chair arms. Without that screen the shields were bound to fail.

It hadn't been easy for Barclay to clamber into the access port for the failed shield projector. He'd almost blacked out from the pain in his ankle. Every ounce of willpower he possessed he focused into remaining conscious. Then he'd slowly begun replacing the burnt-out circuits.

The port shuddered about him. He barely heard the red-alert klaxon screaming in the corridor outside.

Slamming home the final component, he powered up the unit. "Come on, baby, work," he crooned as he tapped the final controls.

Engineering was a disaster area. Panels had been opened for repairs and left hanging. Jury-rigged units were plugged in all over. Geordi jumped one such unit, hoping that the hissing sound it was giving off wasn't a sign of impending doom. He gained the main engineering panel and took in the status.

The field stabilizers were dying. As the latest mines approached, another of the control boards shorted. The emergency backup came on line, then started signaling its impending failure. The main lighting was pulsing in time with the rapid bursts from the core.

"She's gonna blow!" one of the juniors yelled.

Geordi hit his communicator. "Field containment failure imminent," he reported as evenly as he could. His fingers whirled across the panel as he tried desperately to bring one more backup—any backup—into play before the fields shattered.

The bridge buckled and the lights dimmed. The bloodred emergency lighting came on, then faltered.

"Forward shield four back on line," Worf reported. "Shield strength up to forty-one percent. Field containment failure now eight seconds." Then, with considerable satisfaction: "Device detonation—now!"

There was one final shaking of the gravity compensators, then a sudden silence.

Picard let his breath out again. The emergency lighting died, and the main lights returned. The viewscreen—still engulfed in the snowstorm—showed no computer-enhanced targets.

"The gravity mines have ceased transmitting," Data reported from Ops. "Gravitational stresses now normal."

"Geordi here," came a very relieved report. "Field containment is reverting to normal. We'll be back up and running again in a few moments."

"When can I have impulse power?" Picard demanded.

"Impulse power? Captain, I don't think that this is a good time to plan a trip."

"We don't have any option, Geordi." Picard was still grim, despite the elation all about him. "With the Preservers' power now gone, that platform holding open the tunnel through the nebula will shut down."

"Uh-oh . . ." Geordi had obviously forgotten about that problem. "I'll have half-impulse in about thirty seconds, Captain."

"Good enough." Picard glanced at Data. "Any readings on the tunnel?"

"Not precisely," the android answered. "The generator platform does appear to have closed down."

"Ensign," Picard ordered Ro, "lay in a course for that tunnel. Maximum speed. I don't want to be trapped in here, but I've less desire to be caught inside that tunnel as it collapses."

"Laid in," Ro reported.

"Engage as soon as impulse power comes on line." Picard gave Riker a glance. "We're cutting this terribly fine, Number One."

"Don't we always?" asked Riker.

Managing a slight smile at this, Picard nodded. "It does seem to be a bad habit, doesn't it?"

"Impulse power up," Ro reported. There was a whine of power as she engaged the drive. The view of the planet on the screen shifted as the *Enterprise* came about.

"Two minutes to the tunnel at this velocity, Captain," Data reported.

"Will we be in time?" asked Picard, his voice tense.

"It is impossible to be certain," replied Data. "We have never encountered a science akin to this before. The tunnel may have already closed. The generator may have residual effects, and it may still be open. Sensors provide no information at all."

Riker shifted uncomfortably. "We may have dropped down a rabbit hole and pulled it shut above us," he muttered.

"We're not trapped yet," Picard said with more confidence than he felt.

"Let's hope not," agreed Riker.

They watched the screen tensely. The main cloud grew larger and larger. The beautiful swirls of color grew and danced across the interference on the screen. Picard desperately hoped that they would not have to watch it for the rest of their lives.

"I am picking up sensor readings on the tunnel," Data finally reported. "It is still there, but it is showing definite signs of weakening."

"Take us in, Ensign," Picard ordered.

"Aye, sir."

Data half-turned. "Captain, if the tunnel should collapse while we are inside it—"

"I know!" Picard barked. The ship would be annihilated in an instant, ripped apart by the tachyon fluxes. But if they didn't attempt it, they would be trapped inside the nebula.

There was a haven of sorts for them on the world at its heart. Data had assured him that it was in no danger from the termination of the Preservers' machines. It would proceed now on its own path, and find its own destiny. He'd done his best to ensure that the Prime Directive had been upheld. There was still time to return to the planet instead of taking this risk. Should he be risking the lives of all aboard in this potentially suicidal dash?

He knew there was little choice, really. They all had families and responsibilities back in the galaxy outside. And if they returned to the world they had just left, it would be for the rest of their lives. They would be isolated there, forbidden by the Prime Directive to interact with the natives. It was better to take this chance.

In the tunnel they seemed to crawl along. The mad whorls of color fluxed and flowed about the ship. The patterns on the screen were almost hypnotic. Greens, ochres, magentas, scarlets, blues, and whites pulsed and skipped about the *Enterprise*. Picard wished he could relax and enjoy the show, but every nerve-ending in his body ached with the tension and uncertainty of this passage.

"Shield integrity falling," Worf reported. "The power drain is starting to tell, Captain."

"Hold course," Picard ordered. "Data, what do you read on tachyon strength?"

"We are currently still safe from their effects, Captain," the officer replied. "But the tunnel is definitely constricting about us. The strength of the fields restraining the radiation is falling. It is merely a matter of time before the lingering effects of the Preservers' equipment fails under the stresses."

"How long?"

"Unknown, Captain."

Even though he'd been expecting this answer, Picard was still disappointed. After everything, they could still be trapped and obliterated in a split-second collapse.

The light show went on about them, oblivious to their problems.

"Normal space ahead," Data reported. "We will be exiting the tunnel in fifteen seconds."

They were the slowest fifteen seconds of Picard's life. The last vestiges of the nebula slipped past them, like colored paints draining down a sink.

"Protocloud behind us," Data announced. "We are back in conventional space."

Picard stood up. "My congratulations, everyone," he said loudly. "Now let's see about getting this ship back to normal, shall we?"

"No rest for the wicked," muttered Ro. She glanced back at the captain and then stiffened as her eye fell on Worf. "What are *you* supposed to be?"

Worf glared at her. "I am impersonating a magical Earth being," he growled. "Do you have a problem with that?"

Ro managed somehow to keep a straight face. "No. Absolutely not. No problem at all."

"Good."

VOLKER and Kirsch stood in the marketplace and stared together back at the smoldering pit that had once been the town's castle. The explosion had created a column of fire and smoke that was now dying down again. A fine rain of dust was falling over the town.

"Sodom and Gomorrah indeed." Volker sighed. "What a waste of a fine building."

"Perhaps it's a symbol," suggested the scholar. When Volker frowned, Kirsch explained: "The old duke was notoriously corrupt, my lord. Perhaps fire from heaven really was needed to mark an end of his ways. If you use this right, it could help the people to accept you as the new duke."

Volker's mind turned over the possibilities. Yes . . . there was something in what this scholar was saying.

from the

. And he had

the reins and

like the way you

er becoming one of my

e no guarantee that I will

definitely an improvement over

lord. I would be most happy to

ell, we've plenty of work to do." He made

to begin, though. He stared over the smoking

. "I wonder if they were really what they claimed

be?"

"I have a few theories," Kirsch offered. "I *always* have theories."

"Well?"

The new adviser shrugged. "They may have been angels of God. After all, didn't God send angels to warn Lot and his family to flee Sodom before its destruction? And does not the Apostle Paul speak of people entertaining angels unaware?"

"Angels?" mused Volker. "Well, perhaps so. But they claimed to be from our world. From some other continent." He rubbed his chin. "If that's true, then I think we'd better build a few ships and take a look at the rest of our world. If we share it with the likes of beings like Lukas and Dieter, then I want to know where they are. We must be ready if we ever have to deal with them again."

Beneath the rubble, the Preserver fragment was satisfied. The work was exhibiting progress once again. There had been a short time—a mere seven hundred years—where it looked as if the experiment might have failed. The human colony had suffered badly when exposed to the native reptilian species. It had been thought that the presence of creatures they believed in—the dragons of their folklore—would stimulate their growth and progress. In the event, the reverse had occurred. Curiously, it looked as if progress had been restored to the world, thanks to the accidental contact with other humans from outside the experiment. The obsolete equipment had been a small price to pay.

Had this compromised the composition? The fragment couldn't tell, not being in contact with the rest of the Preserver Union. But the influence was removed, and the experiment was back on track. All that it could do was to observe and record, waiting the day when the Union contacted it again for details.

The fragment settled down to its duties, willing to wait as long as it must. Now it had at least the age of discoverers and adventurers to look forward to on this world.

In the briefing room, Picard glanced about the table. Riker, Deanna, Geordi, Data, Beverly, Worf, and Ro looked back. He felt an air of peace, despite the horrendous list of damage to his ship that had been compiled. They were on their way to Starbase 217, which was gearing up to help with the repair work. They were limping along at warp three, but the engines were holding.

"I've spoken with Randolph and Hagan," Riker reported. "Apparently they were the only two members of the poachers left on that planet. It was always a small operation. They're more than willing to name the rest of the gang back on Earth, so we can close this out now."

"And the recent wave of art forgeries will die out with the collapse of the scheme," Data added. "The real Federation Security will be most pleased with our conduct."

"What about the people of that world?" asked Beverly. "Will they be okay now?"

"It's hard to say," Picard answered. "But with their isolation again, they will at least have a chance to make their own progress."

"It's just a damned shame about having to destroy the Preservers' machinery." Riker sighed. "And we didn't get a hold of that map of the other Preserver worlds. Randolph told me he kept it in his room at the castle."

Picard knew how disappointed Riker had to be. He himself had desperately longed to see that map. "Yes. But at least we know that there *are* other worlds they seeded out there. Perhaps the next one we discover will hold a map, also. Who knows? I feel certain that one day we will run into them."

"If I could offer a suggestion," Data said. Picard nodded. The android continued: "The existence of the tunnel through the nebula suggests that the Preservers were keeping access to the planet open. It is therefore not unlikely that they mean to return. If a monitoring station is set up in this vicinity, it is possible that we may detect their approach one day."

"An excellent idea, Mr. Data," Picard agreed. "I'll note it in my report. And while they're waiting, the station could get a really good, long look at the protocloud evolution." He stood up. "I am commending everyone involved for his or her work on this mission," he added. "Thank you, one and all."

As the room began to empty, Beverly came over to him. "How are you feeling, Jean-Luc?" she asked. "Any aftereffects from all of your adventures on the planet?"

"Merely a slight sunburn," he assured her. "How about the casualties on the ship?"

"They're doing well." Beverly smiled. "Lieutenant Miles's arm is mending well. Reg Barclay is screaming about being kept in bed while there's still work to be done."

Picard chuckled. "Oh, and I meant to ask you. I saw Smolinske's name on the sick list. But there was no mention of any injuries. Could you enlighten me a little?"

"It's preventative medicine," Beverly explained. "She seemed to feel that a week in my isolation room just might give Mr. Worf time to calm down."

POCKET
BOOKS

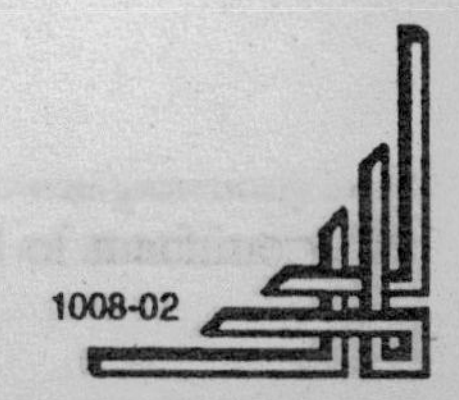